Initiation

Sex Wizards, Book 1

Alethea Faust

Published by Alethea Faust, 2022.

To Geo, my first reader.

Acknowledgments

This story would have never made it to print if it weren't for my partner Geo Sauer, who read the first draft of Initiation with crossed legs and a blush. Without his endless support and understanding, this series would have ended before it ever really started.

Then there's the special kind of friend who listens to your musings about sexy magical theory without batting an eye. So thank you Jo O'Brien for not only supporting this sex epic, but for giving Dom a face (or at least a really sexy torso).

To the amazing band of smutpeddlers who have taken me under their wing and helped this anxious newbie - I seriously cannot thank you enough. Sierra Cassidy, Dakota Brown, Vera Valentine, Mx. Alex, Dominique Marks, Serena Silverlake and Nouh Bdee - I'm so happy to have found my people.

But there's one person who is the true hero of this story, and that is the person who took this dyslexic writers words and corrected all of them. This entire series was edited by Rebecca Scott. To learn more about her talents and how she can help your writing endeavors, visit her website at: www.bee-scott.com/proofreading

Last, but certainly not least, a huge thank you to my readers, but specifically to B Scott, LBMatt, botanicalmysts, R'lee, SortaVulcan, Lila, Sydney, Ace_Of_Clubs, Matt, Cheryl Terra, "Cancassi's Favorite," Azamir, Nora, HypnoStory, Peter, sylvershade, B.K., Melody Diaz-Musgrave, Jill Rafferty, Angie U, Jaye-Anne, Kate W. and the rest of my Patrons who have supported me through this journey. Y'all are seriously amazing and I would have never gathered to courage to put this story out there without you.

Author's Note

This queer erotic fantasy novel has a kink-based magic system, and as such, contains explicit adult content. As this story crosses a wide range of kinks of varying degrees of intensity, applicable chapters will have a description at the top showing what type of play is included in the chapter as well as any other applicable warnings.

Welcome to the Crux

A *bjuration: The school of magic that blocks, banishes, or protects. Casting methods include rope bondage, domination, and submission.*

IT'S TAKEN ME FOUR full weeks to reach the wizards' towers in Straetham.

Four full weeks of soggy mountain passes and wetlands. Of being crisped by the spring sun, eaten by mosquitoes and leeches, and nipped by the meanest horse south of Airedale. The sketchy caravan I hitched a ride with managed to get me here, though they bled me of every last red cent in the process.

I must be out of my godsdamned mind.

The towers stick up from the ground like the fingers of a buried giant. They're *huge*. Bigger than anything in Airedale by at least four stories. Each one is so unique and grand I can't imagine what must have gone into building them.

One is styled like a fortress of red stone. Another seems to fade away into mist, even though it's a clear day. I count nine in all, but the grandest is the main tower that juts up from the rest like a beacon. It's made of a curious white stone that skitters with color - a moving rainbow.

On my long road here, I learned that everyone south of the Hobokins calls it the Crux.

The gate to the courtyard is open. The drawbridge is lowered across the sparkling, water-filled moat. The bridge is wide and welcoming, yet I can't bring myself to cross it.

I feel my threadbare clothes and every hole in them. After four full weeks, I'm ragged and dirty, grit so ingrained that I don't know how I'll get clean again. Every bug bite and burned patch of skin reminds me that I'm not meant for a place like this. I'm just some idiot country boy who's stumbled down the godsdamned mountains on the word of a woman I don't even *know*. I have nothing - no money, no name of any consequence. Only the letter from Allisande.

Four weeks is a lot of time to think on *that* particular uncertainty as well. When Allisande had hired me, I thought it would be a standard escort through the woods. With bandits scouting the roads, it wasn't unusual for folks to hire me to get them safely from one place to the next, but Allisande was far from my usual patronage. Well dressed, with fiery red hair and blue eyes that seemed to pierce right into me even as her smile warmed me from the inside out. She was beautiful, and just from the way she spoke I could tell she wasn't from some nowhere place in the mountains.

I hadn't expected such a class looking woman to really even talk to me during the trip, let alone *sleep* with me, but after I chased off a group of goblins from our camp one night, she'd been grateful. And had been very forward in showing her gratitude. Near demanding, actually, and I wasn't about to say no to those lush red lips.

It had been a whirlwind of a fuck, all adrenaline and teeth and sweat, but I do remember her distinct little "oh" of surprise when I finished.

It wasn't until we went to part ways at the edge of the woods that she handed me a sealed letter. "In case you want a change of scenery," she had said, giving me that little half smile that had made my insides go all funny in the first place. Then, she had kissed me on the cheek and headed down the road and out of my life.

It was a letter of introduction to the wizards' towers in Straetham, claiming I'd be a promising adept. Written on thick, expensive parchment, dated and signed with her name. A personal crest was seared into one corner, and even I know enough to recognize a wizard's seal.

It had stalled my heart in my chest, reading that. I'm the son of a hunter and a mother I barely remember save that she taught me my letters and how to plant things right so they would grow. How the hell did magic make it into *my* bloodline? Magic only exists in the blood of the rich, the royal, and the reputable, and I'm barely one of those things! It felt unreal, and for some time, I pretended like it was.

The letter stayed tucked in my pocket while I thought on it. Then on the shelf in the cabin while I thought on it some more. Then it went into my mother's old plant journal, and I stopped thinking about it for a while.

But my priorities changed after the accident that broke my arm. I set it as best as I could, but it didn't heal right over the winter. When you start to run out of salted meat and pickled vegetables a month before spring, a change of scenery starts looking real good. And what good was a forest guide and hunter who couldn't draw a bow anymore?

Then again, what good is a coward who's traveled for four godsdamned weeks just to turn tail at the *godsdamned* drawbridge?

"Excuse me."

I nearly jump out of my skin. Gaping like an idiot, I'm blocking the main thoroughfare. I step aside and a woman in dark robes brushes past me. I see a flash of colors on her cuffs, but don't have time to wonder what they mean before she asks, "Are you lost?"

The question makes me bristle. I muster my courage. Even if I feel out of place, I'll be damned if I let someone else tell me I am. I didn't travel four weeks to turn tail now.

"No." I hand her Allisande's letter.

The woman's eyes widen as she brushes a thumb over Allisande's seal. She must read the letter twice because she's quiet for a long moment. It gives me time to take her in. She's probably a few years older than me, a southerner with skin as brown as fresh tilled earth. Curly black hair hangs wild around her face, just brushing her shoulders. She's beautiful, with high cheekbones and full lips that I'm getting distracted looking at. But when her shrewd brown eyes focus on me, a knot of uncertainty tightens in my gut.

"This is dated over a year ago."

"I was busy 'til now."

The woman opens her mouth to ask something else but decides against it. "Well, come on then," she says, all business. She continues her way across the bridge, her robes billowing behind her. I hesitate for only a second before I follow.

Inside, the courtyard is more a garden than the wizard rallying area I was expecting. A small pond rests near one wall, shaded by dripping willows. Fruit trees dot the grounds, and this time of year they're all starting to bloom and make the whole yard smell sweet. A gravel path cuts through the grass to the main entry of the Crux. I spot other wizards eating lunch in the shade, or reading a book by the pond. There's even a couple engaging in the most ambitious form of tongue wrestling I've seen in some time.

"Your name is Dominai?" the lady-wizard asks me. She doesn't slow her pace as I gawk. I wonder if she used some sort of magic to learn it before I remember that Allisande had named me in her letter. I clear the embarrassment from my throat.

"Yeah, that's right. Most call me Dom."

"I'm Galiva," the woman says. "I assume Allisande tested you for magical aptitude?" The blank stare I give her is answer enough. "I take it that you've never studied magic in any official capacity."

"You'd guess right," I say. "Allisande just recommended I come here."

Galiva opens the door to the Crux and gives me a look that could scour a pot. "Not just anyone can do magic," she points out, like I don't already know that. "You study it to perfect it, but without the spark, you won't make it that far. And since Allisande isn't here to vouch for your aptitude in person, I'll have to."

Inside of the Crux, the stained glass windows and white stone columns look expensive enough to feed a village like Airedale for a lifetime. I feel something like vertigo when I step in, a tingle in the hairs on the nape of my neck. It even smells different, like magic is somehow infused into the incense that wafts from censers on the wall.

"And what happens if I fail?" I ask and try to blink the fog away.

Galiva shrugs. "You won't be able to study as a wizard, but if you're looking for work, there may be other places for you here. We rarely turn people away if they walk across our drawbridge."

That comes as a surprise. "Awful generous of you."

Galiva shrugs again and leads me down one of the many halls that branch out of the Crux. "Since Prince Thermilious became *King* Thermilious, a certain amount of stigma has been put onto the magical community. We aren't exactly drawing crowds across our drawbridge." She says his name like it leaves a sour taste in her mouth. Even as far as Airedale, I had heard about the young King's dislike of magic, though I hadn't realized it would have an impact on recruitment.

Galiva leads me to a small but modest room. There's nothing in it save for an empty desk and a bed stacked with fresh linens.

"You can store your things here. This room will be yours for the time being."

It's a relief to toss my heavy pack on the floor, though I set my unstrung bow down a little more careful. Galiva gives me that scrutinizing look again.

"You need a bath," she declares, and she's right. There's only so much cold creeks and rivers can do for a person. I don't even take offense to the implication that I stink. "Follow me."

She leads me down a twisting stair at the end of the hall. Even before we reach the bottom, I feel hot steam. A whiff of clean-smelling soap follows right after. Galiva disappears into a side room before returning a moment later with a towel and a neatly folded bundle of clothes. She sees my questioning look and says, "You've been traveling for some time and your clothes don't look like they'll make the trip back if it comes to that. Just take them."

I grab the bundle with a small murmur of thanks. I'm not normally one for handouts, and these definitely aren't some threadbare garb. She's given me a clean linen shirt and durable gray breeches that are better quality than any of what I own. "Take your time and meet me in the main atrium when you're finished. You remember the way?"

"I think so," I say, immediately wishing I had been paying closer attention.

Galiva looks me over and her expression softens. I think she can tell I'm a little overwhelmed. "Up the stairs and to the left, and then your second right. Follow the incense. You can't miss it."

I run a hand through my hair and smile. She returns it and the change it makes on her face is startling. She goes from beautiful to radiant. Her eyes rake over me one more time, and I see something like curiosity in her gaze.

"Enjoy," she says before sweeping back up the stairs.

I watch her go and let out a long sigh, hardly able to believe I'm actually *here*. There are a lot of rumors about wizards. One is that they work fast, and that's definitely no lie. I made that first step across the bridge and entered a new world. Swept into the heart of the Crux in the blink of an eye.

And it's *hot* down here. Steam thickens the air, wafting up from the nine pools that are carved straight into the white stone. They're all different sizes, and while they're all clear, some have a tint of color in the water. Faint greens and blues. I don't know one from the other, but fortunately, all seem to be empty.

The one in the back glows a clear blue, and it seems as good as any. I check around before I strip my clothes off. I'm not keen on the idea of a public bath, but even less when I'm carrying four weeks of filth on me. I'm sticky and gritty enough that my boots and socks try to stay stuck. Galiva's not wrong about my clothes either - there are holes in the elbows of my shirt big enough to fit my fist through.

I plunge my foot into the water only to jump back with a yelp. It's as frigid as a spring runoff. I feel a little betrayed and kick my ragged clothes over to the steaming pool next to it before I slide into the water quick. A little too quick. The water is almost *too* hot, but I can't stop a groan as the grime of travel starts to loosen. The heat is pure relief on my travel-weary body and, not for the first time, I blame my da for never teaching me to ride a horse.

For a second, I just sit there and think about what it must be like to do this every day. And if I pass whatever this aptitude test is, I actually *could*.

There's a bar of soap on a small tray at the pool's edge along with some bottles of sweet-smelling liquid. A steady trickle of water tells me the baths filter water out and in. As good as the bath feels I don't want to make Galiva wait, and I've got a ways to go before I'm clean. I make good work of it.

I just start to scrub the dirt that's caked itself into the skin of my ankles when I hear footsteps coming down the stairs. A man steps into the baths, barefoot and walking a little tender. He pads over to the ice bath across from me, loosening the tie of his robe from around his waist.

Thick black hair hangs loose around his handsome face, falling past his shoulders. He's got warm russet skin, a strong jaw and a lean build that makes me wonder how gangly he'd been as a teenager before he grew into himself. An idle smile plays across his face, and he looks like his thoughts are as far away as Airedale. He doesn't seem to notice me as he gets to the edge of the ice bath and lets his robe drop.

I barely stop a gasp.

His back and ass are a mess of red welts, some raw enough to look like they had been bleeding. Under the new, I see the bruises of older lashes, as if he's been whipped with a belt. He steps into the pool and sinks up to his waist, letting out a shuddering gasp that fades to a groan of pleasure. He relaxes into the chilled water, a smile spreading over his face. He seems awful happy for someone who had the shit beat out of him recently.

As if he finally feels my gaze, he opens his eyes. He looks a little surprised when he sees me. For a moment, he simply stares, like he's trying to decide if he recognizes me. His hand drifts to his necklace - an elaborate thing with four strands full of different colored marbles and rings. He toys with one of the beads.

"You're new?" he asks, his voice holding an accent I can't place.

"Just in," I say. I try to sound casual, like I haven't seen the massacre that is his backside.

The man sinks a little further into the pool, water lapping over his chest. "Do you know what school you'd like to study?" he asks.

It only seems polite to answer, though I don't even know what schools there *are*. "Dunno. What'd you choose?"

"I'm an evoker," he says. "Nuanced and challenging, but very worthwhile."

My stomach drops a little. I don't know much about magic, but I've heard the rumors of how it's done. Blood and sweat, some claim. Others say it is some sort of ritual. Either way, I'd bet my last copper that's how his back got like that. What's so nuanced about getting the shit whipped out of you?

I shake the thought off and grab my towel before pulling myself from the pool. I don't want to leave, but having someone else down here makes it a little less welcoming. Besides, I'm clean and have made Galiva wait long enough.

The man watches me through heavily lidded eyes, that same satisfied smile spread across his face. Something about his attention makes my stomach squirm, not unlike Allisande's effect on me. Maybe it's a wizard thing.

"See you around, yeah?" he calls as I gather my things.

"Maybe so," I say before hurrying up the stairs.

GALIVA IS WAITING IN the main atrium, just as she said, but she's not alone. She's talking to a rather severe-looking wizard. He's older than me, swarthy with a big build, though he's far taller than he is wide. His short hair is dark with flecks of gray touching his temples. In his hand is Allisande's letter. He glances up as I approach, suspicion evident on his face.

"You'll let me know how the test goes?" he asks, but he's talking to Galiva.

"Of course," Galiva says while her eyes give me a good once-over, a grin quirking her lips. The man tucks the letter into his pocket. I debate asking for it back, but he disappears down the corridor before I can get a chance.

Galiva smiles, and motions for me to follow her. "Have a good bath?" she asks and leads me down yet another hall and up a winding staircase.

"Best I've ever had," I say, and it's the truth. "It's a hell of a perk."

Galiva chuckles, and I gotta admit that I like the sound of it. "It's not the only one," she says. "Magical study is challenging, but most find it very worthwhile."

The hall we emerge on is lined sparsely with doors. If there is anyone behind them, they're either too quiet to hear or the hall is witched into silence. Galiva opens one of them and ushers me inside to a sparse room. It's nothing but stone walls and floors with a window in the corner. It's empty save for a heavy wooden cabinet and a couple of chairs.

"So, Dom," she says and closes the door behind us. "Do you know what a magical aptitude test entails?"

There's something mischievous twinkling in her brown eyes. She wears a smirk that promises secrets. It makes me as nervous as I am excited.

"I'm sure you're gonna tell me."

She chuckles. "How about I explain as we go? Take off your clothes."

Heat floods my face. "What? Why?"

Galiva discards her robe carelessly over the back of one chair. Underneath, she's wearing tight riding breeches that hug the curve of her hips, high boots, and a flowing cotton shirt that she's rolled up to her elbows. "Because we're going to have sex," she says matter-of-factly.

I gape at her. Allisande was beautiful, but Galiva is about three cities out of my league. "W-what?"

"If you're not comfortable with intimate contact, there's still a place for you if you have magic in your blood, but this will turn into a very different kind of aptitude test. Are you averse to sex?" she asks, sounding a little amused.

I clear my throat, realizing that she's serious. "Oh. Well, no. I'm definitely alright with that," I say, and the thought of being able to touch her rich brown skin makes heat run straight to my groin.

"Good," she says. "Then take off your clothes."

Her eyes crinkle with a hint of wicked pleasure. I'm sure I'm red as the setting sun, but I lift my shirt over my head. My breeches go next, but when I get to my underthings I give her a questioning look. I'm more used to doing things in the dark, but the late afternoon sun shines through the window like a spotlight. The amused tilt of her head is all the answer I get, so I discard those next. I shiver as goose-flesh breaks out over my bare skin though the room isn't cold.

"Good boy," she says and something in her voice makes the heat in my face flood to the rest of me. "Now, there are a couple of things you need to know as we do this."

I watch as she circles around me. She's also got a multi-strand necklace, filled with the same marbles and rings, but this close I can see that they're *glowing*. A low, gentle light. She toys with a pink marble, and it flashes before the light in it winks out. A curious tingle spreads over my skin, but it's gone so quick I could believe I imagined it. "The first is that we can stop at any time," she says. "I will check in regularly to be sure you're alright. If you are ever uncomfortable, say the magic word and I will stop."

"What's the magic word?" I ask.

"Stop." She chuckles as I flush a degree hotter and walks behind me, one finger trailing over my shoulder. The touch is a shock, but not an unwelcome one. I shiver. "It seems mundane, but it's a powerful word in the Crux. If you violate a stop, you'll be expelled immediately, understand?"

"Right, got it."

"Good." She gives me a gentle shove to the center of the room. "Now wait there."

Galiva walks to the large cabinet and opens the door. She pulls out a large pillow and tosses it at my feet. I blink at it and when I look back at her, she's pulled out a small black cloth and a long coil of rope.

"Now, the second thing to remember, especially for this spell, is that you are safe," she says as she approaches me. "You may be nervous, but know that the spell will fail if you are genuinely afraid. Hence the first rule - stop me if you ever feel that way."

"Right," I say. This close, I can smell her - a mixture of rosewood and musk. Unseemly thoughts cross my mind as I catch a flash of cleavage through the loose v of her shirt. "What spell are we casting?"

There's an idle smile playing on her face, but her ministrations are all business. She drapes the black cloth over my eyes before tying it tight. "We're casting a protection barrier," she says. "One that shields against being seen as well as being attacked. Primarily abjuration with a bit of illusion. Does that sound alright to you?"

"I suppose," I say and blink against the blindfold. "What goes into that?"

"I am going to bind you with these ropes, we will cast the spell, and I'll release you," she says, and the soft rope glides over my shoulder. "Agreeable?"

I whistle and run a hand over my face, feeling the scruff on my chin. I wish I'd had a chance to shave. This is not what I was expecting when I heard the words "aptitude test." Not to say that it doesn't sound like a good time. Way better than anything I had expected.

"Sounds fine to me," I say, wishing I could see her face. I'm trying to be casual even though the thud of my heart has to be loud enough for her to hear.

"Good," she says and I hear the smile in her voice. "Remember the most important rule?"

"To say stop if I'm uncomfortable."

"Good boy."

She takes one of my wrists and guides it behind my back before doing the same to the other. I feel the glide of the soft rope over and under my wrists before she pulls tight enough to bite, though it's not tight enough to cut off blood flow. I stamp out the reflex to pull away as my bum arm twinges at the angle.

She's unhurried as she weaves the rope up my forearms before she does something that makes the ropes bite a little tighter. The ropes allow for a bend in my elbows, but she moves up to my biceps and binds them as well. When she cinches them tighter a sharp pain jumps up my right arm, wringing a gasp from me.

"Are you alright?" she asks. Her warm fingers trail over the ropes and brush my skin in feather-light touches.

"Old injury."

Galiva's fingers freeze. "Where?"

"Right arm. Broke it a while back and it healed funny."

"Humerus?" she asks, her hands landing on my weakened bicep. At a glance you wouldn't notice it, but the muscles there don't sit right, stretched in the wrong way. Pulled as it is, it must be obvious.

"Yeah."

"Apologies. I should have asked before we started. It's been some time since I initiated someone," she says and sounds a little ashamed. She immediately loosens the ropes around my biceps and wrists. It's just enough that she can readjust my arms so they're laying on top of one another behind my back, wrist to elbow. "Better?" she asks.

"Yeah. Thanks."

"Any other injuries or ailments I should know about?" she asks, her hands resting gently against my shoulders.

"Sore from travel, but nothing serious."

"You've eaten and had enough water?"

"I've taken good care of myself," I say, and it's true. The caravan that brought me to the outskirts of town had been generous with their lunch. That, and I'm not about to have her stop now. Already my nerves thrum with anticipation.

"Good," she says before resuming her careful binding. It feels like she's using the whole roll of it just on my arms, but she leaves my biceps alone. The ropes drape over my shoulders and wrap under my bound forearms. When she pulls, my chest is forced out to accommodate the strain as my shoulders are pulled back.

"Still alright?" she asks, her hand resting against the ram-rod straight small of my back.

"Yes." My voice comes out a little higher than I intend. I clear my throat. With the blindfold, I'm aware of every brush of air against my bare skin, every quiet footstep Galiva takes around me. Then her hand is on my shoulder, pushing me to kneel. I don't resist and my knees land on the soft pillow.

She spreads my knees apart with gentle prods before she loops rope over one thigh and under my shin. She slides the soft cord behind my legs and pulls tight before doing the same to the other leg. She doesn't use nearly as much rope as she used on my arms, but it's still effective. I shift again and realize I can't unfold my legs from their kneel.

Her gentle ministrations leave me panting. The unhurried glide of her rope would be calming if I wasn't so heated up already. I've never had someone take control away from me like this. The fact that it seems a little dangerous, a little reckless to let someone I've just met do this only stokes the fire. I don't think I've ever been so randy in my life.

The ropes around my shoulders pull tight every time I draw in a breath, and while it's uncomfortable it doesn't hurt. I've lost track of how long it's taken, but my knees start to ache despite the pillow I'm kneeling on. I try to lean back to give them some relief, but I can't go far without risking toppling over.

A quiet groan escapes me before Galiva's fingers glide through my hair. She grips near the roots and pulls my head back. Though I can't see her through the blindfold, I know she's smiling above me. I can hear it as she asks, "Are you alright?"

There's a strange thrum of energy between us. I hadn't noticed it so much while she was binding me, but with nothing but the ropes and her hand on me I can't ignore it. I swallow when I realize how hard I already am. If it wasn't evident before, it certainly is now.

"Good. I'm good."

Galiva's chuckle washes over me, but it's not mocking. "Glad you're enjoying yourself," she says, a quiet purr. "Are you ready for the next part?"

I nod and feel the thrum of energy pulse. "Good," she says. Her touch disappears, and over the thudding of my own heart I hear her behind me. I swear she's trying to keep her footsteps quiet to keep me guessing. There's a rustle of cloth before things go quiet again.

Then her hand is on my back, pushing me hard. I yelp as I'm pitched forward, but Galiva's strong grip on the rope harness around my arms stops me from slamming against the stone. She gently lowers me down, and my knees scrape against the stone as I try to find a place for them. Eventually I just lay flat on my front, my ass lifted a little by the pillow. The parts of me that touch the stone find it cold and rough.

My cock throbs as Galiva pushes my knees apart once more. "Now, you don't strike me as the adventurous type," she muses. "So I'm sure this will be new for you."

I'm about to protest - I traveled all the way from the high hills to get here, didn't I? But then I feel her hands spreading my cheeks apart. Something cold and wet slicks my ass, teasing my hole as if giving me a second to say stop. When I don't, she eases her finger *into* me. A strangled sort of groan escapes me as Galiva thrusts gently, first one knuckle, then a second.

"Alright?" she asks.

"Fucking hell - it's fine," I gasp. This definitely is new, but the chills it sends up my spine are anything but unwelcome. She takes her time, leisurely exploring before she curls her finger and hits *something*.

I groan and don't recognize the deep, guttural sound that comes out of my throat. "Feels pretty good, doesn't it?" She adds a second finger, stretching me gently. My answer is lost to a long moan. She teases me for a long moment before slowly withdrawing her fingers. I can't stop a groan of disapproval.

But I'm not empty for long. Something cool and smooth glides in to take her place. I moan as the slightly curved object settles against that sweet spot inside of me. Every shift of my hips sends a thrill of pleasure up my back.

"Still alright?" she asks again.

"Yes!" I don't understand why she's stopped. Against the cold stone I'm trembling, both from the strain of the ropes and my need for her to keep going. Between us, the crackle of energy is stronger now. The static before a lightning strike.

She grabs the rope harness and pulls me up enough that I can get my knees under me again. It's a struggle. She chuckles as I finally settle back into a kneel, grunting as the thing inside of me shifts. Her fingers rake through my hair, and I lean into the touch, my mouth dry.

Something brushes my hard cock, making me jump in surprise. With the blindfold on, every sensation is new and unexpected. Galiva slips something over my length. It's cool and smooth, snug without being tight. It hugs the base of my cock gently. The energy seems to concentrate around it, tingling over my already straining erection.

Galiva's expert fingers give me a few good strokes, but when she stops just shy of my release, I want to scream. "For the gods' sake, Galiva, please!"

She chuckles and says, "I'm not needlessly torturing you, you know. The more energy, the stronger the spell."

That may be true, but there's no doubt she's enjoying herself at my expense. My knees and shoulders ache, but my cock is hard as a rock and she's barely *done* anything to it. The strong tingling of the ring she's put there certainly isn't helping.

But Galiva has mercy on me. I feel the warmth of her bare skin as she straddles my waist. Her arms drape behind my neck, legs spread on either side of mine. I realize what she's doing the second before she sits down. The wet heat of her slides down the length of my erection. I don't know when she took her clothes off, and I don't care. The feel of her takes the breath out of my lungs.

She rolls her hips against mine and gives an appreciative little sigh. I feel her clench around me and can't stop a needy little groan. Then she starts moving, and the thing inside of me presses against that sweet spot relentlessly with every rock of her hips. She starts slow at first, but she gradually speeds up as she drives herself further onto me. I feel her arms tighten around my back, her knees braced on either side of my lap as she rides me.

She presses her lips against my neck as her moan joins mine. She trails gentle nips up my jaw before she finds my lips, kissing me hard enough to steal what little breath I have left before dragging my lower lip between her teeth. I can feel her smile as she works her hips faster, riding me until I'm teetering right on the edge of release.

"Galiva," I gasp, hoarse with need.

Her lips smile against my cheek and she gives a few more thrusts, her pace quickening. "Let's finish it together then," she says, her own voice thick with pleasure.

Then, I feel it. The sweet heat of her ripples around me as she cries out in pleasure. Muscles contract, heat surges, the door opens, and I strain against the ropes as I follow her into bliss. The ring around my cock sparks, adding one more wave of sensation on top of the pleasure that courses out of me in desperate spurts.

And then the static tingle is gone, replaced by a pulsing sort of warmth. I can't tell if it's coming from the ring or from Galiva. She rests bonelessly on top of me, her arms still draped behind my neck.

When she lifts the blindfold, I blink owlishly in the light of the room. She smiles at me, the roots of her hair damp with sweat. I groan when she pulls herself off of me, feeling wetness drip onto my thigh. My legs are numb save for my knees and shins, which hurt like a son of a bitch from kneeling. I didn't even notice it until there was nothing else to focus on, and frankly I'd be happy to do that all over again in spite of the discomfort.

Galiva reaches down and pulls the ring from my cock. Under our mixed fluids, I see that it's made of the same white material as the Crux itself. Colors flash inside of it, clean and white like little star-bursts. "Congratulations, Dominai," she says. "You just cast your first spell."

She frees me quickly from the ropes, untying knots with the speed of long practice. I groan as I stretch my legs out in front of me and jerk when the thing still inside of me shifts. I rub the rope marks on my arms and there's the sting of pins and needles as blood rushes back into my feet proper. I sit up slow before Galiva presses her chest against my back. She drapes her arms over my shoulders and holds the stone ring up in front of me.

I take it between my fingers and feel it thrum with our combined energies. A small laugh escapes me as I watch the light spark and dart inside of it. I don't understand it, but somehow, we've made *magic*.

Introduction to Evocation

Evocation: The school of magic that taps into and manipulates energy. Casting methods include impact play, sensation play, and pain play.

THE REST OF THE EVENING passes in a blur. Galiva takes me on a quick tour of the Crux, though in my exhausted haze I'm not sure how much I really take in. After she finishes taking me around to the different towers I must get bad at hiding it. She steers us to the mess to help me grab dinner. Then she sends me to bed with a kiss on the cheek, a promise to come get me tomorrow morning, and my first spell hanging on a leather string around my neck.

Even though I fall asleep in a new bed, I fall asleep as quickly as if I were home.

Maybe it's the magic in the towers, but my dreams are vibrant. In them, I'm walking through the familiar pines and aspens of the Hobokins, bow in hand. Sun dapples through the trees, and over the sound of the nearby river something big shuffles through the underbrush.

I freeze. It could be a good haul, and winter's always just around the corner. A head appears - a deer, but the antlers are all wrong. Black horns curl down like a ram's.

I crouch behind a shrub to nock an arrow, ready a shot. I take careful aim to pierce through the side into the lungs and heart. I

22

don't much like this part, but my aim is good enough to at least make it a quick death.

Yet before I can loose, the earth under me gives. I swear and look down as the grass and dirt turn liquid. It sucks me in faster than quicksand. It's like water but it holds like stone as it creeps up my legs, my hips. It captures my arms as it sucks me in to my chest.

A tendril snakes over my mouth, gagging my shout of panic. More settles into my ears, covers my nose, constricting, suffocating. I thrash against it, but I'm held fast, like the ground is trying to swallow me whole. I look up and see a woman silhouetted against the sky. Pale and dark-haired, with ram's horns that curl just under her pointed ears. She looks down in alarm before the ground covers my eyes, plunging me into black.

I wake with a jolt and realize that someone is knocking on my door. I swear and rub the sleep from my eyes, the flash of panic from the dream already fading.

"Coming."

It takes a second to untangle myself from my blankets, but I manage and stumble out of bed. My toe immediately finds its way into the corner of the desk chair, and I swear as I yank my trousers on and throw open the door.

Galiva greets me with an amused smile, fully awake and dressed. "Sleep well?" she asks.

"I wasn't done, but yeah." I rub my face, wiping a flake of dried drool from the corner of my mouth. "What time is it?"

Galiva snorts. "It's nearly second bell. You've almost slept through breakfast."

It's unusual - I'm not normally a late sleeper, but I still feel like I have another hour or two in me. But at the mention of food, my stomach growls.

"Right," I say. "Give me just a second."

I stumble back into my room and grab my shirt, shaking the creases out of it as best as I can. I pull it on and comb my fingers through my hair. A pitcher of water and some mint leaves have made it onto my desk, along with a bowl, soap, and a straight razor. Magic? Or just a very quiet servant? With how hard I slept, someone may have slipped in without me noticing.

I make use of everything but the razor, letting my scruff stay for another day. I don't want to keep Galiva waiting any more than I already have. I open the door again just as Galiva pulls something from behind her back.

"Congratulations," she says as I take the black bundle. I unfold it to reveal a long robe, not unlike her own. "It's official. You've been accepted as an adept."

It's a light, airy fabric that's so soft it feels like water against my fingers. By far the finest cloth I've ever felt, let alone *owned*. I look at her in shock.

"Seriously? That's it?"

"You cast a spell, didn't you?" She pokes at the ring hanging from my neck with a smile. "You've proven you have everything you need to start studying at the Crux," she says. "You have magic in your bloodline, you're open to new experiences, and you're not an asshole."

I can't stop a small laugh at that, my face heating as I rub the back of my neck. She motions me to follow as she sets off down the hall. I pull on my robe and fall into step beside her.

"But being accepted is the easy part. Now you need to decide what you want to study."

My mind's already reeling with possibilities. It still hasn't quite set in. I can do *magic*.

"Everything."

"That's quite a declaration," she laughs. "Maybe start with one before you try to tackle all eight." She leads me to the nearly empty mess hall. A large table has been laid with an assortment of food but it's pretty picked over. A few people have even started clearing away what remains, but Galiva pushes me forward to grab a plate before they finish.

I quickly grab my fill with an apologetic grin to one of the cooks. A couple sausages, some cold scrambled eggs and a few pieces of bread and cheese. There's even tea, fresh brewed and sitting in steaming decanters. Fucking hell, I could definitely get used to this.

I pour a mugful before going to join Galiva at one of the long empty tables. I assume she's already eaten because she's only grabbed a dark cup of something that somehow smells bitter and sweet at the same time. She sips at it and allows me to eat in peace, which I try not to do too enthusiastically. Just going off of how she holds herself, Galiva's not from a nowhere place like Airedale. I don't want to be rude, but I'm so hungry that I can only eat so slow.

"How did you decide what you wanted to study?" I ask. The more I think about it, the wonder is starting to turn to dread. Gods know I didn't travel for four weeks just to suck at this. I want to learn, but there's so much I don't know. I'm hard-pressed to figure out where to begin.

"Originally tried for divination but I changed my plans. I went through a couple before I settled on the one I wanted to master first," she says as she sets her mug down on the table. "I've been pretty pragmatic about it. I thought about all of the times I've felt helpless, and sought out the magic that would have given me recourse."

"What schools did you settle on?" I ask and take a bite of egg.

Galiva tugs at the sleeve of her robe. It has three stripes of color around the cuff - gray, orange, and red. She points to the gray first. "Abjuration," she says. "Which you've already had a taste of. It's a versatile school, and a good foundation to build off of. Spells can be cast to protect, ward, or deflect various effects and ills."

She points to the orange next. "Evocation," she says. "The manipulation of energy for a specific purpose. Predominantly offensive spells. If you want to be a battle-caster, you'd consider this school." She points to the red next, and hesitates just a second before saying, "Corpimancy. Magical healers study it."

Galiva must see the thinly-veiled panic on my face because she reaches across the table and puts a hand over mine. "Relax," she says. "You don't need to make a decision *today*. Until you narrow down what you want to focus on, you'll act as a conduit," she says.

The blank look I give her makes her chuckle. "It's the role you played in the spell we cast. Minus some conjuration spells, you usually need at least two people to cast anything. I was the one weaving the spell - the caster - while you were acting as the conduit to channel it into the focus," she says and points at the white ring on my necklace.

I roll the focus between my fingers, making the light inside of it dance. Galiva reaches into her shirt and pulls out her own necklace for me to examine. It's got three strands on it. The bottom two are packed full while the shortest strand only has a handful of glowing beads on it.

"How the hell do you keep track of them all?" I ask.

Galiva leans her cheek against her hand, a fond smile on her face. "You can feel it," she says. She trails her fingers over the marbles on the short row and lifts up one that has a sheen of red. "A healing spell - strong enough to mend broken bones." She picks up another from the second row that flickers pink. "A practical barrier spell, so I don't need to worry about bearing your child after yesterday."

Heat rushes up my neck as I clear my throat. I'm a little embarrassed to say I hadn't even thought of that.

"That reminds me," she says. She pulls one marble from the second string and hands it to me. "A protection for you. We've all been checked, and I made sure to check you before we started yesterday, but here's an extra assurance. It will ward you from transmissible diseases you might encounter during your studies."

An awful polite way of saying I won't need to worry about the drip or syphilis, but I'm grateful for it all the same. "Thanks," I say, and string the marble onto my own necklace. The unique energy it gives off is very different from the spell we cast yesterday. Warm and clean to the cold, hard barrier of my first spell.

The cooks have almost finished clearing away breakfast when someone else comes into the mess hall. A tall woman dressed in the usual black robes. She's willow-limbed with porcelain skin, her face barely peeking out from the messy black hair that hangs to her shoulders. But the most startling feature are the horns that rise from the tangle. They're shined black and sprouting just over her temples to curl under her curiously pointed ears.

I blink in surprise. An ovisari. They're solitary folks, favoring only the highest, rockiest peaks of the Hobokins. I only ever saw one come through Airedale and I'm a little shocked to see one this far away from the hills. She looks tired as she shuffles over to a decanter to pour some of the same black liquid that Galiva's enjoying. When she turns, her face surges up from my half-remembered dream.

I lean across the table and point to the woman. "Who is she?" I ask.

"Hmm?" Galiva follows my eyes before turning back to her drink. "Oh, that's Margeurite."

The woman looks up as if she's heard us, and with how those ears flick around like a cat's, maybe she did. She makes for us, her eyes wide with alarm. I open my mouth to say something, anything, but she beats me to it as she slips into the seat beside me.

"I must apologize," she says. Her voice holds a heavy accent, and she forms each word carefully. "I did not mean to intrude on your sleep. I hadn't realized I had wandered into someone else's dream."

I realize I'm staring. She's stunningly beautiful. Her face is angular, sharp and not quite human. Dark brown eyes watch me, and it takes me a moment to notice the pupils. Horizontal like a goat's. On her right horn, she has two gold rings wrapped near the point that curls under her ear. A delicate gold chain threads between them.

"No offense taken," I say, a little belated. "You just surprised me, is all."

Galiva takes another drink from her mug. "Dream walking again?"

The horned woman gives a small, slightly sad smile. "Always searching," she says. "But for some reason, your dream drew me in. It's Dominai, isn't it?"

I nod and her curious eyes search me before she settles on the colorless sleeves of my robes. I can't help but notice that hers have stripes of blue and purple. "Have you considered studying divination?" she asks.

"I'm not sure yet," I say. I don't know what divination entails, but if it's with *her,* I'm certainly willing to try it. "Maybe you can give me a demonstration?"

Margeurite's smile turns sly. "Tomorrow morning then. Second bell," she says. "I'll be in the divination tower. Fourth floor, third door on the right."

I commit it to memory and try not to grin like an idiot when I say, "I'll be there."

Margeurite's smile grows. "See you then." She gets to her feet, taking her cup with her. Galiva waits until she's out of the room before she raises an eyebrow at me.

"Subtle as a brick," she says with a grin. "Have fun, but just... be careful with divination."

"What's wrong with divination?" I ask, still watching the door Margeurite left through.

"Nothing," Galiva says. "It's just not everyone's type of magic."

I watch the door Margeurite went through like I can still see the outline of her. "It might be my type of magic."

Galiva's laugh snaps me out of it. "Though you're having no trouble finding casting partners, I have someone I want you to meet."

ONCE I'M DONE WITH breakfast, Galiva leads me to the evocation tower. It is a sturdy building, made of red stone that shines like moving mica. We walk up to the second floor before she leads me to a particular wooden door and knocks.

A moment later, a man opens the door with a smile as he leans against his door frame. It takes me a second to realize it around the round spectacles he's gained, but I recognize him. It's the same man I talked to in the baths yesterday. Fully clothed with his hair pulled back, he looks like a different person. Gods but he is handsome. I can't help but imagine this version of him naked, too.

He moves a little gingerly, but he's far more lucid today. His hazel eyes are clear and focused as they look at Galiva over the tops of his glasses. "I'm afraid I can't help you with whatever harebrained spell you want to cast today," he says. "I'm still sore from a bout with Adan."

Resting on the door frame, I see that the sleeve of his robe only has two colors; gray and orange. Abjuration and evocation.

"That's why I brought you a present," Galiva says. "Meet Dominai. Dom, this is Olbric."

A present? I give Galiva a sharp look, but Olbric's face lights up.

"Good! It's good to meet you - officially, that is," he says brightly and offers me a hand. "I apologize if I was rude yesterday. I was a little...floaty."

I'm not sure what that means, but I take his hand and shake it. "No problem." As tempting as evocation sounds, I saw what Olbric's back looked like. I'm not sure if that brand of magic is a good choice for me. I'm not keen on pain.

Galiva has other ideas. "If he's amenable, I thought you could give Dom an introduction to evocation. He was a great conduit for our protection spell yesterday. I'm helping him branch out."

Olbric looks all too pleased by that. "It would be my pleasure," he says. "There's a lower caliber spell I've been needing to re-cast."

"Lower caliber," I repeat. "So my back won't look like I've spent a day at a whipping post?"

The second it leaves my mouth I'm afraid I've said something offensive, but Olbric laughs. "Not to say you won't have a few bruises and welts, but I'm not going to put you through anything like what Adan cast with me." His grin is mischievous as he says, "I'll be as gentle as evocation allows."

Both of them look to me for my answer. I shift from one foot to the other. I'm not sure about this. I don't understand why one would willingly seek out pain - even if it is for magic. Even so, my curiosity gets the better of me. Maybe there's more to it than that? Once again, I'm struck by how much I still don't know.

"Alright," I sigh. "I'll try anything twice."

Olbric's smile widens. "Then follow me."

He leads the way further into the tower. We go up a few more flights of stairs before we emerge onto one of the top floors. I've never been in a building taller than a barn, and seeing the view of the courtyards through the arrow slit windows makes me whistle appreciatively. This floor is another row of rooms, similar to the one Galiva took me to the day before. Casting rooms, I realize. Safe, private places for spells to be worked.

Inside, this one has a lower ceiling that is decorated with various metal chains and rings. They hang from strong wooden cross beams that are set into the mortar. Unlike the one Galiva took me to, this has a couple of comfortable-looking chairs sitting by a cold fireplace.

In the corner's a familiar sight. Another large cabinet that makes my guts twist uneasily as I imagine what sort of... things are inside.

Olbric comes over and helps me out of my robe while Galiva takes a seat in the corner. "You're," my voice starts a notch higher than I mean it to. I clear my throat and try again, "You're not going to help?"

Galiva twists one of the spells on her necklace between her fingers. She falls gracefully into one of the chairs, one leg hooked over the arm. Even fully clothed, I feel my face heat as I stare. "I'll watch this time," she says with a wink, and my face gets even hotter. "Olbric is a good teacher."

Olbric sets my robe on the chair next to her before he claps his hands together. He throws open the cabinet doors. "Now, since you worked an abjuration spell yesterday, some of this won't be new to you. Abjuration and evocation often go together."

I try to rub the blush from my face. "Why's that?"

Olbric makes a careful selection before he pulls out a coil of rope. "Unless you're setting a spell to be remotely activated, you actually need some manner of barrier or protection built in to safely cast the spell yourself. Imagine trying to pick up fire to throw it. You could do it, but you'd get your hand burned without some protection. The interplay of abjuration and evocation is much the same," he says. "You're comfortable being tied?"

"Makes it so I can't run away, right?" I say, but the joke falls flat.

Olbric puts a hand on my shoulder. "We don't *have* to do this. As a conduit, it's important that you enforce your own limits."

I sigh and run a hand through my hair. "I don't even know what those limits *are* yet," I mutter, feeling like a rank novice.

Olbric's smile is full of understanding. "That's alright. It's what - day two for you?" he asks. "You're learning. But know that if at any time, for whatever reason - you say stop, I *will* stop." He slaps the coiled rope lightly against my shoulder. "I only like to hurt the willing."

I chuckle and rub my hand over my face. "Alright."

"Good," he says with a white-toothed grin. "Shirt off, please."

I flush. Of course that's a requirement. No one at the Crux seems ashamed of their nudity, so I push my own uncertainty aside as I pull my shirt off and toss it onto my robe. At least he doesn't make me take the rest off. Yet.

Olbric takes my wrists and guides them together in front of me. Carefully, he weaves the rope around them, though I notice he doesn't pull them as tightly as Galiva had. The knots aren't as intricate either, but they're deliberate enough that I know they must be significant. Then, he tosses the end of the rope through a larger ring that hangs from the ceiling. He pulls until my arms are cinched up over my head.

"Is that alright?"

My bad arm twinges, but it's no worse than yesterday. "Fine," I say.

I'm playing it cool, but the truth is, my heart's already thudding. A mix of nerves and anticipation. Olbric ties the rope off on a little ring that's drilled into the ground. He gives it a strum with his fingers before he deems it acceptable.

"Now," Olbric asks, "Have you ever been with a man before?"

I clear my throat and realize he might have asked *before* he tied me up. "No," I say. Not unless you count that one time with the herdsman's boy when we were lads, but I have a feeling he's talking about more than just innocent fondling.

Olbric's eyes widen as he looks over at Galiva. "You brought me a virgin?"

Galiva snorts and I hear her quiet little, "Definitely *not* a virgin," but Olbric doesn't seem to be listening. He grins from ear to ear as he grips my chin and tilts my gaze up to meet his eyes.

"Do you have an objection to it?" he asks. His hazel eyes are intense with excitement, but there's a kindness in them as well. I shiver and I'm not exactly sure why. Godsdamn *wizards*.

"I - no," I say, but he must sense my uncertainty.

"What did I just say about stopping?" he asks.

"I know, I know," I say and flex my hands under the ropes. "I'm alright with it - really. I've just... never done it before."

"I promise I will take good care of you," Olbric says. "I've worked with adepts and masters alike, and I'm told I'm very attentive. But I'll warn you - evocation can have a way of making you... lose yourself. I will check in with you regularly, and I will ask twice to be certain that you're certain."

"Right," I say, though my guts are still a knot of nerves, and maybe a little bit of excitement? It's hard to figure out where one stops and the other begins.

Olbric smiles and strokes his thumb across the scruff on my jaw before coming around behind me. His hands are warm, his grip strong on my hips.

"Relax," he murmurs into my ear. "I will walk you through everything I do as I do it. I'll try and explain what is happening and what you're feeling, but there's always a level of variability. At worst, the spell will fail and nothing will happen. Some folks just aren't tuned for evocation, and that's fine."

I draw in a breath and let it out slow, trying to calm my racing heart down. "Right. Okay."

Olbric's breath brushes against my neck as he reaches around for the buttons of my trousers. He undoes them one by one before pulling them down and off, taking my boots and socks with them. My undergarments go next, and gooseflesh prickles over my skin in the cool room.

But then his warm hands are back, stroking over my ass and back before sliding around to my stomach. My cock twitches in response, and it's not long before his hand slides there too. His grip is firm and he gets right to business, stroking me to attention. I groan as I sink into the ropes.

"Evocation isn't just pain, though it can be an essential element," Olbric says. "What you take in pain, your spell will give in force. The more pain you are able to endure, the more forceful the spell will be." All the while his hand continues to stroke my length, fingers expertly teasing a little liquid from the tip of my cock. He gives the head a little pinch, and I bite back a moan.

"But to be able to endure the pain, it has to be tempered with something else," he says. His hand is gone for only a second before he slides a stone focus around my cock, and then another. "The juxtaposition of pain and pleasure is what gives you *power*. Generate enough power, and you can get multiple castings of a spell at a time. So," Olbric says, his lips brushing the shell of my ear, "I wonder how many I can get out of you?"

I shiver as he slips two more focuses down the length of my erection. I'd swear they're smaller than the one Galiva used. They seem to constrict, keeping me hard even as he withdraws. Olbric rummages through the cabinet before he returns with a leather flogger under one arm, a bottle, and a glass bulb.

I almost wish I was blindfolded. Yesterday, everything had come as a surprise. Today, the anticipation is near unbearable as I wait to see what he'll do. I twist in my ropes, shifting a little to try and keep my eye on him as he circles slowly around me.

My suspicion is well-warranted. As soon as I lose sight of him, his hand cracks against my ass in a stinging slap. I jump away, but the ropes stop me from going far.

Olbric chuckles. "I do like a dancer," he says. His hand lands against my ass in two more stinging slaps - one right after the other. They don't get any lighter, and I yelp. "And a singer!" he crows. I hear

Galiva chuckle and can't stop a begrudging grin. Olbric sounds all too pleased, and hearing him laugh helps me relax a little.

Then his hand is a vice on my hips, holding me still. He holds out the glass bulb in front of me so I can get a good look at it. It's different from the one that Galiva took out of me yesterday. Wider, for one thing, and shaped like a teardrop. I swallow when I notice a glowing focus sealed in the center.

"See this?" he asks. "I had this made special. And I'm going to put it inside of you."

I'd figured, but hearing him say it makes my cock throb. The size of it is daunting. I'm so distracted by it that Olbric's wet fingers surprise me when they slide down my ass. I jump, but his hand grips my thigh to hold me still before he resumes. One finger slips in and then a second. His digits spread and stretch me out, gentle and thorough. It sends chills of pleasure down my spine, and I can't stop a moan as I relax around the intrusion.

I rest my head against my arms as I savor the slow thrust of his fingers. He seems to enjoy the gentle attentions, his teeth scraping my shoulders and neck as he toys with me. The slow thrust and twist of his skillful fingers leave me panting and squirming.

"Are you alright?" Olbric asks. I nod, but his hand cracks against my ass, hard. The sudden shock of pain jolts me back into myself. I jerk away, but his fingers hook inside of me, his other hand grabbing my hip hard enough to bruise. "I need a verbal answer."

"Yes!" I shout as he spanks me again, another stinging slap that fades to a prickling heat.

"Good."

Then his fingers are working again, plunging deep. He's no longer slow and exploring. It borders on painful as he finds the sweet spot inside of me and focuses on it with undivided attention. I groan and arch my back, not sure if I'm trying to pull away or push towards him.

I feel the fabric of his trousers and his firm erection underneath rub against my skin. His hand tightens on my hips to anchor me in place before he spears a third finger into me. I grunt as I'm stretched further, but the discomfort is quickly eclipsed by pleasure. He's done a right job of getting me worked up, and he hasn't scared me enough to make me stop yet.

Energy crackles along the focuses and down the length of my cock without warning. I shout in surprise and arch back against him. "The fuck?"

Olbric smiles. "Ah, you're starting to charge the focuses," he says. "Feels different when there's more than one, doesn't it?"

If by 'different' he means it feels like a static shock directly to my cock, then yes. But I don't have time to think on it for long as he delivers one, two, three slaps to my ass in quick succession, hitting my right cheek on the same spot every time. Then his fingers pull free of me, and I moan at the loss. I stand there, shivering, waiting.

"Don't worry, I won't let you stay empty," he says, and I feel the glass bulb slide down my crack. It's cold against my slick hole, but he doesn't give me long to warm it up before he's pressing it into me. I groan as it stretches me to the very edge of pain. But then, it settles inside of me, filling me up. The tapered end flares out so it can't go *too* deep, but the sheer girth of it makes me doubt I could push it out if I tried.

"Now, be sure to keep that in," he says. "It's one of my favorites, and I would hate for it to break."

I feel the plug shift as Olbric touches the flared base. A tremor travels into the bulb and suddenly the thing is *moving*. It feels like the bulb has dissolved into so many glass balls, all of which are rolling around inside of me.

The sensation is near overwhelming. I cry out and grab the ropes for support. A drop of sweat falls from my nose as the thing wrings a shuddering moan from me.

Then Olbric is in front of me, cupping my face so I have to look up at him. "Are you alright?" he asks, his thumb brushing my lower lip. I blink the fog from my vision, my tongue thick. "Dominai, I need your answer."

The bulb continues to twist, and I arch as the focuses crackle again. I can't tell if it hurts or feels amazing. Is there a difference anymore? "I'm alright," I gasp. *"Fuck,* I'm fine."

Olbric smiles and he grips my hair roughly, yanking my head back before kissing me hard. I meet him, mouth open, wail half out that he swallows like candy.

"Good," he says. "Because now we actually begin."

"WHAT?"

Olbric chuckles and circles behind me. "The second you say stop, I will," he promises. There's a breathless moment, a second of anticipation. Then the flogger connects with my back.

The first strike stings like a hundred little needles before fading to a dull throb. I grunt and arch away. Reflexively I try to escape the next strike, moving as far as the ropes will let me, but the bulb chooses that moment to change direction even as it ups the intensity. Olbric brings the flogger down, and the fight goes out of me, my cry quickly fading to a moan. I cling to the ropes like a lifeline, waiting and tense for the next one.

My blurred eyes land on Galiva, sitting quietly in her chair. She bites her bottom lip, her fingers twirling one of the focuses on her necklace. I meet her eyes just as the third strike cracks against my ass. The focuses around my cock spark in response, wringing another cry out of me. Another strike falls in the same place, making the already stinging points throb. But Olbric doesn't focus on one spot for long, and his pace speeds up when I don't call stop.

The next one snaps against my thigh and stings in an entirely different way. I yelp and lift my foot to try and soothe the spot, but it makes the bulb shift inside of me. It wrings a very different type of shout from me and I stamp my foot back to the ground. Olbric chuckles before he strikes again.

As kind as he had seemed, Olbric is *relentless*. Strike after strike lands against my back, my ass, my thighs. Each strike stings, but I realize I've given up all thoughts of stopping. I stand braced to accept each lash. It never stops hurting, but the sensation of pain gets tangled up with everything else. The bulb inside of me never stops moving, sending wave after wave of sensation through me. The focuses around my cock spark at random and never fail to catch me by surprise. I grip the ropes that are now doing more to keep me upright than keep me contained.

Just as Olbric warned, I feel like I'm losing time. I'm adrift in the waves of sensation, pleasure and pain melding together until I'm not sure where one stops and the other begins. Soon I start to crave the crack of the flogger and the jolt it sends through the rest of me. With every strike, my skin burns a little hotter. My cock throbs, jutting up wanton and weeping, but Olbric had said that endurance was part of the game and he seems intent to test mine. He cracks the flogger down again and again until I cry out, but even then, he only moves on to abuse a different part of my backside.

A particularly harsh crack snaps me back into myself. I wail, not recognizing the layers of agony and bliss in my own voice.

"Olbric, please!" I shout, though I'm not sure what I'm begging for. I feel stripped bare, my desire exposed for him and Galiva to see. When the next strike never comes, I'm afraid he's going to leave me here like this. Wanting and desperate and unable to do a gods-damned thing about it.

The bulb inside of me stops moving, and I realize that Olbric's hand is on my hips again. Compared to my heated skin, his fingers feel cold as ice. He slips the bulb out of me, and I moan at the loss, fists clenching under my ropes. For a second, there's nothing but the ropes holding me up and the focuses constricting my aching cock. A broken sob of need escapes me.

But he's not done with me yet. The ropes suddenly tighten and I'm forced onto my toes. Olbric's hand snakes around my throat and pulls my head back against his shoulder.

"Are you alright, Dominai?" he asks, his lips by my ear. His voice is thick with desire.

"Yes." I'm beyond alright. I'm desperate, panting and shaking with need, but a vague part of me is glad he's not unaffected by this.

"Are you sure?"

The friction of his skin against my welted and abused backside is bliss. I push against him as well as I'm able to. "Gods yes!"

Then, I feel something warm and slick and hard against my hole. "Do you want this?"

I moan in anticipation. "Olbric, *please.*"

He must decide he's kept me waiting long enough. With one steady thrust, Olbric is inside of me, his sizable cock gliding deep into my well-prepared hole. I can't stop a shout at the sudden stretch, and Olbric buries himself to the hilt, his hips flush against my reddened ass. He hisses in pleasure, rolling his hips once, twice as if to savor the feeling.

It's a brief moment of reprieve before Olbric pulls out and spears me again, hard and deep. I choke on my cry as bliss races through me. Even though it's my first time with a man, Olbric is not gentle, and he's not slow. And I don't care. He's primed me for this and after the pain of the flogger and the stretch of the bulb, his sizable cock is ecstasy.

He thrusts into me over and over, his pace relentless. With every snap of his hips, he drags over that sweet spot inside of me. I hang in my ropes and surrender to him, though I can't imagine wanting this to stop.

His hand slides around my throat and constricts, stern, but controlled. My breath gets short, and a flash of fear snaps through my haze. I choke against his grip as spots start to dance behind my eyes. My blood throbs in my ears, in every welt on my ass and back. But I'm close, I'm so, *so* close.

And when Olbric removes his hand from my throat, I draw in a desperate breath only to scream when he grabs my bruised ass *hard*. Inside of me, his cock swells, and I feel him tense as a low, guttural moan escapes him. His cock pulses and empties inside of me while the focuses around my own spark viciously.

His hand grabs my length, and I'm done for. I howl as the sensations rip my orgasm out of me. The focuses throb in time with the fiery waves of pleasure that course from me. It seems to go on forever, and when it finally abates I'm left boneless and panting, my vision a little fuzzy. My wrists are chafed under the ropes, and I have a hard time getting my shaking legs back under me. Olbric pulls out, and I can't stop a whimper at the soreness of my abused hole.

But then his arms are around me. The ropes go slack, and he's there to steady me. He lowers us both to the ground, and I groan as I lean back against his chest. His fingers gently stroke my sweaty hair away from my face before he reaches for the focuses. I moan as he pulls them off, my cock giving one last feeble dribble.

Galiva pulls a blanket over both of us. Olbric makes sure it's tucked tight before he wraps his arms around me again.

"Congratulations, Dominai," he says and holds the four glowing focuses out for me to see. "You managed to charge all of them. Might have been able to get a fifth if I had thought to put it on."

I give a small, breathless laugh as I start to settle back into my body. My ass hurts where it rests against the cold stone, my back pulsing fiery heat in time with my heartbeat. I should have assumed I'd be sore, but the reality of how much punishment I had been able to take startles me.

"We'll have to try and break that record next time," I say and lean my head back against Olbric's shoulder.

The man cups my face and tilts my head back to look at him. "There will be a next time, then?" he asks as his thumb strokes my cheek. "I was afraid I may have pushed you a little too far for your first time."

I open my mouth to a few false starts before I finally say, "I have never felt *anything* like that. And I'll be damned if I never feel it again."

Olbric laughs, and he looks pleased as his fingers gently stroke through my hair. "I'm so very glad," he says. We fall quiet for a moment, and Olbric seems content to act as a human chair while I get the rest of my senses back. Slowly I extract myself, and Olbric helps me to my feet.

"Is there anything you need?" he asks. "There can sometimes be a sort of... emotional drop after a spell like that."

I pull the blanket a little more firmly around my shoulders. I feel a little lightheaded, but not dizzy. 'Floaty' suddenly becomes the perfect description. "I think I'm alright," I say. "Though I might take one of those ice baths tonight." Olbric chuckles and he gathers my clothes before offering them to me. "And you have four castings of that spell?"

"Yes," Olbric says. "Quite a feat for a first-time adept."

"I want to see what it does."

Olbric looks at me in surprise before he smiles. "Get dressed and I'll show you."

OLBRIC LEADS ME AND Galiva to the courtyard of the abjuration tower. It's a pretty barren stretch. Mostly dirt and scorched grass, with a single sad-looking tree. On the far end, there's a heavy gate and a small bridge over the moat that leads to the forest, where I can see more signs of destruction.

I'm moving a little gingerly. The brush of my trousers against the welts on my ass are a constant reminder of what we've done, but even now the pain is starting to fade. I'm almost a little sorry for it.

Olbric hands me one of the focuses before giving the remaining three to Galiva. "This can be a great defensive spell," he says. "So, if you are ever threatened, it will force back an aggressor. It won't kill them, but it will buy you time to get away."

I worry the focus between my fingers and realize that I have no idea how to release a spell. But then Olbric shoves my shoulders hard, and I nearly topple over in surprise. The focus in my hand reacts instantly. Energy swells and there is a loud *whoomp* as the spell is released. It happens so quick that I barely see it. One second, Olbric is there, and the next he is tossed back, flying about ten feet before he skids to a stop in the dirt.

"Oy!" I shout and rush towards him, dropping the spent focus. Olbric is flat on his back, and he manages a cough before he's able to get his breath back. Then, he starts to laugh.

"You know," he coughs. "I thought adding a breath-play aspect this time might knock the wind out of someone. I didn't realize how effective it would be."

I give a small laugh and offer him a hand up. He takes it, and I remember the feel of that strong hand slowly choking the air out of me. He doesn't appear hurt, but he must have been braced for it. "Pretty damn effective all around," I mutter and pull him to his feet.

"Definitely more force than I expected," Olbric says. "But I suppose I didn't exactly go easy on you. And *that's* why we test abjuration spells before we use them." Olbric walks us back over to Galiva, who looks like she's doing her best not to laugh. He takes one of the three remaining castings from her hand and strings it onto my necklace. "So, use this one with caution. As you saw, you just have to hold it and have a need for it. The focus will do the rest."

I look at the innocent little ring as I nod. Even though it was fun making it, using it could have very real consequences. A spell like that used against the wrong person or for the wrong reason could open up a whole box of trouble. And Olbric had mentioned that this was a *lower* caliber evocation spell.

As we head back inside, I can't help but think that it's no wonder the King is wary of magic. Any sane person should be.

Diving Into Divination

D*ivination: The school of magic that can discern the truths of the past, present, or future. Casting methods include full sensory deprivation, body worship, and edging.*

ONCE WE'RE FINISHED in the yard, Olbric makes sure I'm well taken care of. He brings me down to the baths where he tends to the welts he left. After having me soak in the ice bath until I can't stand it anymore, he makes me sit on the lip of one of the steaming pools before slathering the most stubborn of the welts with healing salve.

His fingers are gentle, but as he brushes a particularly sensitive one I shiver and arch away from him.

"Sorry," he murmurs. "I went a little harder on you than I should have."

I can't help but tease him a little. "So you don't normally beat the sense out of newbies?"

"With adepts, I'm usually far nicer," Olbric chuckles. "You were such a fun conduit to play with that I got a little lost in the spell myself."

My face flushes hot as I let out a small laugh. It quickly turns to a gasp as he rubs salve into the sore spot. Whatever he's using is cool, and as he massages it in, the sting of the welt diminishes, leaving nothing but a gentle tingling behind. I groan and lean forward to rest my head against my knees.

A comfortable silence passes before I murmur, "Thank you."

"It's the least I can do after putting you through it," he says and gives my shoulders a gentle squeeze. "Aftercare is important. Making sure you feel safe and taken care of can help stave off that emotional drop I mentioned."

"Well, you're doing a fine job of it so far," I groan. With his hands gently rubbing my back, I'm halfway to dozing. "But I wanted to thank you for just... walking me through it." I almost let my nerves talk me out of doing something I ended up really enjoying.

"Seduced you into it is more like it, right?" he says, and I can't help but chuckle.

"Maybe a little of that, too." I glance back. Olbric catches my eye and winks. It sends my insides fluttering, and I look away as he gives my back one last go-over. I'm a little sorry when he stops.

He sighs and slips into the steaming pool beside me. I want to join him, but don't want to wash off the salve, so I just dip my legs in. It's hard not to watch him as he gets settled. His hair is down, and he dunks his head back to wet it, slicking the black locks away from his pretty face. Gods, but he's nice to look at. Then he turns his eyes onto me, and heat floods my cheeks as I look away.

"How are you feeling?" he asks. His hazel eyes watch me so intently that I have to fight the urge to cover myself. A silly thing to do - it's not like we haven't seen each other naked. And gods know that no one else in the towers seems self-conscious about their nudity.

"Good," I say. "Feels like I'm floating on air."

Olbric grins and says. "Sounds like I gave you a taste of conspace. I'm glad - that feeling is part of what I love about evocation."

"Conspace?" I ask.

"It stands for 'conduit space,'" he says. "And it's a pretty common experience when working spells that deal heavily with pain."

I settle comfortably against the lip of the pool, pulling one leg up to rest my cheek against my knee. "Yeah? Why's that?"

"Pain does strange things to the mind," Olbric says, his face lighting up a little as he explains. It's obvious that he enjoys this - not just doing it, but the theory behind it as well. "Everything we're doing with evocation makes your body scream 'danger, danger! Knock it off!' but your mind, ever the responsible one, starts sending out this heady, euphoric feeling to try and get you through that pain. It can happen with intense exercise, too - which, let's be real, that's just a different type of torture."

I chuckle at that. "Never thought of it like that, but I guess you're right. I did some hikes in the Hobokins that left me feeling a little like this."

"Ah, so you really are a masochist if you go climbing up mountainsides for fun," he says.

That startles a laugh out of me. "Maybe I am," I say. "So what does that make you?"

Olbric leans back against the lip of the pool with a grin, his black hair falling over his shoulders. "I consider myself an... evocation enthusiast," he says. "I enjoy casting it, but I will fully admit that I am a sucker for pain."

"Does that mean I get to be the one with the crop next time?"

The man chuckles and glides through the water towards me. He rests his chin on the lip of the pool as he looks up at me. "Not a chance, adept," he purrs. "But give it a few more months, and then we'll talk."

I flush at the heat in his voice and rub the back of my neck. I'd been joking, but the idea of him on his knees at my mercy makes my cock twitch. I force the thought away. Gods, this place is starting to get to me.

"How long have you been here?" I ask, quickly changing the subject.

Olbric folds his arms and rests his head against them, floating on his front. I try my best not to stare at the swell of his ass, but it's a losing battle. "I came to the Eastern Tower just before I turned 19, so about five years ago now," he says. "I transferred to the Crux about a year later."

I whistle at that. "Long time."

Olbric shrugs. "Doesn't feel like it. There's... a lot to love about this place. It makes it easy to stick around."

His eyes slide closed, an idle smile on his face. I can't help but stare at him. The folks at the Crux are an attractive lot, but there's something about Olbric that I have a hard time looking away from. His russet skin shines in the gentle light of the baths, his black hair floating in a cloud behind him.

He must feel me staring, because he opens his eyes and grins up at me.

"Still feeling alright?" he asks.

Heat rushes to my face, but I can't seem to look away from him. "Doing great."

"You sure? That drop can kind of sneak up on you. Is there anything you need?"

His concern makes me smile. "I'm alright, I promise," I say even as a yawn catches up to me. "Feels like I'll sleep like the dead though."

Olbric chuckles. "Well, if at any point you start to feel off - middle of the night or no - come find me. It doesn't always hit immediately, and you may never even experience it, but I like to be certain. It's a mindfuck of a thing to let someone hurt you on purpose."

We take our time as we extract ourselves from the bath. Olbric checks my welts again before slathering a little more salve on. It makes me feel pampered all over again, and I can't help but admit that I like how it feels when he touches me.

"Everyone's aftercare routine is a little different, but I like gentle touches after having my ass beat to a blush," he says as he finishes rubbing the salve in. "So remember that for the future."

He gets to his feet and drapes a towel around my shoulders. I huff a laugh as I pull it close. "Yes, sir."

Olbric grins as he wraps a towel around his own waist. "Oh, now that I could get used to."

I chuckle and follow him away from the pools. I'm so relaxed that getting dressed feels like a chore. I pull my trousers on and don my shirt, barely even feeling it when the fabric brushes the welts. Olbric hands me my robe as we make our way out of the baths. We reach the top landing just as the dinner bell rings.

We walk together in a comfortable silence until we reach the main atrium. Olbric rubs the back of his neck. "See you around, yeah? If you're sure I didn't scare you off of evocation, I'd love to cast with you again."

I grin at that. If he was trying to scare me off, he's done a pretty poor job of it. Wizards are a pretty open bunch, so before I can convince myself not to, I press a quick kiss to his cheek. He rewards me with a dashing smile.

"Absolutely."

While Olbric heads towards the illusion tower, I head for the mess hall, my stomach growling. Whatever the cooks have made smells amazing. My mouth waters as I grab a bowl of stew over rice and a fresh slice of bread before I find Galiva in the slowly filling mess hall. I find a seat across from her, and she smiles as I sink into it with a groan.

"You're practically glowing," she says. "Seemed like you had fun today."

I finish swallowing the bite of warm bread before I say, "If this is what studying magic is, I'm an idiot for not coming here the second Allisande gave me that letter."

"There's a little more to it than that," she chuckles. She reaches into her bag and pulls out a small stack of books that she pushes across the table to me. "But here's a couple of things to help get you started."

Once I've eaten my fill, I take the books back to my room, eager to see what they're about. One is a history and introduction to magic that is so dense and wordy that I start to doze halfway through the first chapter. I switch to the second book, which proves to be far more interesting.

It's a book on abjuration and knot magic. I still don't know which schools I'll focus on, but something about the beautiful intricacies of the knots draw me in. I'm so engrossed with it that I lose track of time. When the midnight bell rings, I'm half asleep with it on my chest. I manage to mark my page before I set it on the desk, blow my lantern out, and am asleep the second my head hits the pillow.

I SLEEP SOUNDLY, BUT at one point, I reach that strange, half-waking place where I realize I'm dreaming again. In it, I'm in the baths of the Crux, lounging in one of the warm pools. Steam rises up around me, and bubbles float on the surface of the water before popping out and into the air. Soon, the room is filled with tiny rainbow spheres.

Then Margeurite walks through them, and they part like a curtain to allow her to pass. She's wearing a sheer dress that's more an idea than an actual garment. Her dark nipples show through the fabric along with the little tuft of black hair between her legs. She smiles as she slides into the pool with me, and the sleeves of her dress turn to frothy waves that crest in her wake. She straddles my lap, her fingers trailing gently over my chest.

The ovisari leans close, her curled horn just barely brushing my cheek before she whispers, "Aren't you forgetting something?"

The dream breaks around me as I jolt awake. Light is streaming in through my window. I've slept in. Again.

I'm late.

I swear and quickly clean my teeth before I grab my robe, trying to straighten my sleep-creased clothes as best as I can. I hurry through the halls and take a couple wrong turns before I manage to find the entry to the divination tower. I have to go outside into the main courtyard and veer to the left before the dark stone tower comes into view.

It's smaller than the abjuration and evocation towers, but it's far more beautiful. The stones are a deep purple, so dark they're almost black until the sun hits them. Veins of silver shimmer through the stone like frozen lightning. Instead of the normal crenelations or peaked roof, the top appears to be a glass observatory.

But I don't have time to gawk. I rush inside and up the narrow, winding stairs. Fourth floor, third door on the right, right? Gods, I hope that's right. There's no telling what could be behind the wrong door in a place like this.

Once I find what's hopefully the right door, I run my fingers through my disheveled hair and knock. I give a sigh of relief when Marguerite opens it.

"That was much quicker than I expected," she says with a smile. "I had a feeling you would kick yourself if you slept through our time."

My grin comes out lopsided. "You'd be right," I say. "Sorry - I'm not sure what it is about this place that makes me sleep like the dead."

The ovisari's face is thoughtful as she takes my hand and guides me into the room. "Magic is a trying undertaking. Most of us had an adjustment period when we first started practicing," she says. "And I heard that Olbric used you as a conduit. Evocation is an especially difficult school to jump in to."

"Truer words," I mutter. Though the welts have faded after the ice bath and the salve Olbric used, every step I take still sends little fizzles of sensation from my ass and thighs. "I'm hoping divination isn't as... physically exhausting."

Her laughter is clear as bells, and I can't help but smile. Unlike my dream, Margeurite is dressed in her robes, just as she had been the day before. I wonder if it was me or her who supplied the dress she wore in my dream. I don't ask.

"It is not," she promises. "But that does not mean it is not challenging. Just challenging in a different way."

I look around the casting room. There's nothing but two white pillars in the middle that stretch up to the ceiling. No cabinet, no rings or ropes - nothing.

"You've got me curious," I say.

Margeurite smiles. "Divination is different from evocation and abjuration in that you act as both the conduit, focus, and to an extent, the caster," she says. "There is no spell to take with you when we finish because your body and mind become the spell. It is a magic designed to read the truths of the past, present, and future. You use it to gain insight, discern truths from lies. Some even use it to spy."

"But not you, right?" I tease.

Marguerite's smile turns mischievous. "Not usually. Though sometimes, you cannot help what information you discover while divining. It is not an exact magic."

She leads me over to the two pillars and it's only then I see that they are made from the same shining white stone as the focuses on my necklace. Margeurite runs a hand over one, and the light inside sparks and glows in response to her touch. "This isn't the same as the ropes of abjuration. When you are divining, you are helpless in the purest sense. You will not be able to see, nor move. You cannot hear or speak. You will only have the sensation of touch to ground you."

I reach out to touch the pillar and feel a strange tingle in the tips of my fingers. It's not ticklish or painful. It almost reminds me of the gentle lap of water.

"How do you stop?" I ask.

Margeurite looks pleased by the question. "You have to trust your caster," she says. "Divination is not something you ever want to do alone. You would have no one to release you."

That makes me a little nervous. I don't know Margeurite, but the colors on her sleeve show that she's not green at doing this, and her serene smile is a comfort. I figure that there are far worse places to be than at her mercy.

Her curious eyes are perceptive. "Would you like to try? I will not keep you in for long unless you wish it."

I look at the pillars uncertainly. "What do I have to do?" I ask. I've never done anything but act as a conduit. The thought of casting a spell is as exciting as it is daunting.

Margeurite takes off her robe and folds it before setting it on the lone chair in the room. Underneath, she's wearing a dress not unlike what she had on in my dream, though far less see-through. Maybe I had supplied that part after all.

"You simply have to experience," she says. "If you are divining for more specific information, or dream walking, there is more you must focus on, but for your first time, you only need to open yourself up to the experience."

It sounds easy enough. But if I've learned one thing from the two spells I've helped make, it's that nothing with magic is easy. Though it sure ends up being a hell of a lot of fun. Besides, I won't learn anything without trying it first.

"Alright," I say at last. "I'm willing to give it a shot."

Margeurite smiles and leans up to kiss my cheek. "I will take good care of you, and I'm told I do well by those under my mercy," she says. "Disrobe, please, and stand between the pillars."

I lift my shirt, and feel her eyes on me. My trousers slip down, and I glance back to see her gaze lingering on my ass. She meets my eye with a knowing smile. "He certainly did not go easy on you, did he?"

I rub the back of my neck with a grin. "It wasn't so bad."

"Spoken like a true pain slut," Margeurite says, and that does get a blush out of me. "I've never been fond of physical torture myself." The way she emphasizes *physical* makes me wonder what other types there are. I can't help but admit that I'm excited to find out.

As I pile my clothes on one of the chairs, it strikes me just how quick I've fallen into the swing of things here. A week ago I would have been blushing hot red being naked in front of a woman like Margeurite, but now I strip without a second thought. The fact that everyone in the Crux seems to treat nudity as commonplace certainly helps.

Margeurite takes my hand and guides me between the pillars. She stands me so my legs are slightly apart, my hands resting comfortably at my sides. Even the innocent touch makes me shiver, gooseflesh raising over my arms.

"We will start slow," she says. "I will count five minutes - it won't be enough time for any real spell to be worked, but it will be enough to know if you can handle the restrictions. I will check on you then, and we can decide if you would like to proceed."

I nod, but Olbric's more or less beaten the necessity of giving a verbal response into me. "Right," I say. "I'm ready."

Margeurite's smile is mischievous as she rests a hand on the pillar. "We will see."

For a second, nothing happens. I just start to feel a little foolish when something cool washes over my toes. I look down to see a shimmer of something cover the tops of my feet. It looks like liquid silver, but it's warm and creates a slight pressure as it creeps up my ankles and shins like a living thing.

I shiver as it slides up my thighs before it rolls over my cock like a gentle caress. Margeurite had warned me I wouldn't be able to move, but I wasn't expecting the stuff to hold quite so strong. I can't budge from the waist down, and unease settles in as it moves up my stomach and chest, gaining speed. The silver spreads out and down my arms, and I can't so much as twitch a finger inside of the strange substance.

Margeurite's hand cups my cheek. "You are safe."

The stuff slides up my neck, and her hand moves away a second before the not-liquid rolls over the spot. When it gets to my mouth, it slides between my lips and teeth, pooling until it fills my mouth. It forces my jaws apart, and my grunt of alarm is lost as I'm quickly and efficiently gagged.

The silver creeps towards my nose, and panic flashes through me. For a second, I'm terrified I won't be able to breathe. But even though it tastes like water and holds like stone, I'm able to breathe through it as if nothing is there.

When it's just under my eyes, Margeurite's smile is the last thing I see before I snap them shut. I feel it slide over my eyelids and pool into my ears. There hadn't been much sound in the quiet room to begin with, but now even that is blocked out, plunging me into total silence. I feel it glide over my forehead and come together at the top of my head, encasing me fully. There's a moment of nothing. Then somehow, the floor drops away so I don't even have the sensation of the stone under my feet to ground me.

It almost feels like being submerged - that same sense of weightlessness. Except water doesn't hold like stone. I try to find any give in the silver, try to squirm even an inch, but it feels as if the stuff constricts tighter to keep me in place. I can't open my eyes, can't speak, can't hear. Fear races up my spine when the realization settles in that I am well and truly trapped.

I remember coming across a snake one time in the Hobokins. It had just found a nest of robin's eggs and swallowed them one by one.

I remember the way its body bulged around them and wonder if this is what it feels like to be devoured. My breathing speeds up as I imagine the snake constricting tighter and tighter around me, trying to squeeze the breath from my lungs.

Panic latches onto me. I cry out, but I can't tell if any sound makes it past the silver that gags my mouth. The thud of my own rapidly beating heart is loud in my ears.

Then, something touches me. Feather-light against my chest.

My panicked mind goes to fight or run, but I can't do either. I'm overwhelmed by my helplessness. Completely at the mercy of the gentle hand that strokes down my chest. I feel it as clearly as I had Galiva's during our first spell.

Then suddenly, the silver lifts from my eyes and mouth. I gasp like I'm surfacing water, my eyes shooting open wide. Margeurite is there, her serene face sympathetic. One of her hands is on my chest, while the other reaches out to stroke my face.

I'm just relieved to find that I'm not alone. A dark part of me had been afraid I'd been left there. She pulls the stuff out of one ear with her long fingers. It feels like my ears have popped, and I can suddenly hear again.

"Just breathe," she says, her voice calm and soothing. She draws in an exaggerated breath, and I mimic her. It hitches and shudders in and out at first, but Margeurite's steady hands on my cheek and chest help ground me. By degrees my breath gets a little steadier, my pulse edging back from panic. I'm no less trapped, but I'm far more calm by the time she stands on her toes and plants a gentle kiss against my lips.

"It's overwhelming, isn't it?" she asks.

I give a small, frayed laugh. "You could say that." I can't move my head, but I can glance down. I realize that I'm floating a few inches off of the ground, suspended by the sheet of silver that hangs between the two pillars.

"You don't realize how much you're attached to your senses until you can no longer access them," she says. "Yet did you notice how your sense of touch was amplified?"

"You scared the shit out of me," I admit, and Margeurite chuckles.

"Apologies," she says with a smile. "It is difficult not to surprise someone who can't hear or see you."

I let out another breath, feeling a little foolish. "Sorry," I mutter, but Margeurite's thumb brushes over my lips.

"What you experienced is actually a rather common response," she says gently. "Ask Olbric to tell you about when he decided divination was a poor fit for him." I can't stop a small laugh at the thought of it, though it does make me feel a little better to know I'm not alone. "But now that you know what to expect, would you like to continue?"

I swear quietly, not sure what I want. Part of me is afraid I'll start to panic again the second my eyes and ears are blocked, but then I remember what Olbric had said about endurance giving a spell force. It must be a similar idea here, except the endurance is a lack of sensation instead of an overload of it.

"Will you keep a hand on me?" I ask at last. "I was afraid I was alone."

Margeurite's smile is gentle. "I will not leave you," she promises. "I will count fifteen minutes, this time."

I let out a breath. Five had felt like a lifetime, and fifteen sounds like an impossibility, but I'm nothing if not determined. "Right," I say. I draw in a breath, like I'm readying for a plunge into an icy lake. "I'm ready."

"Just breathe," Marguerite says before she drags her fingers over my eyelids to close them. The silver of the pillars slides back into my ears and over my eyes. Just like before it pools into my mouth, forcing it open once more. I breathe deep and settle into the lack of sensation.

Just as she promised, Marguerite's hands stay on me, grounding me in the silent nothing. Her fingers are a warm comfort as they trace gentle circles over my chest. They trail a line over my arm as she circles behind me. I imagine her smiling at my still-red ass before she starts to gently massage my shoulders.

It feels so good that I would groan if I was able to. My shoulders are still a little sore from yesterday, and my bum arm hasn't been happy since Galiva tied it up, but Margeurite's gentle focus helps some of the knotted muscles relax. She is slow and thorough, her hands careful but firm. I wonder if she can feel me relax inside of the silver, because she doesn't move on until I'm limp under her touch

Her touch travels to my legs, skipping over my welted back and ass. Her fingers feel just as good on my thighs as she massages the muscles that are still tight from my weeks of travel. Her hands glide down to my feet and ankles, and I realize I've never had anyone really touch me there. It tickles a little bit, but her fingers are firm and slow as they massage my feet and toes. It feels amazing, and soon even the little thrills of ticklishness fade as she relaxes all the little muscles and bones I hadn't even realized hurt.

By the time she's finished, I'm limp in the silver, my heartbeat slow and steady. It's almost meditative and, unlike every other spell I've worked, it doesn't seem inherently sexual. But then, she takes my legs and spreads them apart.

I gasp into my gag at the sudden change. I hadn't realized that was possible, but the silver that holds me still doesn't give Margeurite the same resistance. In fact, she seems to be able to pose me whatever way she pleases.

She spreads my legs wide, but not wide enough that it's uncomfortable. I still can't so much as budge, let alone close them. It makes me feel dangerously exposed. Unease starts to creep back in at my own helplessness, but I take a few deep steadying breaths to stamp the feeling back down.

Margeurite's fingers trail up to my arms next, and I can't stop a groan as she lifts them from my side and places them over my head. I hadn't thought I could feel any more exposed, but she's proved me wrong. Galiva had shown me what it was like to be tied up at the mercy of someone, but this is a new level of helplessness that scares me as much as it heats me up.

My cock starts to throb even though it can't so much as twitch. As if she can read my mind, Margeurite's delicate hand slides between my legs to cup my balls and shaft. I moan around the gag of silver, and the thought that she may not even be able to hear how appreciative I am somehow ratchets my desire up more.

My heartbeat is loud in my ears, the only sound in the suspended silence. I tremble in anticipation as she strokes my length to full attention. Yet as soon as I'm hard, she releases me, letting the silver keep my trapped cock erect. Her fingers travel down to gently massage my balls in feather-light, teasing touches.

It's enough to drive me wild. I can't even thrust my hips for more friction, and after a futile moment of trying, I sag helplessly inside of the silver. She hadn't been joking - I am completely at her mercy.

Then, the gag of silver is removed while one ear is freed. "Dominai, are you alright?" she asks. Her voice is barely above a whisper, as if she's trying her best not to startle me. I'm grateful for it. Even her quiet voice seems loud after the silence.

I'm panting, and with my eyes blocked I can't tell if I'm imagining the tingling touches that still seem to graze my body. "I'm alright," I say and the husky growl of my own voice sounds foreign to my ears. "I'm good."

Margeurite's smile is evident in her voice. "Would you like to continue?" she asks. "This time, I will keep count of an hour before

I free you. It is a short time for divination, but it may be enough for you to gain some truth."

It's taken her fifteen minutes to reduce me to a trembling mess. I can't imagine what I'll become after an hour of this. I hesitate, not sure if I can handle it. "You'll keep a hand on me?"

Her voice is a purr against my cheek. "And so much more."

I purse my lips to stop a moan. "Alright," I say at last. "I'm ready."

Margeurite moves the silver to fill my mouth once more, and it stretches my jaw again as it gags me. I let out a moan and realize that I can hear the muffled sound through the silver. That's reassuring. If something goes wrong, I can at least make noise.

"Then I'll see you on the other side," she promises, before my ear is filled once more and I'm plunged back into the void.

Maybe it's because of Margeurite's prepping, but the emptiness doesn't feel as empty this time. It's hard to tell if I'm imagining it or not. I feel Margeurite's hands on my hips, solid and real, but I'd swear that there are others touching me. On my feet, my back, through my hair. Then, there's the whispering.

That I *know* has to be imagined. I can't hear a thing with the silver plugging my ears, and yet it sounds like a distant crowd is talking. A steady stream of almost-words that I can't quite make out. Some of the voices even sound familiar, though no matter how hard I try I can't pinpoint them.

Then Margeurite's hands are back, gliding over my exposed side in a way that makes me want to squirm away. I can't, obviously, and her teasing touch soon settles on my ass. She gently kneads the flesh, and the welts that Olbric left spark with sensation. It's not painful, but it brings back the memories of yesterday. I can't help another moan.

Her hands are soft and exploratory. They stroke over my ass and thighs, taking their time tracing the map of welts Olbric left. Then she grips my cheeks and spreads them.

I shudder in anticipation - folks in the towers seem to only go there for one reason. I expect to feel a finger prod at my still sore hole, but none come. Yet even when Margeurite lets go of me, I'm left spread wide by the silver.

My anguished moan is muffled by the gag, but Margeurite doesn't even pause in her slow, torturous exploration of my body. Her hands return to my chest before I feel the warm lap of her tongue around my nipple. She sucks and lavishes the tender flesh with attention before moving onto the other. Her breath is hot against my skin as she trails gentle kisses and nips down my chest and stomach.

Under the silver I'm shivering, and when Margeurite's tongue darts out to lick the tip of my cock, I'm grateful that the silver is there to hold me up. She takes her time, sliding her lips over my length, but never taking it into her mouth. Her tongue laps up the underside before moving lower to tease my balls. She spreads my legs a little further apart before she takes one into her mouth, sucking gently before doing the same to the other.

I can't focus on anything else. Floating in the sea of nothing, her touch is the only thing keeping me grounded to reality. And even that feels iffy. I still feel the phantom hands, hear the whispers that seem to fade in and out of my awareness, but the one real, tangible thing is her mouth on me. So when it pulls away and her hands rest lightly on my hips, I can't stop a wail.

My chest heaves. Margeurite's fingers stroke gentle circles over my heated skin as she allows me to cool back down. She seems to stay there forever, her lips pressing chaste kisses against my hip bones and stomach. Her tongue darts out to tease my navel, and I laugh miserably into my gag. That's not fair! I can't do a damn thing to stop her from tickling me.

Her hand pats my hip in apology, and then her mouth is around my cock, swallowing me deep. I gasp, my entire body tensing. The wet heat makes me ache with need, my cock throbbing. Her tongue laps the underside of my length as she slides her lips back towards the tip. Her pace is unhurried, and a vague part of me wonders just how much time has passed. It feels like none at all. It feels like an eternity.

Her tongue circles the tip of my cock, and I let out a low, appreciative moan. I feel like I'm right on the edge of cumming, but she abruptly pulls away again. My moan turns desperate, and I vainly try to thrust my hips forward.

She gives nothing but another pat, but it's a mockery of an apology this time. I whimper as I sag into the silver. Time ticks by as my breathing regains a normal pace. The thudding of my heart calms back down, beating in time with the aching throb in my cock.

The whispering has gotten louder, though it's gotten far harder to concentrate on. Especially when Margeurite's hand finally moves again, reaching down to toy with my balls. Everything she does is soft and maddeningly gentle. I almost wish for Olbric's fast-pace, no-nonsense approach to casting, yet the thought of doing that here, with no way to stop, is terrifying.

I feel the heat of her breath against my cock and strain uselessly against the silver before sagging back into it. Accepting it. It's like she was waiting for me to submit. I feel her tongue lap the tip of my leaking cock before she swallows my length again. I moan my gratitude as loudly as I can, hoping it will sway her to be merciful.

I see color spark behind my closed eyes, near pictures that change too quickly for me to make out. Margeurite's lips slide up and down my length and she sucks gently before she swallows my length fully, her nose nudging my stomach. I'm so riled up that it only takes seconds for her to put me on the ragged edge of release once more. Even though I'm braced for it, dreading it, I can't stop a wail as she pulls away again.

Spit slides from the corner of my mouth and down my chin. I'm helpless to stop it. Helpless to do anything. I'm pleading into my gag, begging the void for relief. I feel the throb of my cock from the soles of my feet to the shells of my ears. The phantom voices seem to be laughing while the feather-light touches, whether real or imagined, only help to keep my desire at a stable and unbearable level.

I don't know how much more I can stand. With her gentle sucking and touch, Margeurite has tested my endurance far more harshly than Olbric had. Maybe this is what she meant - maybe *this* is her preferred brand of torture.

Then, I feel something cool between my spread cheeks. I gasp as a slick finger gently prods at me before sliding in. Whatever lotion she is using is cool and soothing, and I moan my gratitude. She is slow and gentle - always - as she presses her finger in a little further, searching for that sweet spot inside of me.

Her mouth swallows me again just as her finger finds its goal. There's no stopping it now. My orgasm comes, hard and fast, and this time Margeurite allows me to have it. I sob into my gag, shuddering as my release courses out of me. It feels so good it hurts, and Margeurite's mouth works around my length as she swallows every drop. It seems endless - just as everything does in the void.

The waves of ecstasy make the colors spark into a full picture, the voices dropping away until only one remains.

It's Allisande.

Her beautiful red hair is lank and dirty around her face. She's wearing the same traveling clothes she had worn through the Hobokins, except now they're ragged and torn. There are lines on her face I don't remember being there, crow's feet reaching out from her startling blue eyes. There's a clank of metal, and I realize her wrists are shackled to the stone wall behind her.

Something catches her attention, and her head jerks up, startled. She looks like she's staring straight at me, but there is nothing but hatred and defiance on her face. A voice comes from somewhere, words garbled like they're coming through water. Distinctly male, though no matter how hard I try, I can't make out what he says. Allisande's mouth moves, and though her words are mottled and a little delayed, I catch some of them.

"-can't keep me locked here forever. It's only a matter of time before the Crux finds out. They'll come for me."

But the vision fades as quickly as it came. Allisande's voice is lost to the void no matter how hard I try to hold onto it. Her beautiful, furious face is swallowed by the blackness. The void suddenly feels empty and so very lonely.

Then the gag is pulled out of my mouth. It startles a gasp out of me, but then I feel Margeurite's lips kiss my cheek. She murmurs something against my skin, but with my ears still blocked I can't hear what she says.

She releases me by degrees. I'm grateful for it as she uncovers one ear and then the next. Our breathing sounds deafening at first, the shuffle of her feet across the floor loud in the quiet room, but I start to settle back into my senses. My eyes are returned to me next, and I blink until I can focus on Margeurite's smiling face.

She must notice the bleak expression on mine because her smile fades quickly. "What's wrong?"

"I saw something. I saw Allisande."

Her eyes go wide, her hand flying up to cover her gasp. Yet under the shock, I see something else. Hope, maybe?

Unease settles further into my stomach as Margeurite works to free the rest of me as quickly as she is able. I stumble as the silver sloughs off of me, but Margeurite is there to catch me. She helps me to sit, the cool stone pure relief against my heated skin.

"Are you alright?"

I rub my face, still feeling the aftershocks of pleasure racing over my nerves. It feels tainted now after what I saw. "I'm fine," I promise. "That was... intense."

Margeurite looks at me with something like awe. "It always is," she says. "But possibly moreso when you break through a non-detection field."

"*What?*"

Margeurite kneels in front of me, her hands resting gently on my shoulders. "We have been divining for any sign of Allisande for some time," she says. "Yet none of us have been able to find any hint of her. Even if she was dead we should have found *some* sign, but for nearly a year there has been nothing."

The unease in my gut sours. The Crux is a big place. I had assumed I would run into her eventually. "I didn't realize she was missing."

"When did you meet her?"

I flush. "It was brief. She wrote my letter of introduction to come here."

Margeurite's face is full of a painful kind of hope. Just by that look, I get the hint that there was something between them. Something more than just casual casting. "When was this?"

"A little over a year ago, I think."

Margeurite's eyes light up in understanding. "Then you very well might have been the last of us to speak to her before she disappeared," she says, and I think that's an awful nice way to put it. There really hadn't been a whole lot of speaking at the time.

But then Margeurite is on her feet, hurriedly gathering my clothes. "We need to speak to Grandmaster Arlon immediately."

EVEN THOUGH I DIDN'T recognize his name, I know Arlon's face. He's the older wizard that gave me the side-eye when I met Galiva in the Crux on my first day. He looks no less suspicious now, and I find myself standing a little straighter under his shrewd gaze.

"You have never delved into divination before?" he asks. His voice is deep, and I think he'd be nice to listen to if he didn't sound pissed off all the time.

"No, sir."

Arlon leans forward on his desk, fingers steepled in front of him. It's only then I notice that the sleeves of his robes are decorated with a rainbow of colors. All eight of them, in fact. "And you're *certain* it was Allisande that you saw?"

"Clear as day, sir," I say. "I'd never forget her face."

Margeurite pipes up. "Dominai mentioned that he met Allisande a little more than a year ago," she says before turning to me. "You laid with her, yes?"

I flush bright red. "Well - I mean, yeah I did, but - "

Margeurite cuts me off. She looks excited, her face hard with determination as she puts her hands on Arlon's desk. "We have had no luck getting Sight of her since her disappearance," she says. "But if Dominai was the last of us to be with her, do you think that is why he was able to break through the non-detection?"

"Assuming there *is* a non-detection, which has not been verified," Arlon mutters, but his brows knit as he mulls that thought over. "It's divination - it's all very inexact. Who's to say Dominai didn't tune into a moment from months ago?"

"Does it matter?" Margeurite demands. "We have found *nothing* of her. Nothing of the past, the present, or the future. He's done what none of us have been able to!"

"Margeurite-"

But she plows on, and I'd been foolish to think the polite little ovisari didn't know how to raise her voice. "Others have gone missing since Allisande. If we can determine who was last with Alix, or Iona, or Marvin, *maybe* we can break through the non-detection just as Dominai did. If divining can gather any clues as to the whereabouts of our missing wizards, isn't it worth it to try?"

"Whoa," I say as the thought strikes me. My vision made it clear that Allisande was being held somewhere, but, "Is someone *targeting* folks from the Crux?"

Arlon lets out a weary sigh, and I can tell he's been mulling that question over for some time. "We're not sure," he says. "It's not unheard of for wizards to go missing on assignment. Accidents happen. Our work doesn't bring us to the safest places - battlefields, disaster areas and the like. But what you Saw certainly lends more credence to the theory."

He falls quiet, and Margeurite is like a taut bowstring beside me. Finally, the older wizard lets out a long breath. "Alright," he says at last. "I will put out a notice asking for anyone who cast with the missing wizards to come forward. You realize some of them won't consent to divination, don't you?"

"That's their choice," Margeurite says. "But I believe that if it means finding the whereabouts of the missing, even the reluctant will at least try."

Arlon nods. "Alright then," he says. "I will leave it in your hands, though I will offer whatever assistance I can in casting. I will send all who come forward to you."

Margeurite's smile lights up her face. "Thank you, Arlon," she says. "If I discover anything else, you'll be the first to know."

She turns to leave, and I move to follow, but Arlon stops me. "Dominai, a moment please," he says.

Margeurite offers a smile. "I'll find you later," she says before closing the door behind her.

Somehow, the office feels a lot smaller without Margeurite there. I try to swallow the lump of nerves that's formed in my throat and turn to look at the Grandmaster. "Sir?"

Arlon's looking at me curiously, a slight frown on his face. "When you first came here, I thought it was some sort of joke - yet another country boy coming for an easy lay," he says at last. I bristle, and it must show on my face because Arlon raises a hand, "And for that, I apologize. It appears I misjudged you."

"Oh," I say and deflate just as quickly.

Arlon gets to his feet, and it's only then I realize how *big* he is. Not only is he tall, but his robes help hide how broad and muscled his shoulders are. I can't help but think he looks more like some sort of soldier rather than a grandmaster of the wizard's towers.

"Those with magical blood usually have a family name that they can give as entry to the towers. Someone approaching us with a letter of recommendation as you did is, well... rare."

"I'm not sure which side my magic comes from, if that's what you're asking," I say. "I assume my mother, but it could be my da was just real good at keeping a secret."

Arlon looks thoughtful as he leans casually back against his desk, though I notice the way his eyes rake over me. I can't help but admit that I'm doing the same. Like we're sizing each other up.

"Where are they now?"

I shrug. I'm not keen on dragging up bad memories, so I make it quick. "Da died a few years back from the fever," I say. "My mother cut out when I was just a kid. Never saw her again."

Arlon only looks more intrigued, but I'm glad when he changes the subject. "What did you do before coming here?"

I rub the back of my neck. It all seems so... mundane compared to what I've been doing here. "Was a forest guide and a hunter," I say. "That's how I met Allisande. I was guiding her through the Hobokins."

Arlon frowns thoughtfully, and it seems as if that expression is a comfortable one for him. "I remember when she left for that trip," he says. "She was heading to our sister tower out east and refused to take a boat. Needed a change of scenery, she had said."

I can't stop a small laugh. At Arlon's curious look, I say, "She said something similar to me when she gave me that introduction letter. I guess we're kindred spirits in that."

Arlon gives a thin grin, and I can't help but wonder if he ever smiles. "And are you finding the change of scenery to your liking?" he asks, words heavy with implication.

In spite of the rocky start, I think I like Arlon. "I regret not coming here the second Allisande gave me that letter."

"It certainly seems as if you're making up for lost time," Arlon says and steps closer to me. My heart thuds when I realize I have to look *up* at him, and I'm no short stack. "Galiva reports that you have been going near non-stop since you arrived. I urge you to caution - new adepts have a tendency to wear themselves out. It can get you hurt."

I feel a little giddy, a little cocky when I say, "I can take it."

"Is that so?" Arlon asks and takes another step towards me. I bump into the wall behind me without realizing I had even backed up. Then, his hand grabs my crotch, his large fingers surprisingly gentle as he massages me through the fabric of my trousers. "Then close your eyes."

I shudder at the touch and grind into his hand even as I do as I'm told. I feel the laces on my trousers tug open before Arlon pulls them and my underwear down unceremoniously. His hands are warm and calloused, and I wonder if my initial thought of him as a soldier isn't too far off.

Something slides over my length, cool and entirely unlike a focus. My balls are slipped between something tight. It almost pinches before they slip through and are able to hang normal. Then, I hear something click, and my eyes shoot open in alarm.

I see Arlon smiling - *smiling*. White-toothed and all too satisfied. And then I look down. "What the fuck?"

Shiny metal covers the length of my cock, though there's a little slit at the end for necessary functions. There's an attached ring that he's threaded my balls through and then locked in place with a cleverly placed silver lock. I feel my half-erect cock throb in protest and realize the purpose of the little device.

A cage.

I look up at Arlon in disbelief as he pockets a little silver key. I take it back. I don't think I like Arlon at all. "That's not fair," I protest.

"It's necessary," he says. "You haven't had an introduction to conjuration, have you?"

I swear and pull up my trousers, fumbling with the laces and blushing hot red. "What's conjuration got to do with it?" I mutter irritably.

"Chastity, Dominai," he says. "And the release that comes after. I have a feeling you haven't cultivated the self-control to abstain without a little assistance."

I open my mouth to protest, but then I realize that he's not wrong. I let out a frustrated sigh and shift from one foot to the other, feeling the weight of the cage. It's not entirely uncomfortable, but I don't think I'll ever be able to really ignore it.

"How long?" I ask.

The smile is back on Arlon's face, and I'm immediately wary again. "Hmm, let's see, you've been here for what, three days? Let's give it five more to give you a chance to rest and reset."

"Five days?!"

Arlon smiles and puts a finger over my lips. I want to bite him, but I abstain. See? I've got self-control.

"Do you want to know the best part of conjuration magic?" he asks, his deep voice taking on that sultry pitch again. "It's that when you do get your release, it's like it's new all over again. So don't worry, Dominai. It will be worth your wait."

Playing Assistant

While casting, a wizard is not constrained to any one school. Some of the most effective spells come from combining casting methods. Combining elements of abjuration, evocation, and enchantment can create powerful and effective spells.

IT'S THE NEXT MORNING when I realize how quick news spreads in the Crux. A notice has already been posted in the main atrium requesting that anyone who had last cast with one of the missing wizards to come forward. When Galiva collects me for breakfast she asks for details, so I tell her all that I Saw.

Her fingers drum down the side of her steaming mug. "I can't believe it. Not that I'm doubting the truth of your divining," she amends. "It's just that you'd either have to be insane or very, very good to try and take on a master wizard from the Crux. Especially one like Allisande."

I think back to Allisande's gaunt face, and my stomach knots with unease all over again. "My bet is on very good," I say. "Whoever it is took her alive."

Galiva swears under her breath. "Allisande was going for full mastery," she says. "She had her stripes for everything but enchantment and corpimancy, and she was well on her way to gaining those as well."

I whistle. For all the change she brought to my life, I realize just how little I know about her. "Then why the hell did she hire *me*?" I ask. "With even just an evocation mastery, she'd have no problem getting through the Hobokins by herself."

Galiva grins at me over the top of her mug. "Knowing Allisande? She probably did it for the company." Her smile fades as she rolls her cup between her hands. "But if all of this proves anything, it's that we're not as untouchable as we thought."

"Maybe I should have stayed with her," I say and set down my last bite of bread and jam. "It... didn't feel right leaving her. We'd made it to the edge of the Hobokins, but the roads still aren't the safest for a lone traveler."

Galiva takes another sip of her drink, a frown on her face. "Do you remember much about that trip?"

I can't stop a grin. That trip was memorable for a few reasons. "Allisande said she'd been referred to me by the innkeep in Airedale," I say. "I remember she seemed... in a hurry. She also asked that we take the less traveled roads, so I assumed she was running from something, but it wasn't my job to ask questions."

"Wish you would have," Galiva says. "I remember her saying that it was no easy decision for her to leave. She just felt like she was stagnating here. Thought that some time away would do her good."

"She didn't talk about any of that," I say. "Was pretty quiet about who she was, though she sure did ask me a lot of questions." I smile as I remember some of the conversations we'd had. The talk that had skirted the lines of inappropriate. It was like she got a kick out of making me blush. "She was nice. Easy to travel with. I think we were on the road little more than a week. It was pretty uneventful until the third or fourth night."

It's one of those memories that stick out. "We were jumped by a goblin band. They're quiet bastards, but the smell of them woke me up in time to get my bow nocked. One grabbed Allisande's hair and tried to drag her off before I put an arrow through it."

Why hadn't a spell released? Surely with her many masteries, she had something that would have helped.

Then I remember the rest of that night. Allisande's fiery red hair haloed by moonlight like some sort of goddess, and I had revered her like she was one. Fueled by adrenaline and relief, it all felt unreal. I'd almost been afraid to touch her pale skin, but then she'd grabbed my hands and guided them around the perfect curve of her breasts. My confidence grew after that, and I remember cupping the back of her neck to pull her down to capture her lips. It had been a thrill like no other when she returned the kiss.

It hits me all at once. I set my mug down with a thud. "Oh shit. She didn't have her necklace."

Galiva's eyes widen, her hand going to her own strands. "Are you sure?"

"Positive," I say. "They're unique-looking things. If Allisande is a master six times over, it would have been impossible to ignore. She *wasn't wearing it.*"

Galiva swears and rolls one of her marbles between her fingers. "Unless we're inside the tower walls, we don't take them off," she says. "Allisande would never have done it willingly. Someone must have taken it."

I lean back in my chair, frowning as I try to puzzle out what could have happened, but it's like trying to make a picture while only having half the pieces. "I wonder if someone in Airedale saw what happened. Maybe Allisande ran into some trouble?"

"That much seems clear," Galiva says through a sigh. She looks just as frustrated as I feel. "But Margeurite seems confident about this new lead." She meets my eyes across the table and smiles. "You did well, Dom. Far better than I can do with divination."

I flush at the praise and take a long sip of my tea to avoid responding.

"And I heard you finally got to meet Arlon?" Galiva asks, but a hint of mischief has entered her voice.

I'm immediately suspicious. "What did you hear?"

Galiva chuckles and gives my crotch a knowing look before she says, "How many days did he give you?"

Good gods, rumor travels *that* fast? I certainly didn't tell anyone, so I assume Arlon's spread the news for me. "Five," I mutter.

"Well hey, at least you're on his good side," she says with a laugh.

"*This* is his good side?"

"If you weren't, it'd be fifteen days instead of five. It's a pretty short time for conjuration, really."

I groan and rest my head in my hands. "What am I going to do for five days?"

"How's your headway on those books I gave you?" Galiva asks only to chuckle when I glower at her. "It's not all fun sexy time, you know. You *do* actually have to study the methods if you ever want to be competent at casting. I'm planning on quizzing you on those two books once you're through them."

I know she's right, but the petulant part of me makes me ask, "Why can't I just be a conduit?"

"You'll never gain mastery of any school if you can't cast a spell," she points out. "Though there's nothing *wrong* with preferring to conduit. You've just been going non-stop since you got here, and for a new adept that can get overwhelming. You can start to agree to things you normally wouldn't." Her grin fades a little. "You can start to regret some of them. I have a feeling that's why Arlon locked you up in the first place."

She's probably right, but I'm determined to be surly about it. The weight of the cage is a constant distraction. My dreams were no less vibrant, and though Margeurite didn't make an appearance in them this time, I woke up with my cock aching all the same. Knowing that any form of release is locked away from me makes me want it even more.

When I glance up, Galiva's looking at me. There's the mischievous twinkle in her eyes again. "How about this," she says. "You strike me as more of a hands-on kind of learner. I'm supposed to cast a spell with Olbric today. You want to assist?"

That perks me up. Even if I'm caged up, it'll still be nice to actually do something. I'd been a little afraid I'd be stuck in my room wallowing for a week. "Absolutely."

OLBRIC IS WAITING FOR us in the evocation tower in the same casting room we had used last time. He's leaned back in one of the chairs, reading a book as he waits, but his face lights up when he sees me.

"Oh good! If you're here, then I get to dole out a beating instead of taking one, right?" He takes his spectacles off and sets them on his book as he gets to his feet.

"Wrong," Galiva says, dashing those hopes quick. "Dom's working a conjuration spell, so he'll be helping me today." Besides, I'm still sporting a few welts from last time.

Olbric's eyes dart to my crotch. "And you want to help cast a spell?" he asks. The doubt in his voice gives me pause. Maybe watching a casting with a cage on isn't the wisest idea.

Galiva waves him off. "Of course he does," she says. "I'm sure he's looking forward to seeing you put in your place after that beating you gave him."

Olbric looks wounded, though there's a playful twinkle in his exaggerated puppy-dog eyes. "Put me in *my* place?" he says. "Bold words for someone I had mewling at my feet the last time we cast."

Galiva spanks him hard, though it's not very effective through his trousers and robe. "I am *also* looking forward to putting you in your place," she says with a grin. "Now shut up and strip."

Their easy banter makes me smile. There's an obvious level of comfort between them. An easy sort of trust. It makes me wonder how long they've been casting together, and I can't help but wonder what that must be like.

Growing up like I did, I didn't have much by way of friends *or* lovers. Life in the woods was usually dull, but after my da died, it became downright lonely. To have someone you can turn to for friendly company and more must be nice.

Then Galiva turns her bright smile to me. "Go grab some rope," she says. I do as asked, but she pushes the coils back into my hands when I try to hand them over. "I'll instruct you," she says. "We're going to tie his hands in front of him."

She helps me find the ends and slides the rope through her hand until we've folded the length in two. "Weave that up his forearms, just like he did with you," she says and hands the rope back to me. "Be sure the ropes don't get twisted."

Olbric finishes disrobing, and I can't help but notice that there are still a couple of faded welts on his ass. Apparently it's not enough to keep him from doing it all over again. He catches my glance, and his grin snaps me back to the task at hand.

I take the rope and do as I'm told. I make a figure eight around Olbric's wrists before weaving it up around his forearms. He watches me with an excited sort of serenity, alert yet calm. When I catch his gaze, he grins and gives me a wink that makes my stomach do a little somersault.

"Not too tight?" I ask.

"You could even go a little tighter," he says and gasps when I cinch the ropes up.

Galiva checks them and makes a quick adjustment to the knot I tied before nodding her approval.

"Not bad, adept," she says with a grin. She takes the loose ends and ties them in a knot before tossing them through one of the rings that hang from the ceiling.

"There's a stack of ten wooden slabs in the bottom of that cabinet. Can you grab them?"

I'm eager to help and find the evenly cut, flat squares of wood right where she said. They're heavy. My bum arm complains a little, but I manage to grab all of them at once and carry the stack over to her.

I can't help but wonder what the hell she's going to do with them, and apparently I'm not the only. Olbric looks at the blocks with a frown.

"Wait, what spell are we casting?" he asks.

Galiva's grin is mischievous. "A containment spell of sorts, but I'm going to add a twist," she says. She sets down two stacks of five blocks at Olbric's feet. She sets them a little more than a shoulder length apart before giving his ass a playful swat. "Step up."

Olbric gives an exaggerated yelp but does as he's told. The blocks aren't huge, but they're big enough for him to stand comfortably on. They raise him up about a foot off the ground but keep his legs spread.

"We're just doing abjuration?" Olbric asks.

Galiva takes the rope and pulls his arms over his head, though not quite as tight as he had done to me. She at least allows him to keep his feet flat instead of putting him on his toes.

"I said there was a twist, didn't I?" she asks before slapping his ass again.

"What kind of twist?" I ask.

Galiva heads towards the cabinet. "When I heard what you Saw, I got to thinking," she says. "I started wondering about precautions we can take, in case someone is targeting wizards. Containment spells are great for that. They stop a potential attacker and hold them prone until you release them."

She pulls out another length of rope from the cabinet before grabbing something else. It's a long pole attached to a sturdy base. But sticking up from the end is a thick leather phallus.

Olbric shifts his weight from one foot to the other on the blocks, his eyes wide. "But containing someone is only part of what we want, right?" Galiva says like a teacher giving a lecture, and I guess she kind of is. "Once we have them, I think I'd like some answers. So this particular containment will add some... necessary pressure that will help us obtain that information."

"So, what, a cage that causes pain?" I ask. It's one thing to make a shield, or create a force blast, but this seems like a complicated spell with a lot of elements to it. Galiva sets the phallus down behind Olbric and adjusts the height of it so it's just barely poking against his ass.

"Even more subtle - a cage that will only cause pain the more you fight it," Galiva says with a wicked grin. "Even though I don't have mastery in enchantment, I'm going to add a bit of it in to try and compel answers."

Olbric shudders. "Fuck, Galiva - you're going to be the death of me," he says. "This sounds ambitious. You think it'll work?"

Galiva takes another length of rope and circles in front of Olbric. She pulls the length tight with a quick snap. "Only one way to find out, isn't there?"

"You've never done this spell before?" I ask and step around to watch her. She starts tying the rope around Olbric's chest, pulling it tight enough that I can see it bite against his skin.

"Not exactly," she says. "I've done spells with similar effects but I've never tried to combine them before. Spell casting is all very symbolic. The ropes and knots reflect the type and strength of the containment. The blocks and phallus will create a predicament for Olbric while casting - the more he struggles, the more blocks I'll take away. You'll see what goes into enchantment, and the pain - well," she says with a wicked grin, "I'm planning on using a cane."

I'm still not sure I understand, but Olbric is already shivering in anticipation, and it sure as hell seems he understands what's in store for him.

"Here, take this over," she says, and I see that she's started an intricate lattice of diamond shaped knots around his chest. I do as told and give an apologetic grin up to Olbric as I fumble through it.

"Wrap under, not over," Olbric says.

I still have a false start before I get what he's saying. It gets easier the more I tie, and I feel a little accomplished when I manage to finish the pattern Galiva started. Though she's not done yet.

Galiva steps up to Olbric, and I watch as she takes a short length of rope and ties it around Olbric's balls. It's not complicated, but it tugs them down and wrings a pained groan from him. Even so, he's already half hard, and his cock only swells as Galiva ties the knot off.

She circles behind him, her hand trailing over his waist. I notice that all of Olbric's witty retorts have been silenced. He watches her with glazed eyes, hands clenching under the ropes I tied.

Galiva takes a bottle from the pocket of her robe and slathers the large phallus before adjusting the height again. Olbric moans and bites his bottom lip as the tip of it pokes into him. Galiva makes sure the base is stable and won't slip away before nodding in satisfaction.

Finally, she pulls out five focuses from her pocket and slides them over his erect length. Olbric's breath hisses through his nose. He stands very still, though there's a distinct tremble in his legs that he can't hide. The blocks he's on may as well be a pedestal, and I can't help but admire the sight.

He's lean and tall, even more so all stretched out like he is. Sinewy muscles flex under the cage of ropes Galiva created. His dark hair is tied away from his handsome face, but a few strands have already escaped. A hint of sweat shines on his forehead, and it makes the heat pool in my groin to see him bound and shivering.

"How's that feel, Olbric?" Galiva asks as she returns to the cabinet. She sorts through a stack of various canes and switches before she finds the one she's looking for. It's a wooden cane, no thicker than my pointer finger.

"Good," he says, a little breathless. He shifts on his pedestal to rise onto his toes before sinking back down. He lets out a little moan as the phallus pushes back into him and rests his head against his bound forearms. "Real good."

"Gods, you're an eager little slut, aren't you?" Galiva asks. The heat in her voice surprises me, but not as much as the vulgarity of her words. "Now, I think you've gotten an idea of the game, but just in case, let me be clear. You lift a foot, you lose a block. You answer my questions, and you get relief from the cane. Got it?"

She trails the tip of the cane over Olbric's trapped erection. He bites back a moan as he worries his lower lip between his teeth.

"Got it," he says.

Without warning, Galiva brings the cane down on his ass in a loud crack. Olbric yelps and jerks, his eyes shooting wide with surprise. It leaves a long, angry red welt, and I realize that Galiva isn't here to fuck around.

My cock immediately stirs, but the metal cage around me is unyielding. I take a seat in Olbric's chair and cross my legs. Staying to watch this may very well be a bad idea, but I'm not about to leave now.

Galiva doesn't go easy on him. Every crack of the cane makes me wince. She hits his ass, his thighs, his chest, and it gives me a whole new appreciation for what an evocation wizard can take. Olbric shouts and curses at each one, and I can't imagine how much that little cane must sting. Red welts start to cross his skin, raw and angry. One particularly sharp crack against his calf makes him yelp and lift his foot to try and soothe the spot. Galiva tsks in mock disappointment.

"I thought you were more resilient than that, Olbric," she says. "You're so eager to get fucked, so let's give that ass of yours what it wants, shall we?"

She reaches down and taps his foot. He lifts it, and she removes one of the wood planks before doing the same to the other side. Olbric sets his feet back down, a few inches lower than he had been, making the large phallus slide deeper into him. He shudders and lifts himself up onto his toes to try and ease the discomfort of it, but Galiva has set up the predicament well. He can't pull himself off of it anymore.

She puts the tip of the cane under his chin. His glazed eyes open, and the knot in his throat bobs as he swallows. The hazy expression on his face makes my groin throb. Even at a glance, I can tell that he's sunk into that conspace he had mentioned.

"How does that cock feel?" Galiva purrs. "Big, right? But nothing your loose hole can't handle, is it?"

Olbric doesn't answer and Galiva taps the cane hard against his nipple. He swears and clenches his eyes shut, but when he opens them again, there's defiance in his hazy expression. He's going to make her wring an answer out of him.

Galiva seems more than up for the challenge. With the undersides of his feet exposed, she focuses the cane there. It only takes a few good thwacks before Olbric shouts and tries to dance away from her, swaying precariously on his pedestal.

"Pathetic," she says. "When did the most infamous pain slut in the Crux come undone under a cane? When did you get so soft, Olbric?"

He doesn't answer, and she removes another plank from under each of his feet. Olbric sinks further down onto the phallus with a muffled cry as he buries his face against his arm. He's fully on his toes now. His calf muscles work to keep him up, arms held taught in their ropes. He won't be able to do it forever, though. There's already the tell-tale tremble of fatigue in his strained limbs.

The cage pinches a little tighter around me. Olbric's face is a mask of anguish, his chest a map of welts. Even so, his erection strains hard and red under the ropes and focuses. A thin trail of liquid weeps from the tip, and I can't seem to look away from it. I wonder what it tastes like.

Galiva's strikes become less frequent and more calculated. She focuses on his inner thighs until it's a field of fiery red lines. All the while, she's talking to him. "Who's mewling now? Do you like that, you little slut?"

"Yes!" Olbric shouts and Galiva stops her assault. She strokes the tip of the cane down his flushed face.

"Good boy," she says. "Have you had enough yet?"

I can't help but admire his stamina. He's endured almost an hour of this, and there's hardly a spot of skin left on his ass or thighs that isn't hot with welts. He'll be sitting gingerly for days. I know I would have stopped some time ago. Even watching is near unbearable, though for an entirely different reason.

Olbric shudders, and I see his warring thoughts play out on his face. He draws in a few deep breaths before his resolve hardens again. He grimaces and buries his face against his arm. Galiva's grin is full of sadistic glee.

"Yeah, I thought so," she says. "Your hungry ass isn't so easily satisfied, is it?"

Olbric gives a short laugh, like it's some sort of inside joke, but otherwise stays quiet. Then Galiva taps the cane against his throbbing cock, and all humor vanishes from his face. He throws his head back and *howls*. He does something like a pull-up with his ropes, as if that will somehow soothe the sting. It's still not enough to get him off of the phallus, and he's rewarded for that athletic little display by Galiva removing two more blocks.

"Poor little slut. Was that too much?" she asks, and though her tone is mocking, there's concern on her face.

Olbric wails as he's impaled further onto the phallus. He's forced up onto the very tips of his toes now. If he loses any more planks, he'll only have the ropes to keep him off of it. His face is pinched with pain, teeth clenched in a grimace. A drop of sweat falls from his nose. Even so, his silence is deliberate.

I shift where I'm sitting, an involuntary little groan escaping me. A wicked grin spreads across Galiva's face as she looks over at me.

"Come here, Dom."

I shudder at the heat in her voice but get to my feet. My cock throbs inside of the cage. Every step is torture as I walk towards them.

Galiva smiles and gives me a chaste kiss on the cheek before pointing the cane at Olbric's leaking cock. "Would you like to suck him?" she asks.

"Fucking hell, please," Olbric moans, voice thick with wanton desperation. "Please, *please*." His hips give a feeble thrust, his cock bobbing. It's a tempting sight, but it's his begging that undoes me.

Even with five focuses snug around the base of his erection, half of his length is still free. I crouch in front of him as Galiva strokes her hand through my hair.

I'm a little self-conscious. I've never been on this side of things before. What if I'm rubbish at it?

Tentatively, I grab his length and lap the liquid from the tip. It's warm and slightly salty. Olbric's shuddering moan washes over me, and the sound makes gooseflesh break out on my arms. He arches towards me with a plaintive little whine. He's sizable, both in length and girth, and for a moment I'm not quite sure how to go about it. I run my tongue up the underside of his length, teasing the skin that is exposed between the focuses.

The desperate little noises he's making are doing nothing to help me. My trapped cock aches, but I grow a little more confident at his reactions. His hips thrust feebly, a quiet chorus of "please, please" falling from his lips. I take pity on him and pull his head into my mouth.

I feel the fight go out of him. He cries out as he sinks fully onto the phallus. His calves tense, feet trying to lift himself back up, but he only succeeds for a moment before he falls onto it again, fucking himself on the length of it. His body jerks when Galiva snaps the cane against his ass again. "Do you want to cum, Olbric?" she asks.

This time, his answer comes fast. "Yes!"

Galiva reaches down and tugs the cleverly tied knot to release his balls. Olbric wails, layers of agony and bliss in his voice. I redouble my efforts, bobbing up and down the length of him, lavishing the underside with my tongue. I grip the base and feel the focuses spark under my fingers.

It rips a scream from Olbric. His cock swells in my mouth before it erupts. It catches me by surprise, but I don't pull away. The taste of him fills my mouth, salty and hot. I swallow before I can think to spit it out, a flush of heat and embarrassment washing through me. It's a few long moments before he's finally empty, spent and shuddering on his pedestal. I keep my mouth around him until I'm sure he's finished, and even then, he whimpers when I pull away.

For a second, I can only look up at him in awe. Five glowing focuses are around his softening length. He hangs limp in his ropes, beautiful and defeated. Galiva's hands are gentle as they slide over his abused flesh. A shudder runs through his body, so strong I'm afraid he might come apart. Galiva adjusts the phallus and pulls it out of him, wringing an exhausted moan from him.

She carefully loosens the ropes, and I'm glad I stayed kneeling, because I have to catch Olbric as he stumbles from the pedestal. I help him sink to the ground. He lays against me with a little groan, his head falling against my chest. His skin is hot to the touch, and the weight of him is doing nothing to stamp down my arousal.

I try to ignore it as best as I can. I still have four days left, after all.

"You're alright?" I ask and brush the loose, sweaty strands of hair away from his face.

He blinks hazily up at me and gives a grin that makes my stomach do a funny sort of twist. "Peachy," he says, voice thick. He pulls his bound arms to his chest and closes his eyes again, letting out a long breath. I think he's started to doze as Galiva kneels down and begins untying the ropes from around his arms.

"Thanks for your help," she says with a smile.

"Anytime," I say. "That was... very informative."

Galiva chuckles quietly and goes to grab a blanket from the cabinet before draping it over Olbric. He moans quietly as she slips the glowing focuses from his length, but otherwise doesn't stir. After a moment, his breathing starts to even and deepen, and I realize he's dozed off.

"Want to help me one more time to test one of these?" she asks.

I look down at Olbric, and I'm not sure how to extract myself from under him. I'm not sure if I want to. And not because I'm afraid of testing the spell. He's a comfortable warmth against me, and I'd deny him a pillow if I got up.

Galiva sees my hesitation and chuckles quietly. "Later, then," she says and leans down to press a kiss against Olbric's forehead. He groans quietly but doesn't open his eyes. "I'm afraid I double-booked a bit today. Would you mind taking over aftercare duties? I have to meet with Margeurite." She doesn't sound particularly excited about the meeting.

"Of course," I say, though I give her a curious look.

Galiva's grin is lopsided. "I was the last person to be with one of our missing wizards."

I've gathered her dislike of divination and give a sympathetic smile. I can see how it would not be for everyone.

"Ah. Good luck," I say. "It should be a cakewalk after some of the stuff you do in here."

Galiva's grin evens out a little. "Thanks. I'll let you know what I See - if anything."

"IT'S NOT A CONTEST, you know," I say.

Olbric's teeth chatter even as he grins at me. He's submerged up to his neck in the ice bath, his welted skin turned even redder from the cold. He's endured far longer than I was able to the other day.

"S-says you. I'm t-trying to beat a p-personal record."

I chuckle as I roll my eyes. "Of what? How many cold fits you can stand?" I say before a particularly strong shiver overtakes him. "Because it looks like you're winning."

He chuckles as he pulls himself from the water. I offer him the towel from my lap, but instead of wrapping himself in it, he lays it out on the ground. He sprawls out on top of it, his bare back and ass to the air, head pillowed on his folded arms. The welts seem to have faded in the cold. Either that, or they've just blended into the rest of his cold-reddened skin. A few still stand out in tender-looking lines.

"Since Galiva's foisted her aftercare duties off on you, it's time to put that lesson I gave you the other day to use," he says and motions to the little glass bottle resting by the lip of the pool. I pick it up and scoop some of the gel into my hands. I hesitate for only a second before I carefully brush it over one of the worst of the welts on his ass.

He gasps, arching a little before sinking against the towel with a groan.

"You're alright?" I ask.

"Oh, I'm great," he moans. "Just a little sore, but no one ever said a good time had to be comfortable."

I chuckle and start to rub the salve into his skin. His shivers slowly subside, his skin warming under my touch. I coat his back and ass and thighs, taking my time with it. It does seem to help. The marks stop looking quite so angry, and Olbric certainly seems to enjoy what I'm doing.

He groans quietly as I touch him, only to twitch when I hit a particularly sensitive spot. Gods, but he's awful nice to look at. He's got an idle smile playing on his face as he lays with his cheek pillowed on his hands. Completely content as he drifts down from the high Galiva gave him.

"Would you believe that there was a time I couldn't *pay* Gal to take a cane to me?" he says.

"After all that, I honestly can't," I chuckle. "Looked like you two were having fun."

Olbric slowly rolls over, biting his lip as he lays his sore backside against the towel. I can't help but notice that his cock is half hard. "I love the kind of fun that hurts the next morning," he groans.

I can tell he's still floating, and it doesn't seem right to be sitting here doing nothing. Instead, I grab his hands and try to work the warmth back into them. They're the only part of him that seem to want to stay cold. His long fingers are calloused and scarred, but his nails are kept neatly trimmed and taken care of.

"Evocation's not kind on your hands," he says when he notices me looking.

I rub some of the salve into his knuckles. There's no welt marks there, but I figure it can't hurt. "I thought you said abjuration stops you from getting hurt by the spell?"

Olbric shrugs. "It does for the most part," he says. "Making magic is one thing, releasing spells is an entirely other thing. When you're firefighting, your focus can slip. Sparks graze your hand, you feel some blow-back in your joints."

I wince as I massage his palm. "That sounds intense."

Olbric chuckles. "It *is*. That's what makes it so incredible."

When I switch to his other hand, I pay some extra attention to the joints of each finger. "Have you been in a lot of fights?"

"Plenty," he says. "I'm usually sent out for part of the summer on bandit patrol on the main road through the Hobokins. Also broke up the New Year's mob that happened last year - that bard will never be allowed in Straetham again."

I chuckle at that and can only imagine what havoc that must have been.

"But wizards are a pretty harmonious bunch, so I've never had a firefight outside of sparring," he says. "With luck, I never will."

"Yeah?" I ask. "Why's that?"

Olbric blinks as he looks up at me. "You know how rock beats shears and shears beats paper and so on?" I've never heard the expression before, but I get what he's saying and nod. "The only thing that beats magic in a fight is magic."

For some reason, that makes a chill run up my spine. Seeing the spell released in the courtyard makes me wonder what sort of damage two well-armed wizards could do. Not just to one another, but to everything around them.

"You never fight with other wizards?" I ask.

"Oh, we squabble plenty, but it never ends in a firefight," he chuckles.

"Y'all must be a pretty close-knit group, then."

Olbric tilts his head, amused. "It's hard not to be close when you're all fucking one another."

I laugh at that even as heat rushes to my face. The man meets my eyes as he gives me a look of pure mischief. But I don't have a chance to react before he lurches up to capture my lips in a searing kiss.

The intensity of it makes my head spin. I'm too shocked to pull away, so I guess it's a good thing I don't want to. Inside of the cage my cock throbs, lust surging hot through me. Olbric nibbles my lip as a frustrated groan breaks free.

He chuckles and presses a chaste kiss against my cheek. "Such a shame we can't get a little closer right now," he purrs, and my cock gives another wanton throb. "Guess we'll just have to wait until you're freed."

I barely stop a whine as he lays back on his towel. My body feels hot, and no matter how hard I try, I can't seem to rub that heat away from my face.

"I fucking guess," I groan.

Olbric just laughs.

The Devilish Boar

T he next morning, I sleep in until a little after first bell. The sun is well into the sky when I open my eyes, and the first thing I feel is the tightness of the cage pinching around my cock. I groan as I kick my covers off. It takes a few long minutes, but the feeling gradually starts to fade.

This bed is so comfortable that it's hard to will myself out of it, but I manage. I'm not used to lounging around, as tempting as it is. As I get up, I notice that another set of clothes has been laid on my desk. They're not much different than the ones Galiva gave me a few days ago, but the idea of having two good sets of trousers to choose from boggles my mind a bit. I pull the new set on just as someone knocks on my door.

My fingers pause in tying my trouser laces. Galiva had said that I had the morning to myself, but maybe it's Olbric? I can't help but hope so. I tie my pants closed and pull my shirt on before I open my door.

To my surprise, it's Arlon. The last of my morning haze jolts out of me as I look up at the giant of a man. He grins, showing just a sliver of white teeth.

"Good morning, Dominai," he says. "I wanted to check in to see how you were doing."

"Oh." Inside of the cage, my cock jumps. "Um... it's not rubbing if that's what you mean."

Arlon's grin turns sly. "I was asking in more of a general sense, but I'm glad to know where your mind is. How are you settling in?"

I rub the back of my neck, my face heating. "I'm doing good," I say. "I... like it here." It feels like an understatement. "Quite a bit."

"I'm glad to hear that," Arlon says. "It seems that you're fitting in well. Galiva and Olbric both tell me good things."

That catches me off guard. "Yeah?"

"Surprised?" Arlon asks. "You shouldn't be. Word travels fast in the Crux - especially when it's concerning such a willing newcomer."

I flush at that. I guess I hadn't realized folks would be talking about me, but now that I know, a knot of worry twists in my gut. Arlon snaps me out of it when he asks, "Do you have any questions? I know just how overwhelming this place can be to those not used to it."

A small laugh bubbles out of me. "It sure is, but not in a bad way."

Arlon looks amused. "How so?"

My grin comes out crooked. "Airedale is a pretty prude town compared to... all of this," I say. "But it's been easier to adjust than I thought it would be."

Arlon hums at that. "Some take to magic easier than others," he says. "Just remember that if anyone asks you to do something that you're not comfortable with, you are always allowed to say no and have that no respected. You're also allowed to stop a spell at any time, for any reason. We don't force or coerce magic here."

"Of course," I say. "Galiva made that clear, but no one's done anything that's made me want to stop."

The Grandmaster gives an approving nod. "Good." A shadow of a grin crosses his face, "Though that look you gave me when I locked you up made me wonder if I'd pushed you a little too far."

I laugh as I try to rub the blush from my face. "You definitely caught me by surprise," I say. "But I think I can handle it."

Arlon's smile is sharp. "Only three more days to go."

It's an effort to bite back my groan. Inside of the cage, my cock throbs, just to remind me that I can't use it. Fucking hell, and two has felt like a lifetime in this place. "Yes, sir."

Arlon chuckles, and the deep sound shivers through me. "If you need anything, I'm always available," he says. "I'll see you soon, Dominai."

THAT EVENING, I FIND a secluded corner in an alcove on the first floor. I'm not exactly hiding but godsdamn, if I see one more sly glance aimed at my crotch I feel like my face is going to catch fire. It's damn near impossible to forget the cage is there, and I sure don't need folks reminding me. Every shift, every adjustment already does that.

I'm hoping the history of magic book Galiva gave me will help. It's been a dry read so far, but I'm finally starting to get into the parts about magical theory. It's way more interesting than struggling through a long, dry history lesson that I only half pay attention to. The more I read about mixing schools and materials, the more things start to click with what I've already done and seen.

For a bit, I can almost forget the cage. I'm just about to give it up and get an early dinner when Galiva rounds the corner.

"There you are," she says. "I've been looking everywhere for you." She looks a little flustered, her hair wilder than usual.

"What's wrong?" I ask and snap the book closed.

"What do you mean?" She puts on an easy grin, but she's not fooling me. I raise an eyebrow, and she must realize it's a lost cause. She sinks into the chair across from me.

"The casting with Margeurite was a bust," she mutters. "A disaster, actually."

"Shit, what happened?"

"I panicked - like I always do with divination," she mutters, frustration pinching her face into a scowl. "Margeurite got me out, but I pulled something trying to fight the silver. Arlon made me spend the night in the infirmary."

"Hell - I'm sorry Gal. Are you alright?" She waves me off and sinks further into the chair. "For what it's worth, I panicked when she first put me under, too."

Galiva rubs her eyes. "Sure, but this wasn't my first time," she says. "Every time I've tried, it's always the same. It's just that *this* time, there's actual stakes riding on the success of the spell."

I lean back in my chair. "Have you ever cast divination with anyone but Margeurite?"

Something like resentment flashes across her face. "No."

There's enough bitterness in that single word that bad blood must exist. Surely that has to have some effect on casting.

"Maybe you should try with someone else?"

Galiva frowns up at the ceiling and it sort of seems like I'm not the first person to suggest this to her. "Maybe," she says, but it's that kind of maybe that sounds more like a no.

"How's Olbric?" she asks, quickly changing the subject. I won't push the topic if she doesn't want to talk about it. If there's one thing I've learned, it's that folks here respect boundaries.

"He's fine," I say. "Miffed that you left him." Though not that miffed. He sure seemed to get a kick out of riling me up while knowing I couldn't do a damn thing about it. "I took him down to the ice baths. He stayed in longer than I thought possible."

Galiva's snort of amusement drains some of the tension out of her. "He's such a masochist," she says. "Shame I can't do it again today - beating up Olbric is good stress relief. Shame you're working a conjuration, too. You'd also be good stress relief."

I chuckle at that. "Blame it on Arlon," I say. "What else do wizards do for fun? Besides casting, that is."

Galiva shrugs. "Some go into town," she says. "There are some decent taverns. A couple gambling houses, too, I think."

I sit upright at that, and Galiva gives me a curious look. "Gal, my cock is locked in a cage, Olbric seems keen on driving me insane, and I think I've maybe read ten pages since I've had it on," I say. "I could *really* use a drink."

Galiva chuckles and runs a hand over her face. "Alright, fine. But if we invite Olbric, he won't stop trying to drive you insane."

I don't have to think on that decision long. "Nah, he should come."

Maybe I'm a masochist, too.

WHEN IT'S TIME TO HEAD out, I meet Galiva and Olbric in the main atrium of the Crux. They're not alone. The newcomer stands with their back to me, and long white hair cascades down in an elaborate knot. When the wizard turns to greet me, I can immediately tell they're not human.

Long, pointed ears poke through their fine hair and startling copper eyes look me over. They offer a friendly smile, their face beautiful and genderless. Gray, white, and green ribbons are sewn around the cuffs of their robe. Underneath it, they wear a finely made ruffled collar shirt and black trousers with shiny black boots that go nearly up to their knees.

"Dom, this is Cancassi," Olbric says by way of introduction. "I just found out that they passed their transmutation mastery. I figured this would be a good chance to celebrate."

Cancassi offers me a hand, and I take it. There's an extra joint on each of their long fingers, but their grip is strong.

"A pleasure," they say formally, voice softly accented and deeper than expected.

"Same," I say intrigued. I realize I'm staring and tear my eyes away. "Sorry, I'm not trying to be rude. I've just never seen one of your kind before." Don't even have a name for them, I realize.

Cancassi grins, looking none too surprised. "I understand that you are from the north. I would be more surprised if you had encountered one of my kind before," they say. "I am of the Maeve. We come from the islands west of the mainland."

I don't know what a Maeve is, and it feels rude to ask, but Cancassi seems friendly enough. The four of us leave the Crux together, heading into town on the main thoroughfare. The Crux hovers on the edge of town, and it's about half an hour walk to get into the bustle of Straetham proper.

Even though it's early evening, the market is still busy. Folks are out and about hawking their wares, and I'm a little overwhelmed by the offerings. This is definitely no small town market. There are rolls of lustrous fabrics, goods from distant lands, foods that I can't even *recognize* though they make my stomach growl to smell.

As we make our way through town, Olbric points out a couple of stalls. "Galiva will say that the shop in Hilltop has the best meat pies in town, but she's a dirty liar - Mabel sells them right there," he says. He waves to a plump woman who smiles at the sight of him.

I laugh, but Galiva doesn't rise to the bait. It's only then I tune into the quiet conversation her and Cancassi are having behind me.

"Have you expressed your concerns to her?" Cancassi asks.

Galiva sighs. "Sort of," she says. "After this last attempt, I told her I wasn't going to cast with her again. She took it like sour grapes."

"Yes, well, Margeurite is nothing if not proud," Cancassi says. "But I think it would do her good to hear the specifics of what went wrong."

"Like she'll listen," Galiva says with no small bit of frustration in her voice. "She keeps insisting I'm overreacting."

But my eavesdropping is interrupted as we reach our destination. A large tavern and inn rests right on the edge of the market. The doors and windows are thrown open to welcome the early summer air, and I can hear the plucking of a mandolin over the din of voices. A spiky boar with a red apple in its mouth winks down at us from the large sign that reads *The Devilish Boar*. I do a double-take and realize that that's no apple.

Olbric sees me staring and nudges me in the ribs. "You know, I think you'd look rather dashing in a ball gag," he says. "Maybe I'll try one on you next time."

I swat his arm away, yet I can't help but grin as I walk into the tavern. The energy of the place is infectious. In Airedale there was a small dive you could go to for a drink, but it was nothing like this.

There's a long bar top where a skilled tender is taking orders and tossing out drinks. Serving maids hurry about the room, bearing trays ladened with beer steins and bowls of what appears to be hearty stew and fresh-baked bread. In one corner of the large common room, there's a bard on a raised stage. She starts in on a bawdy song that the group closest to her immediately join.

We find an empty table in one corner. Glancing around the busy room, I notice we're not the only wizards in attendance. There are a few other black robes, and though some of the faces are familiar, I don't know their names. It seems to be a popular haunt for the folks of the Crux.

A serving maid comes over to our table and gives us all a bright smile. "What'll it be?" she asks.

My gut sinks when I realize I don't have a single coin to my name. I spent every last cent I had getting to Straetham. Olbric jolts me out of my thoughts.

"Beers all around," he says. "And I'll take a bowl of stew. Dom - you want one?" I open my mouth to decline but Olbric grins, "I've got tonight."

I let out a sigh. "Sure," I say with a smile. All of the food at the Crux is good, but it's also very... clean. Mostly fruit and grains and vegetables with very little meat. Nothing sounds better than a hearty bowl of stew. "Thanks."

Olbric bumps his shoulder against mine. "We've all been there," he says. "You have to be at the Crux for a month before you start to get a stipend."

"A stipend?"

"Of course," Olbric says. "Our spells and services are worth good coin. It only makes sense that we see some of that."

"The only reason that you have to wait a month is to be sure you actually want to study magic. You wouldn't believe how many folks cut out after the first few days." Galiva gives me a sly look as she leans into her chair. "Doubt that'll be a problem with you."

"'Course it won't - I'm sort of locked in at the moment," I say, my grin coming out crooked.

Olbric laughs while Cancassi gives me a curious look. "Arlon has him working a conjuration," Galiva explains.

"Ah," Cancassi says sagely. "I am sorry for your temporary loss."

I don't admit that I'm counting the hours until it's off, but the thought is pushed aside when our serving maid returns. She has the handles of all four drinks closed in one hand and a tray with four large bowls of stew in the other.

Olbric scoops his mug up. "A toast then," he says. "To new mastery and new adepts."

Our mugs clink, and I take a long drink. The beer is malty and cold, and paired with the stew, it's the perfect distraction. I've never been much of a talker, and I don't do much of it as I eat, but I enjoy listening to the rest of them. At times, it's like they're speaking a whole other language of magic and casting that I'm just starting to understand. It's enough that I even forget about the cage for a while.

After we finish our meals, our serving maid comes back with another round of beer. Conversation has floated around Cancassi's transmutation mastery, but I finally have to ask, "What exactly do you have to do to earn your mastery?"

Cancassi takes a sip from their fresh mug, long fingers curled almost all the way around the stein. "It can vary, depending on the school you're testing for, but usually it's a twofold process that you undertake with Arlon," they explain. "First, you have to cast a spell of your particular school with him acting as the conduit. The challenge is that it has to be a spell of your own making. You're allowed to mix schools, but the dominant effect must be the school you are testing for. If you are successful at that, then Arlon will cast a spell with you as the conduit." They chuckle and take another long drink of beer. "And he is a ruthlessly efficient caster."

I can almost feel the heat of Arlon's hands, see his amused smile after he'd locked the cage around me. An errant shiver rushes through me.

"Yeah, I'd believe that," I say. "What does transmutation magic entail? It's modifying matter, right?"

"Correct," they say. "I actually created my spell with Arlon in mind. You've seen how strong he is, so I thought I would try to harness that into an enhancement spell. It took a lot of trips to the saddler."

The beer must be going to my head. "I'm sorry, did you say a *saddler*?"

Cancassi's grin turns mischievous. "I did," they say. "With transmutation especially, materials are important. My idea was to harness the strength of, say, a draft horse into a spell that a person might use to enhance their own strength at a needed time. So, I used Arlon's own natural strength, along with a specially made leather driving harness, shoes, tail and other adornments to create the spell. I'll say - Arlon made quite an impressive beast of burden."

Olbric looks simultaneously aghast and impressed. "You did not," he says, scandalized.

"I sure did," Cancassi says with a pleased smile. "If he thought the spell would fail, I'm sure he would never have agreed to it. But as it is..." Cancassi clicks their tongue and tugs at the green band around their sleeve. "Besides, I think Arlon rather enjoyed embracing his inner draft horse. I certainly enjoyed watching him do it."

I can't stop a small, amazed laugh and shake my head. "I can't even imagine," I say. Some might call Arlon imposing, but I think that's too nice of a word. He takes the breath out of a room when he stands up. I have a hard time picturing him naked, let alone trussed up like a carriage horse.

Cancassi turns those curious copper eyes to me and grins. "The harness is adjustable - I would certainly be willing to cast the spell again, if you're interested."

I flush at the thought. Heat shoots through my gut and into my trapped cock. I avoid answering by taking a long drink of my beer.

"I'm sure after all that, Arlon didn't go easy on you," Galiva says. "I remember thinking I was *so clever* when I was testing for my evocation mastery until he started in with the cat-o-nines on my ass."

Now it's Cancassi's turn to take a drink. "Where the hell do you think I've been for the past two days?" they ask. "He's had me in the dungeon since Saturday. Put me in an adjustable iron gibbet, with a plug and phallus locked *in* me on top of a cage around my cock. There was always someone monitoring me, of course, but he would come down every couple of hours and change my position to be gradually more and more uncomfortable. But the end result is the strongest shape-metal spell he's ever cast, so there's that, at least."

"I guess I can't complain too much, then," I mutter. I'm trying to imagine it, but the thought of Cancassi naked must be distracting me. How did they accommodate a plug, a phallus, *and* a cage? Unless the phallus was in their mouth? I frown into my beer as a moment of quiet passes. When I look up, all three of them are watching me, looking amused.

"I can see you doing the math," Olbric says slyly.

I open my mouth to protest, even though that is *exactly* what I'm doing.

"Don't tease him," Cancassi says. "Neither of you knew when you first met me, either."

"Know what?" I demand.

Olbric grins over the rim of his beer. "Cancassi is intersex."

"Wait, what sex?" I ask, even more confused now.

Cancassi laughs at that. "Humans call the Maeve intersex," they say, "but I say we're simply efficient. We only have one sex, and our parts are more or less a mix of the two that humans typically possess."

I blink, at a loss for words, though I find myself looking a little more closely at Cancassi. Under their robes, I see a hint of breasts under the ruffle of their shirt, but their face is beautiful and impossible to put into either one gender. Then I catch their curious copper gaze and Cancassi winks, sending my insides scuttling about.

Godsdamned *wizards*.

Do I have that effect on people?

I doubt it.

"I could show you later, if you like," Cancassi says, and I flush red all the way to the tips of my ears.

"Nope," says Olbric, with a distinct slur in his voice. "He's mine later."

"You're drunk," I say with a grin. "And I'm no one's later. Chastity, remember?"

Olbric's finger trails up my leg, and his smile is just short of obscene. "That just means you can't orgasm. There's still plenty of things I could do to you."

I shudder at his touch, my breath hitching as my cock throbs in its cage. "You're the fucking worst."

"Not yet, I'm not."

Galiva slaps Olbric on the shoulder. "Leave him be," she says, amused. "Arlon's trying to keep him from wearing out and neither of you are helping."

They laugh and the conversation meanders to other things. I was a little uncertain of Cancassi at first, but I like their quick wit and sense of humor. They're relaxed and open with Olbric and Galiva, and I gather that the three of them started at the Crux around the same time a few years ago. Even though I'm the newcomer, Cancassi doesn't talk down to me and answers my questions with clear and polite answers. All of them make me feel welcome, and by the end of the night, I'm laughing and joking with them.

By the time the three of them pitch in to pay our tab, Olbric is thoroughly drunk and Galiva has a grin that just won't go away. Cancassi seems relatively unaffected, and I don't realize how much I've had until I stand up. I sway a little, but end up helping Olbric out of the tavern and down the road back to the towers, a hand around his waist. I can't help but think he's hamming it up just so I'll hold him, but I'm not about to complain.

When we reach the Crux, Cancassi wishes us a good night before disappearing towards the illusion tower. Galiva kisses my cheek. "Do you think you can get him up to his room?" she asks and Olbric mutters something like, "I'll take you to *your* room."

"I'll manage it," I say with a grin and give Olbric a pinch to get him moving again. It has the opposite effect I'd hoped for. Olbric moans and presses up against me, his nose brushing my neck in a way that makes my skin ripple.

Galiva chuckles and shakes her head. "Goodnight," she says, before heading towards the abjuration tower.

"You're second floor in the evocation tower, right?" I ask. Olbric nods before gently nipping at my neck. I swear under my breath, wishing now more than ever that I had the damn cage off.

"That is quite enough of *that*," I say before bodily scooping him up. Olbric yelps, his arms flying behind my neck. My bad arm twinges but holds.

"You make me feel like a dainty lady," he slurs, grinning widely as he rests his head against my shoulder.

"Dainty, you are not," I say with a breathless laugh as I carry him up the stairs. It's a fortunate thing that he's not on one of the higher floors. He's maybe an inch taller than me, though probably weighs about as much. I'm doing pretty good, but as we get to the second-floor landing my bad arm spasms, sending a jolt of pain down to my wrist. I set him down with a quiet hiss. Olbric stumbles as he regains his feet and looks at me in concern.

"You alright?" he asks, lucidity entering his drunken haze.

"Fine," I say and clench my fist a couple of times to try and get the muscles sorted out. Olbric frowns before taking my good hand and leading me down the hall. The door to his room clicks open as we approach, and I barely have time to see the glowing focus around the handle before he pulls me inside and closes it again.

His room isn't so different from mine except it's a little bigger and far fuller. His desk is covered with stacks of neatly noted parchment and inkwells. A number of quills and charcoal pens rest in an old jar. I notice with a little bit of jealousy that his unmade bed is bigger than mine - maybe a perk of mastery? Above it on the windowsill are a few sweet-smelling plants next to a little globe that glows with a soft golden light.

The door is barely closed before I'm shoved onto the bed. "Wait - Olbric," I protest, but he doesn't pounce on me.

As much as I don't want to torture myself with the cage on, I'm a little disappointed. Instead, Olbric reaches into one of the drawers of his dresser and pulls out a silvery cloth. In the dim light of his room, it glows under his touch. He sits down next to me and takes my bad arm.

"Where does it hurt?" he asks. There's still a haze of drink in his eyes, but underneath it he's very serious.

I slip off my robe and roll up my shirt sleeve to show him the twitching spot in the muscles of my arm. Every spasm sends needles down to my elbow, but Olbric's fingers are gentle as he touches the spot. He takes the cloth and wraps it around my arm like a bandage, tying it off before kissing the knot. A comfortable heat radiates from the cloth, and I sigh as it starts to relax the twinging muscles.

"This might come as a surprise to you, but I know a little something about soothing pain," Olbric says with a lopsided grin. I chuckle at that and meet his eyes for a moment, feeling my heart thud in my chest. Not just because I want him - I definitely do - but he's looking at me in a way that feels like he's trying to find something hidden in my face.

But then he smiles, and I see how *very* drunk he still is.

"How did you hurt it?" he asks as he pulls me to lay down. His bed is big enough that it can fit us both - barely. "Since I can't have you to myself with that cage on, you can't leave until I get a story." He hooks one leg over mine to prove the point, his head resting on my chest.

I chuckle and try to find a comfortable spot to rest my arm. I end up settling it around him before I start in. "Before this, I lived just outside of Airedale up in the Hobokin mountains. I worked as a hunter and a forest guide. Helped folks get through the woods safe," I say.

Olbric chuckles sleepily. "Of course you did," he says. At my look, he says, "Bloodline wizards don't usually come so ruggedly handsome. Imagining you holding a bow is a pretty picture."

I snort. "And no longer an option for me," I say.

"Why not?"

I sigh and run my fingers down his arm. "It happened last fall and it never quite healed right. A wolf had been spotted outside of

Airedale. Farmers had lost livestock, travelers and caravans had had a few close calls and were scared to go through the Hobokins. There was a reward out for its hide. My pay had dried up thanks to the damned thing, so I thought I'd hunt it down."

"Foolish thing to do," Olbric mutters.

"Would have been if I'd failed," I say. "I tracked the wolf to the flatirons - a jagged, rocky part of the mountains that skirt the main road. It's not a kind area. The bluffs are steep and unstable and easy to hide in. But I found her just a second after she found me. She leapt at me from a higher bluff, and she probably would have killed me if my bow hadn't been nocked. But I heard her snarl when she jumped and got an arrow up just quick enough to shoot."

"Fucking hell," Olbric says, and I'm a little pleased to have impressed an evocation wizard.

"It was a lucky shot," I admit. "The damn thing was rabid. She was skin and bones, but that didn't stop her from trying to get at me. My shot killed her quick enough to stop her from biting me, but didn't do anything to stop her body from knocking me off of the cliff. I fell about twenty feet and landed poorly. I'm lucky I got away with nothing but some scrapes and a broken arm."

Olbric settles a little more comfortably against me. "Luck-touched," he mutters. "I'm glad. You wouldn't be here, otherwise."

I grin and look down at him to see him already starting to doze. I settle in, realizing I'm stuck here for the night. With Olbric's warmth against me, I can't be too sore about it.

"Yeah, me too."

Creating a Conjuration

Conjuration: The school of magic that creates matter out of thin air. Casting methods include periods of chastity and masturbation.

ON THE FINAL MORNING of my chastity I wake up at dawn, just like I used to in the Hobokins. I stretch, feeling better rested than I did all last week. I hate to admit it, but maybe I did need the break from casting.

The sun is just brightening the sky, so it's too early to go to Arlon's office. As eager as I am to get the cage off, I doubt he'll be inclined to unlock it if I wake him up. Instead, I get dressed and head to the mess hall to grab a quick breakfast before going down to the baths. This early it's abandoned, and I'm glad for it. Gives me a chance to ease into the day on my own terms before other people enter the mix.

Of all the things I've had to get used to in the Crux, being around folks all the time has been the unexpected challenge. In the Hobokins, I'd talk to people maybe once a week when I went into town. Now, unless I've locked myself away in my room, I'm rarely alone in the towers. I'm not complaining, but it can get a little exhausting being around folks all the time. For now, I take advantage of the rare moment of solitude and take a spot in my favorite pool in the back.

I take my time to bathe and shave before I simply slide back into the water and enjoy it. I must be there an hour before I hear someone else come down the stairs. It would normally be my cue to leave, but when I look over, I see that it's Cancassi.

And they're naked.

"Can I join you?"

"Of course," I say.

I try not to stare, but it's a losing battle. Cancassi moves like a dancer, long limbs elegant and poised. Their long white hair hangs free of its braid. It stops at their slender waist, dripping over their shoulders to partially cover the small mounds of their breasts. Their porcelain skin glows with sweat, and I can't help but wonder what they were doing before this. As they step into the pool, my eyes are drawn to their soft cock that's haloed by a little tuft of white hair, but it disappears under the water as they sink in with a sigh.

"Early morning?" I ask and blink hard as I force myself to refocus on Cancassi's face.

"More like a late night," they say and sink up to their neck. "I was helping with an enchantment spell in the dungeon."

"Gods, all night? That sounds daunting."

Cancassi chuckles. "Not so much for me. I was simply assisting in casting. For Thaddius though, almost certainly. But testing for mastery isn't supposed to be easy."

I rub a wet hand over my face. "I'm sure it's not. Magic's more complicated than I ever imagined. I'm having a hard enough time just narrowing down which school I want to study," I admit.

"Have any struck an interest?" they ask.

My grin is crooked. "That's the problem - they *all* have. At least all the ones I've tried so far."

Cancassi chuckles. "Maybe you should get a taste of all of them before you decide," they say. "Which schools haven't you delved into yet?"

I think back and count it off on my fingers. "I've tried abjuration, a bit of illusion, evocation and divination," I say. "I'm about to finally get *out* of conjuration. I've seen a little bit of enchantment, but haven't tried it. And I haven't tried transmutation or corpimancy."

Cancassi's grin turns sly as their foot brushes mine under the water. "Well, then let me formally extend an offer to give an introduction into transmutation."

Even the innocent touch makes me shiver. After five days, every brush of bare skin against mine is enough to light my nerves up. Cancassi's grin widens as they slide their foot up my leg to nudge the metal cage.

"You get this off today?"

My breath hitches. "Yeah."

"Good," they say. "Later this week then? I would very much like to get you into that harness. I hate that it's just collecting dust."

I hope it's not just my desperation that makes me say, "Deal."

Cancassi smiles. "It's a date."

ONCE FIRST BELL RINGS, I head towards Arlon's office. It might still be a little early, but I'll take my chances. Cancassi's less-than-innocent touch helped nothing, and I'm starting to get desperate.

I'm almost to the Grandmaster's door when someone calls my name. I nearly groan, but when I turn I see that it's Marguerite. She hurries to catch up to me, robes billowing out behind her. As she gets close, I see the dark shadows under her eyes. She looks exhausted.

"You're alright?"

She gives a tired smile. "I'm fine," she says. "You are kind to ask."

I give her a searching look. She looks anything but. "How's the divination going?"

She lets out a huff that reminds me too much of the goats my da had kept. "Slowly," she says. "And very frustrating. None of the wizards last with our missing people are divination wizards. It makes gathering more information very difficult."

I remember the half-heard conversation between Galiva and Cancassi on the way to the tavern the other day. It makes me wonder if others have declined to cast with her. Marguerite had been attentive and understanding with me, so I'm not sure what happened to cause the rift between her and Galiva.

"Would you be interested in going into the silver again? I wonder if we can't find a little more information." Her face is so full of hope that I don't feel right denying her. I've got no problem with divination. Quite the opposite, actually.

"Of course," I say. "Though it'll have to be later this week. Saturday?"

Marguerite looks a little disappointed, but she nods. "Saturday it will have to be. Thank you, Dominai," she says, and gives my cheek a quick kiss before sweeping back down the hall.

The innocent kiss makes me flush with warmth. I rub the spot, grinning from ear to ear as I make my way to Arlon's door. I lift my hand to knock, but pause. My guts twist with anticipation. I don't know what's in store for me with conjuration, so I straighten my robe and take a breath before I knock.

The Grandmaster's deep voice answers from inside. "Come in."

I open the door, and Arlon looks up from the papers on his desk. "I assumed I'd see you today," he says, amusement coloring his tone. "And how has your chastity been?"

"Frustrating," I admit.

Arlon gives his close-lipped grin, but I see a hint of wicked pleasure hidden in his face. "Come in. Close the door behind you."

I do as asked, my pulse already racing. Arlon is unhurried. He finishes scribbling whatever it is that he's writing before he gets to his feet.

"Come. I'll give you a demonstration on conjuration," he says and motions for me to follow.

I didn't notice it the last time I was in here, but there's a door on the far end of his office. He leads me through it and down a winding stone staircase. It opens up into a large space, the lights dimmed to just brighter than a candle flicker. It's cool down here and more cavernous than I would have thought. It takes me a moment longer to realize that we're not alone.

"Morning, sir," a woman says brightly from where she's seated by the stairs.

"Good morning, Ambra," Arlon says. "How is Thaddius?"

"Holding on well, sir."

"How many have been down to use him?" Arlon asks.

Ambra does a quick count. "Three so far," she says. "Cancassi spent most of the night with him. Fey came down after, and then me, of course."

It takes me a moment to see who they're talking about. A naked man stands a little further in the gloom. He's locked in a wooden pillory, forced to stand bent at the waist. There are holes in the wooden framework for his head and hands, but I can't get a good look at his face due to the leather hood that's covering his eyes and ears.

A curious sort of gag is fastened into his mouth. A circular metal ring that keeps his jaws forced open. I watch him shift from one foot to the other, a quiet, tormented moan spilling from him along with a trickle of saliva.

Oh, so *this* is where Cancassi had been.

"That's not nearly enough for a domination spell," Arlon says. "Maybe we should move him to the courtyard for others to use."

Ambra's smile brightens. "I'd be happy to, sir. Keep him in the pillory?"

"Yes, but not the stand. Let him stretch out a bit," Arlon says, though judging by his grin, it won't be a mercy. I shudder and wonder exactly what he means by 'use.' Going off the gleam of liquid sliding down the man's leg, I can guess.

Ambra goes to the pillory and unlocks the wooden frame from the stand before pulling Thaddius upright. The man gives a surprised shout but stands, shivering as Ambra ties a leash to the collar I hadn't noticed around his neck. She gives him a tug, and he blindly follows, stumbling only a little as she leads him. They make their way up the stairs, and out of sight.

"Enchantment," Arlon explains. "In this case, a spell that can dominate the will of an individual. Thaddius won't be done with it until he begs for it, and he's always had a bit of an ego. I imagine a couple of hours in the courtyard as a public plaything will do him in."

I remember Galiva's mocking words to Olbric during the last spell they had cast. "Humiliation," I say, my mouth dry.

Arlon gives me an appraising look. "A necessary component," he says. "Enchantment plays with the mind, and so you must play with the mind of your conduit. I'm sure Thaddius wasn't expecting to be moved. Depending on the desired effect, hypnotism is also an effective enchantment method."

Arlon touches one of the glowing globes that rest in sconces along the wall. All of them immediately brighten, casting light into the dungeon. It's... actually kind of nice. There are comfortable chairs set about as well as various casting components. A number of whips and crops hang against one wall, and a large bed rests against the back. There's even the iron gibbet Cancassi mentioned.

"How have you been spending your time this week?" Arlon asks, snapping me back to attention. He leads me to the back of the room, towards the bed that stands in front of three large mirrors.

"I've been shadowing Galiva and Olbric," I say. "That and reading some of the material she's given me."

Arlon nods in approval. "Good," he says. "And has anyone touched you?"

"Not really, other than Olbric and Cancassi teasing the crap out of me," I say, wondering at the odd question. Does conjuration magic mean I'm not allowed to be touched?

Arlon tsks and pushes my robe off of my shoulders before draping it over the back of a chair. "They were being kind," he says. "That desperation can make for a powerful conjuration spell. How did it feel watching the spells that Galiva cast and knowing you wouldn't be able to find your own release?"

I run my tongue over my lower lip as Arlon starts to unbutton my trousers. "Maddening," I say, a little breathless.

Arlon grins, and I see a hint of teeth. "You don't know maddening," he says. "Not yet."

Suddenly, I'm on the bed without really knowing how I got there. In spite of his size, Arlon is *fast*. I struggle to sit up, but he holds me down, overpowering me with an ease that scares me. He pins my hands over my head with one of his own, his free hand exploring my chest. He must see the fear on my face, because he slows down, gently stroking my cheek.

"The cardinal rule applies everywhere in the Crux," Arlon says. "Even with me. You say stop, and I *will* stop. That is a rule we don't tolerate being broken."

I let out a breath. "Right."

I knew I would get the cage off, thought I'd maybe get a lecture, but I hadn't expected to actually cast with Arlon. Yet the promise of an out puts me at ease, and the thrill of fear turns to excitement.

Gods know I'm just as curious about the Grandmaster of the Crux
as he seems to be about me.

I scoot my hips to help Arlon pull my trousers the rest of the
way off. He doesn't bother with my shirt. Instead, he pulls me up and
turns me so I'm kneeling in front of him, my back flush against his
chest. I'm put on full display in front of the mirrors and can watch as
he runs a large hand down my chest and stomach before toying with
the cage around my cock.

"Look at yourself," he orders quietly.

I swallow, my face reddening in my reflection. Other than
glimpses in ponds, I realize I've never really gotten a good look at
myself. Not like this - splayed out and half-naked.

My mussed auburn hair falls onto my face, covering one green
eye. I've never really noticed them before, but I have a dusting of
freckles over my sun-tanned face to match the ones on my shoulders
and arms. Years of wandering the Hobokins have left me with wiry
muscles and more than a few scars. My cock looks small inside of
the cage, and I flush even brighter. Olbric is right - I'm not like the
bloodline wizards here. There's a rough edge about me that's missing
from the rest of them.

Except Arlon.

Arlon seems to read my mind. "Oh, but you are an impressive
one," he says, and I see him watching my reflection appreciatively.
His hand trails down between my legs, pushing them further apart.
"You should feel no shame having no name to put to your magical
lineage. Not all of us do, and we're usually more powerful for it."

I shudder as Arlon's strong fingers caress my hips and ass, his
breath hot against my neck. "Speaking from experience?"

Arlon chuckles as his teeth graze my shoulder. "No one expected
an unnamed bastard to rise to be Grandmaster of the Crux, and yet
here I am," he says. "But that was years ago now, and you are one of
three non-bloodline wizards to appear since."

His uncertainty about me suddenly makes a lot more sense. "I would never have known if Allisande hadn't told me," I say, but whatever follow-up thought I had is lost when Arlon leans me forward. He pushes my chest against the bed and lifts my ass up.

"Lucky that she did," Arlon says as he spreads my cheeks apart, wringing a moan of anticipation out of me. My cock throbs inside of the cage, which only aggravates my desire more. "I think you will do well here, Dominai. So long as you don't wear yourself out in the first month."

I feel his breath against the small of my back before his tongue darts out to taste my skin. His teeth follow, nipping gently. My freshly washed skin is still sensitive, and I break out in gooseflesh as my hands fist in the covers of the bed.

"Temperance is something you will have to learn," Arlon says. "There is power in delaying gratification - *especially* with conjuration."

Arlon's fingers twine through my hair before he pulls my head up, forcing me to look at myself in the mirror. I see his grin reflected at me before he dips behind me. He takes his time, leisurely exploring as if I'm just a new toy for him to play with. His tongue darts over my tender flesh, traveling up the bridge of skin from my still-trapped balls. He nibbles gently, teeth scraping the inside of my thighs and scrotum.

Then, his tongue is at my ass. My eyes shoot wide in the mirror, and I jerk in surprise. He tightens his grip on my hair and holds my ass still as his tongue circles the pucker of flesh. I can't stop a moan. I've gotten used to the fascination with my ass here, but this is certainly new. Then he pokes his tongue *into* me, and I make a rather undignified noise of surprise. I feel the huff of his laugh against my skin.

Under his commanding grip I can only watch, seeing the haze of pleasure fall over my reflection. I've never been a vain person, but even I can admit that it's arousing to see. The cage around my cock feels impossibly tight as his tongue prods and teases me until I want to scream at him to *get on with it*. I grab the cover of the bed and press back into him.

As if on cue, Arlon pulls away. I moan at the loss, but I'm not left waiting for long. His tongue is quickly replaced by a finger, slicked with lotion. I bite my lip and press wantonly back, spearing myself on his digit. He finds the sweet spot inside of me with a hunter's precision and massages it with one finger, and then a second. His fingers are large, and even with two I feel full.

He works them slowly, moving with a leisure that is completely at odds with the burning need inside of me. After a week of deprivation, the stretch of his fingers coax the fire back to life with ease. Every touch feels new; every teasing nip and kiss against my shoulders and back, every slow, gentle slide of his fingers into me.

Suddenly, he pulls me up to kneeling once more, my heated back pressed against his chest. "Look at yourself," he growls, his voice thick with pleasure. I can feel his erect cock against my back and can tell he's enjoying this slow torment.

I do as told, and a hard shiver runs through me. My face is flushed with more than just embarrassment now. Arlon is a shadow behind me, holding me with an arm around my chest, his fingers seated deep inside of me. Inside of the cage my cock is leaking, a thin stream of liquid oozing from the trapped tip.

Arlon twists his fingers, and my hips jump, making the cage rattle. It's *maddening*, but at least his godsdamned pace picks up. He spears me steadily, working his fingers in and out, always curling just enough to drag across that sweet spot. It sends ripples of pleasure through my body, and yet, as good as it feels, I doubt I can finish with the cage on.

He fondles my captured balls with his free hand and squeezes a third finger into me, spreading me wide. I reach back and grab his neck, tossing my head back with a shout. The initial stretch burns a little before fading to a throbbing sort of heat as I relax around the intrusion. He is slow and meticulous, exploring and stretching my hole thoroughly. And here I'd thought the cage was maddening, but *this* is a new level of torment.

A moan rattles out of me as I try to push down on his fingers, but he stops me, his arm tightening in a commanding grip around my chest. I've never been overpowered like this. I feel trapped, helpless, even though it's just his hands holding me. I realize that Arlon could do this for days, keeping me teased and desperate, all the while holding the key to my release. I'm shocked to find that a part of me *wants* that.

He's right. There is something in delaying gratification - as tortuous as it is.

I hadn't realized I'd been resisting him until I submit, sinking against him with a desperate moan. "Arlon, please," I gasp.

"Not yet," he says and pulls his fingers from me.

I feel empty. My cock aches, and I wiggle my hips as if the friction of the cage will do anything to ease it. It doesn't, of course, and Arlon chuckles. He tugs my shirt off and tosses it aside. He doesn't take his clothes off - doesn't even get rid of his robe, but in the mirror I see him release his sizable cock from the slit in his trousers. His powerful hand lands on my hip as I watch his reflection slick a good amount of lotion over his length. It swells under his grip, and I'm suddenly very grateful for the amount of time he's spent stretching me.

"I am going to fuck you, Dominai," he says, his deep voice rumbling through me. "And only after I am satisfied will you have your freedom." He turns me sideways to the mirrors and bends me forward until I'm on all fours, his hand fisting in my hair. "And I want you to watch."

I'm intimidated by the size of him. Olbric was well-endowed, but Arlon's cock is proportional to the rest of his large body - both in length and girth. I feel the tip of his cock prod at my hole before the head of it eases in, and as big as he looks, he *feels* larger. The stretch of him makes me whimper. I grip the covers and bury my face against the bed. He stops, only a couple of inches sheathed inside of me.

For a second, I think he's stopped to give me a second to adjust. Yet even after I relax around him, he stays still. I swear and pull my head from the covers and open my eyes, realizing that keeping them open is going to be harder than I thought.

As soon as I focus on my reflection again, Arlon resumes. I watch him push into me, inch by tortuous inch. He goes slow, obviously aware of his size, and I'm grateful for it. Even the gentle treatment makes me feel like he's going to split me in half. He eases in until his hips are flush against me and lets out an appreciative little hiss of pleasure.

"You are so very tight," he groans and rolls his hips, and my whole body shifts with him. "Are you alright, Dominai?"

My hands clench in the covers. His cock is big, bordering on painful, but the longer he's in me, the easier it is to relax around him. I rest my head against the bed, face turned towards the mirror.

"Yes, sir."

"Good."

Slowly he retreats, almost to the point of pulling out before he thrusts in again only incrementally faster. His strong hand keeps me pinned to the bed as he works himself into me at his leisure. I feel stuffed full, and watching his cock slide in and out of me only seems to enhance the feel of it.

He must read the pleasure and torment in my reflection, because he speeds up and slows down accordingly, never moving fast enough to hurt me or finish me off. With the cage on, I doubt I could any-way. At least with Olbric I had the focuses to stimulate my cock, but now the cage keeps my pleasure locked just out of my reach. Each thrust reminds me that I can't finish until Arlon lets me. The slow drag and thrust of his length is as much bliss as it is torture.

After what feels like a lifetime, he pulls out. I shudder in relief, but he only re-applies more lotion before easing back into me. It's that casual show of control that breaks me. He really is going to do this for days, keeping me on the edge of desperation until I'm sure I'll go mad with it. He'll keep me down here and use me for his pleasure, just like Thaddius. As helpless as I had been in the silver, Arlon wields a very different kind of control, but it holds just as strong.

I wail and slump against the bed. Arlon stops, and I open my eyes to see that he's fucked me even closer to the mirror. I look at my own flushed face, hazy with desire and defeat. My cock is making a puddle below me, and all the while, Arlon kneels behind me, a smile of perfect control on his face. Only when he locks eyes with my reflection does he start again.

But even Arlon must have a limit. Or maybe he found a shred of mercy in that stony heart. Either way, he starts to speed up. My legs are shaking, and with one particularly hard thrust, he pushes me flat on the bed, his hand yanking my hair. I shout as he snaps his hips, thrusting into me again and again. I feel split open, rent apart, and yet when Arlon finally groans in release I'm still whole enough to feel his seed fill me.

He pulls out with another groan of pleasure, and my hole twitches at the loss. I shudder as I feel a trail of wet follow him, sliding down between my legs. I feel used and dirtied, and *godsdamn*, if it doesn't do something to me. My cock throbs, swollen and red inside of the cage. Then something cool and round slides against my stretched ass.

"Arlon, please," I beg. I can't take anymore. He's taken me right to the edge of my endurance, and a stop is just behind my teeth.

"Hush," he says gently and holds the little silver key out for me to see. I'm transfixed by the sight of it. I realize I would do all manner of unseemly things to get it. And Arlon can tell.

In the mirror, his toothy smile is reflected at me. "It's just the focuses to contain the spell you're about to conjure."

I shudder as he presses the little ball into me, and then another. Two more follow, and it only does a little to fill the emptiness he's left. "I recommend you pull them out as you find your release," Arlon says. "Don't worry - the spell should still get caught by them."

I shudder and sit up as Arlon's strong hands turn me to face the mirror full on again. He reaches around me and slips the key into the lock on the cage. There's a quiet click, and just like that, it's off. A week's worth of torment, gone in an instant. My cock springs up, hard and leaking. I reach for it, but Arlon stops me with a look, that iron control still holding strong.

"The manner of the spell you conjure is dependent on what you focus on while casting," Arlon says. "But I have a feeling you're too damn distracted to focus on much. So, just do what feels good, and we'll see what comes of it. You are both caster and conduit with conjuration."

"Right," I breathe. But even then, I don't move. Arlon's eyes hold mine before he looks to my straining erection. He reaches out, but doesn't come close enough to touch. Even as I strain towards him, he keeps his fingers just shy of contact.

His chuckle rumbles through me like music. "I think you're ready."

Then, he pulls away from me, leaving me alone on the bed. I feel cold and exposed, yet in the dim light, I can see Arlon watching me.

I don't care. Let him watch. I don't intentionally put on a show, but I'm sure he gets one all the same. After I broke my arm I had to switch to using my left hand, which had been a rather frustrating adjustment. I've long gotten used to it by now and I grab my cock, already slick with precum. After five days and *all of this*, I'm so sensitive that even my callused fingers feel like bliss.

Watching my reflection is more arousing than I would have imagined. I watch the slide of my hand up and down my cock, see my thumb stroke over my head. All the while, Arlon sits in a chair behind me, a grin on his face.

It doesn't take long. I know how to take care of myself. Other than Allisande, I wasn't exactly getting solicited back home. Airedale is a prudish sort of town. Folks keep to themselves, and when they do come together, it's quick and full of shame and disappointment. Wood nymphs want no business from the likes of humans, and other than a few caravans a year, the roads aren't exactly busy. There was a lot of time to get to know myself.

I feel my orgasm building, and it's a bit of a surprise to see my reflection tense so obviously. I've never thought about what I must look like when I cum.

When my gut tightens and my pulse sings, I do as Arlon said. I find the string attached to the focuses and pull. My orgasm rips a shuddering moan from me, and I jerk as each ball slips out of me. Normally I'm pretty quiet about it, but it's been a godsdamned week, and Arlon's heated gaze is burning a hole into me. I moan until I run out of breath as ribbons of white erupt from my cock, coating my hand and the bed in front of me.

It's the type of orgasm that empties me, leaves me lightheaded as it goes on and *on*. I stroke myself until it starts to hurt, and when I'm finally spent, I collapse into the mess I've made. I don't care. I'm so tired that I feel like I could fall asleep right here.

Vaguely, I feel the focuses taken from beside me. I hear the rush of water from somewhere in the room and a moment later, Arlon returns with the four focuses, cleaned off and shining.

"It appears that you were successful," Arlon says as he presents them to me. "Are you alright?"

It takes a minute to find my voice. I'm sore in ways I never thought I could be, exhausted and spent. But under all that, I'm satisfied. The ache of need that's followed me all week is gone, and in its place are four glowing focuses. I take them and roll them in my palm.

"Fucking hell, I'm fine."

Arlon chuckles and offers me a basin of water and a towel. "Conjuration is very personal. I'm curious to see what you made." It'll be another trip to the baths, but I make use of the wash basin for now.

As I finish cleaning myself off, I realize that Arlon's wanting us to test the spell *now*. I groan as I go about collecting my discarded clothes. It takes some time to find them all - my shirt somehow made it halfway across the room. I gather them and take my time putting them back on. Arlon's kept me waiting a week - he can wait a few damn minutes while I get my pants on straight. He watches me with faint amusement on his face.

Once I'm relatively put back together, though definitely walking a little tender, I grab the gently glowing focuses. Arlon puts a hand on my shoulder.

"We'll test it outside," he says. "Unless it's divination, we always test outside."

Of course we do. I don't know what I've made, but I made it well and thorough. Even I can tell the spell inside of the focuses is strong - whatever it is.

"We'll go to the conjuration yard," Arlon says.

He leads me up the stairs and out of his office. We pass by the open doors to the main courtyard, and I see a group of people assembled. My stomach jumps when I realize it's Thaddius in the middle of them.

The group around him are chatting and laughing, like there's not a naked and bound man in front of them. I only catch a glimpse, a quick flash - but I see Ambra at the center of it with him. She has her boot on Thaddius' back, forcing his face into the dirt while another woman roughly tugs at his cock and balls. His anguished moans fade as Arlon leads me further into the Crux, towards the conjuration tower.

The tower itself is made of blue-gray stone, but we only dip into it for a second before we emerge out into the back yard. It's much like the evocation yard except the grass is lush and the tall stone wall that hems it in is decorated with vibrant, thorny vines that are unlike anything I've ever seen.

"Don't touch those," Arlon warns. "I'll have to get help to cut you out."

The barely-open bulbs on the vines turn to watch us as we step into the center of the yard. Arlon stands just behind me.

"Have you ever released a spell before?" he asks.

"Once, with Olbric," I say.

"Good," Arlon says. He leaves one focus in my hand and takes the other three for safekeeping. His hand lands on my shoulder as he says, "This will be no different. Whenever you are ready."

I draw in a breath, suddenly nervous. What if I've conjured up something useless? Or worse, something dangerous. Arlon had gotten me well and worked up, so who's to say I'm not about to destroy something?

Arlon squeezes my shoulder, a steady comfort. "It will be alright," he says gently.

I roll the marble between my fingers and plant my feet. I take another breath and hold the focus out in front of me. The spell lets loose.

The energy rushes out of the focus in a flood of silvery light. It swirls in front of us before condensing into a form. Four legs, a massive head. The silver wolf shakes itself as if just waking up.

I stagger back into Arlon with a gasp, a fear I didn't realize was still there surging up. It could be a copy of the wolf I killed. The same golden eyes, the same silver fur. But she's no longer starved and mangy. Those eyes aren't glazed with delirium and hatred. Instead, she looks at me expectantly, as if waiting for something.

"It's alright," Arlon says again and keeps his hands on my shoulders. "I'm guessing that wolves have some significance to you?"

I can't take my eyes off of her, just waiting for the creature to spring. But she doesn't. She starts to look a little bored and sits on her massive haunches, tail sweeping across the ground. I swallow and say, "Yeah, they do." This one in particular.

"This is your creation," Arlon says. "It will obey you - whatever command you give it. You don't need to fear it."

I steel myself and clear my throat. "Walk along the wall."

The wolf bounds to her feet and goes to lope the perimeter of the yard. I can't look away from her. She's graceful - not at all like the lumbering, jerking gait of the creature that had attacked me. I draw in a steadying breath before saying, "Come here."

I tense as the wolf pads over. *Godsdamn* she's massive, but she only comes to sit in front of me. Slowly, carefully, I reach my shaking hand out. She leans forward to sniff my fingers, and I can't stop a small, awed laugh. I close the distance and put my hand on her head. Her fur is warm and soft and very real as I skritch her head gently. She leans in and closes her golden eyes as if enjoying the touch.

"Well done, Dominai," Arlon says, and I can hear the approval in his voice. "Conjuring a familiar is an essential of the school, and you managed it on your first try."

The wolf nudges into my hand, more insistent, and I kneel down to give her a good scratch. "I had a good instructor."

Arlon chuckles, and I glance back to see him smiling, showing teeth and all.

"You should rest," he says at last. "You've earned it."

Courage and Corpimancy

C orpimancy: *The school of magic that controls the forces of life, death, and healing. Casting methods include piercing and blood-play.*

"HOW LONG DID THE WOLF stick around for?" Galiva asks over dinner that evening.

"A while, I think," I say. "She followed me back to my room. Curled up on the foot of my bed and fell asleep. I took a pretty long nap, but by the time I woke up, she was gone."

Galiva beams at me. "That's great, Dom!" she says, and I can hear the pride in her voice. "It took me weeks to find my familiar."

I flush at the praise and look down at my cup. "Arlon did all the work - I just finished it," I say.

"No doubt he put you through it, but by the very nature of con-juration, *you* did the work," she chuckles. "How's it feel to have sur-vived your first week?"

I take a sip of water from my cup to hide my grin. I'm still sitting tender thanks to Arlon, but even now I shiver thinking back to this morning.

"It feels like I should have been doing this years ago." While I was guiding, I was just existing. Working to build enough resources to get through yet another winter and nothing more. "It's strange, I feel... sharper, somehow. Like I've been asleep and I'm just now waking up."

Galiva smiles at that. "The Crux has a way of doing that. I noticed it when I came here, too," she says. "Do you miss the Hobokins?"

I sigh and lean back in my chair, pushing my empty plate away from me. I wouldn't mind another helping of the leafy greens and fish the cooks prepared, but I don't want to be greedy. I'm still getting used to this whole three-meals-a-day thing.

"Not the woods specifically. I miss the quiet though," I say. "And I miss hunting."

Galiva glances at my bad arm. "Olbric's a dirty gossip. He told me how you broke it," she says and rests her chin on her hand. "Ironic that your familiar is a wolf."

I snort. "Not just a wolf - *the* wolf. The damn thing looks just like it."

Galiva hums thoughtfully. "You know, some theorize that familiars aren't so much straight conjuration as they are a summoning," she says. "Maybe this is your wolf coming back to thank you."

"*Thank* me?" I repeat. "I killed it."

"But it was rabid, wasn't it?" Galiva asks. "That's not a kind disease. And there's no curing it. Did you know a rabid animal can't drink? It would have been confused and in pain. Imagine if you were separated from your pack in such a state? I think you did it a mercy."

I fall quiet. I've never thought about it like that. When I find the three charges of the conjuration on my ever-growing necklace, I could swear I see a golden eye looking back at me from inside the little marble.

"Maybe you're right," I say at last.

Galiva gives me an appraising look, and I can see something working behind her eyes. I take another sip of water from my cup and wait for it to come out. Finally, she says, "How would you like to be able to shoot a bow again?"

My hand goes to my bad arm, rubbing the knot of twisted muscles. I'm sure I look like a deer. All wide-eyed surprise.

"I'd like that," I say, which is the understatement of the year. I'd been terrified to leave my da's cabin in the Hobokins without a means to protect myself. Looking back, that's part of why it took me so long to do it. I had to muster up the courage.

Now it's Galiva's turn to look uncomfortable. "I have my mastery in corpimancy," she says. "But for an old injury like that, I would have to cast the spell directly *on* you."

"So what? I've pretty much done nothing but conduit since coming here."

Galiva winces and says, "Yeah, well, there's a reason that there are only three corpimancers in Straetham right now - including Arlon. It's... not easy to be a conduit for. It pushes endurance in a way that even evocation can't compare."

At the beginning of last week I might have jumped in without question, but I've learned a lot in the time I've been here. "What kind of endurance?"

"Pain. Among other things," she says.

"Right." I fall quiet as I think about it. At worst, I won't be able to hack it and the spell will fail. At best? I might be able to shoot again. "I can always stop, right?"

"Always," Galiva promises.

I steel myself and let out a sigh. "Alright," I say and give a lopsided grin. "C'mon and hurt me, Gal."

THE CORPIMANCY TOWER is small. It's only three stories instead of five or six like the others. As we walk up the dimly lit stairs to the top floor, I notice that it feels different than the other towers I've visited, too. Calm and subdued, like there's an extra weight in the air. Even in the evenings the towers are usually occupied, but we're alone as we head down the hall. It's a little eerie.

Galiva opens the door to a casting room and ushers me inside. Just like the rest of the tower, there's not much in here. Other than a wooden table and a cold fireplace, it's empty. Not even a cabinet.

When Galiva touches one of the globes set into the wall, the room brightens to a warm glow. A pack is slung over her shoulder, and as she sets it down I hear the slosh of liquid. She takes off her robe and rolls up her sleeves.

"Go ahead and take your shirt off. Get comfortable," she says and waves me towards the table.

I do as I'm told and tug my shirt up before hopping onto the table. On second thought, I snatch my shirt and bunch it up to use as a pillow. I'm not sure how comfortable you can get on a bare wooden slab, but I do my best.

I crane my neck and look over as Galiva unpacks a jug of liquid, a clean cloth, and a neat little leather case. I'm nervous, but I try not to let it show as she carries the stuff over and sets it on the table beside me.

"We can do this one of two ways," she says. "I can leave you free during the spell and trust you to stay still, or I can strap your arm down."

A nervous laugh bubbles out of my throat. "Fuck, Galiva, way to romance me." I look at the leather case and say, "Maybe strap it down."

Galiva kisses my cheek, and I feel a leather strap slide up through a slit in the wood that I hadn't noticed. She gently rubs the muscles in my bad arm. When she finds the atrophied knot, I hiss as the spot twinges under her fingers. She lays my arm down before tightening the belt just below my elbow.

"Some spells don't necessarily need the energy of sexual release to be successful. With corpimancy, the energy created from the casting itself is usually enough to finish a spell." She gives a wry grin and adds, "Not to mention, I doubt you'll be able to get it up unless you're a particular brand of pervert."

That startles a genuine laugh out of me. "And are you that particular brand of pervert?"

Galiva winks and says, "I got my mastery in corpimancy, didn't I?"

She flips open the leather case and reveals rows of sharp little needles. They're about as long and thick as a small porcupine quill, made of polished metal with tips that look sharp enough to pierce flesh. All in all, there are about 20 of them in the case.

I stare up at her, and my fear must be evident. "We don't have to do this," she says. There's sympathy in her voice and maybe a tinge of regret. Does she feel bad for even mentioning it? For dangling the possibility in front of me?

I draw in a steadying breath, trying to stamp the fear down. "What exactly are you going to do with them?"

Galiva takes the fingers of my bound hand and slides a focus down each one like a ring. "I'm going to use them to pierce the skin on your arm," she says. "I'll arrange them in a particular way to draw the energy to the poorly healed area. Whatever excess there is will go into the focuses. If I do it right, I'll be able to use the spell to heal fresh breaks."

I let out a long sigh and clench my eyes shut. It will hurt. I know it will hurt, and yet I'm considering it anyway. Galiva waits for my answer, her fingers gentle as they stroke through my hair.

"Fucking hell. I won't know how bad it is until I try it, right?"

Galiva chuckles and says, "That's one way to think of it."

"How do you think of it?"

Her answer surprises me. "It's euphoric," she says at last. "It hurts, sure, but that gets drowned out after the first few needles. It's like going into conspace but even more pronounced. It's... a very different kind of bliss from other types of casting."

"You make it sound kind of nice."

"And for some of us, it is," she says. "Too many are so turned off by the idea of it that they don't even try. I think there's a lot of good that can come from corpimancy, but fear keeps people away."

I draw in a few steadying breaths, like I'm about to go into the silver. It helps calm me down a little bit. Helps me be certain.

"Alright," I say at last. "Let's do it."

Galiva kisses my cheek before she takes up the cloth. She soaks it with the contents of the jug, and I get a whiff of the heady scent of alcohol. She cleans my arm thoroughly, her hands firm but gentle. The liquid cools as it evaporates against my skin. Galiva uses the rag and alcohol to clean her own hands before she picks up the first needle. I have to close my eyes.

Her fingers pinch a piece of skin on my arm and she asks, "Do you want me to tell you when I'm doing it, or do you want me to surprise you?"

I swear under my breath. I'm not sure which will be better or worse, but if I know, I'll brace against it. If it's anything like the silver, it will only make adjusting harder.

"Surprise me," I say at last.

I can hear Galiva's smile. "As you wish," she says. There's a weighted pause, a breath of anticipation. I grit my teeth, and a second later the needle pierces through my skin in one smooth, surprisingly fast movement. I let out a shuddering breath as the pain follows swiftly on its tail, sharp and hot, before settling to a throb.

"First one done," Galiva says. "Are you alright?"

"So far," I say even as Galiva pinches another fold of skin between her fingers.

"Good," Galiva says before the next one slides through me. My shout of pain is trapped behind clenched teeth. It's like the initial sting of a wasp with none of the poison after. A jolt of adrenaline followed by a strange, foreign throb. Another needle follows shortly after, but I'm ready for it this time. The pain isn't as much a surprise as it is an inevitability, and I let out a low moan.

With each new needle, the initial sting becomes less noticeable. No, that's not right - it's always noticeable, but the part of me that's supposed to translate it as pain stops working right. When Galiva puts another in just above my elbow, I gasp and arch off of the table a little. It's not pleasure - not exactly, but it's just close enough.

"Still good?" Galiva asks and there's a calm serenity in her voice. It reflects the tranquil feel of the tower like a mirror.

"Yes," I whisper. "How many more?"

A moment's pause. "Twelve," she says. "Though you're already starting to charge the focuses."

I give a short, wavering laugh. "Oh, good."

Galiva chuckles and catches me off guard with another needle. My eyes shoot open in surprise. I blink and realize my vision has gone a little fuzzy, like looking through shallow water. Galiva looks down at me, a smile on her face.

"Do you want to watch?" she asks.

I swear and try to imagine it, but even the thought makes me queasy. I can kill and skin a deer without issue, but seeing needles driven through my own skin hits in a very different way. "Nope, not ready for that yet," I say, voice tight.

Galiva laughs and kisses my cheek again. "You're doing wonderful," she says before easing yet another needle through me.

It's almost like falling into a trance, though very different from the silver. Different even than the conspace I experienced with Olbric. I'm still definitely grounded to reality here, but there's a weightlessness all the same. It's not the same as evocation, where you temper the pain with pleasure. Here, I have to find pleasure in the *pain itself*. I feel a sort of giddy relief that my body can not only withstand the pain, but *relish* it.

Galiva is calm and gentle, completely at odds with what she's doing to me. Another needle penetrates me, and I let out a shuddering sigh of not-quite-pleasure.

"It's strange, isn't it?" Galiva says. It sounds like she's talking to me from far away. "Corpimancy is the magic of the body, and you learn so much about your own while doing it."

Another needle slides in, and my whole arm feels as if it has a warm weight pressed against it. The atrophied muscles underneath the needles shiver. I feel the ripples all the way in my bones, from my shoulder to the tips of my fingers.

I've lost count, but I feel like we have to be getting to the end of her supplies. Another needle slides in, and as it does, something in my arm *shifts*. By all logic, it should hurt. I shout like it does, and for a second, I remember what it felt like when I broke it. That sickening crack, the pain that had wiped every other thought from my mind.

But it doesn't hurt. It's all heat and pressure, as if Galiva's turned my bones to warm clay to be molded. I feel the ache of the twisted muscles straighten out, the lay of my arm relax. I let out a long breath.

"There we go," Galiva says, and I can hear her smile in her voice.

For a second I just lay there, not sure how to react. I'm floating about half an inch outside of my body when I feel Galiva's hand on my cheek. I come back to myself and blink up at her. It takes a moment to get my eyes to focus, and when I do, I see her beaming down at me.

"That's it?" I ask.

Galiva laughs, mirroring my own giddiness. "That's it," she says. She unclasps the belt and grabs my hand. "Squeeze. Move it gently. Tell me if anything feels off."

Her hand is warm, her grip gentle. I do as asked, and for the first time in over a year, there's no pain. No resistance.

"It feels great," I say in awe. I hadn't realized how bad it had hurt, how constant the ache was that I became conditioned to it. Without that pain, my entire right side feels like it's back in balance. I slowly sit up, my head swimming in a way that's not entirely unwelcome.

"Easy," Galiva says. "You still have twenty needles in your arm."

"Oh," I say faintly and look down at the glowing focuses around my fingers. I glance at my arm - it can't hurt now that the needles are in, can it? I blink and see the neat, even rows of silver. They're in four straight lines down the side of my arm. I'm shocked that other than a couple small drops, there's very little blood.

"The line was crooked when I started," Galiva says. "As soon as I saw them shift, I knew we'd done it."

I blink and look away from my arm. "You did it, you mean."

Galiva cups my face. "You had the courage to let me try." She gently eases me back onto the table. "Let me get these out of you."

I lay back and close my eyes. "Thank you, Galiva."

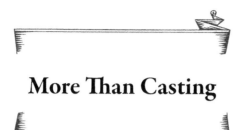

More Than Casting

I have explicit instructions to go easy for the next few days. Galiva cleaned my arm and bandaged it neatly before telling me to find her if any of the needle marks weren't healing right. An inherent risk with corpimancy, she explained.

So I do as I'm told. I stick to my room or the common areas, doing nothing but reading and resting and taking notes. Fortunately, the little wounds heal without issue. By the afternoon of the third day, I take the bandages off and don't even see scars where the marks had been.

Only then do I find my unstrung bow in the little closet of my room. It's traveled with me all the way from Airedale - a silly thing to do when I couldn't draw it. Couldn't even string it. I rationalized it by saying that I'd sell it if I had to, but I'm glad it never came to that. I don't think I would have had the heart to get rid of it. It had belonged to my da, and it's the only thing I have left of my old life.

It rests in my hand like an old friend. Polished yew with a well-worn leather grip. I find my oiled bowstrings tucked away in the bottom of my travel pack. I check one to be sure it's in good shape before I loop it over the bottom notch and take a breath, nerves settling in my gut.

When I couldn't string the thing was when I knew I had to leave Airedale. I had spent *hours* trying every angle and method I knew to try and get the string into the godsdamn top notch, but with my badly healed arm, I just didn't have the strength to do it. It had been the lowest time I can remember. I couldn't hunt, couldn't provide for myself, couldn't *fend* for myself.

Now, I fold my leg around the arms of the bow and set the bottom carefully against my foot. I grab the top with my healed arm and bend it until I can slide the string over the top notch. I make sure it's set into the little groove before I release it with a sigh.

The bow rests taut in my hand, and I can't stop an amazed laugh. It's as easy as I remember it being before my accident. One quick, smooth motion instead of a losing fight.

With growing excitement, I grab my quiver and head outside. The evocation yard isn't being used, but I go through the gates and cross the little bridge and moat to get to the trees beyond. I sure don't want to be in anyone's way.

The tall grass brushes my trousers as I head across the field. I set up a crude target, scoring a circle into the trunk of a tree with one sharp rock before I walk back twenty paces. The grip of the bow is well-molded to my hand, and I take a breath as I draw an arrow from my quiver.

Moment of truth now.

I nock, take the string between my fingers and draw it back to my ear. My heart soars. There's no jolting pain. No numbness. I'm a little shaky, but that's got to be from being a year out of practice.

I take a breath, narrow my sight in, and loose.

The arrow flies true and slams into the trunk of the tree, dead center. I can't stop a whoop of triumph. It's hard to believe. Galiva's done an impossibility, and yet the proof of it is right in front of me. I've done my part to make spells, even released a couple of them, but it's only now it really sinks in. The Crux is making *magic*.

I shoot until the sun starts to set, and my arm is sore by the time I finally stop. I've probably pushed it further than Galiva would have wanted, but it feels good to work the disused muscles. I walk forward and grab my last round of arrows from the hole-riddled tree trunk before storing them back in my quiver. I turn to head back in only to start when I realize I'm not alone.

Olbric sits cross-legged with a pile of torn up grass in front of him. Judging by the size of his pile, he's been there for some time. I'd been so lost in the simple pleasure of target practice, I hadn't even noticed him.

"You're good," he says and unfolds his long legs to stand.

"I'm rusty."

"You call *that* rusty?" Olbric points to the tree. There are very few errant holes. Most are centered right near the middle. I shrug even as my ears get hot.

Olbric chuckles as he walks over to me, kicking at the grass as he does. "I'm glad Galiva was able to help. I hope you're not mad that I told her."

It's only then I realize that he's nervous. He hasn't met my eyes yet, and I can't help but admit that he makes a pretty, demure little picture. I grin as I shoulder my bow.

"Oh, I'm furious," I say. "How dare you share my best tavern story? I'm sure you didn't even tell it right."

That startles a laugh out of him. He looks up, and our eyes lock as I close the distance between us to catch his lips. The kiss is gentler than I meant and lingers longer than I expected. When we finally part, I'm flushed and a little breathless.

"Thank you," I say. "Seriously, *thank you*. Galiva was able to give me back something I never thought I'd have again."

Olbric's arms snake around my waist to hold me there. "I'm glad I could help."

He has that look to him again. The same one he had when I took him drunk and stumbling to his room. Like he's trying to find something hidden in my face. This time, however, it seems as if he's found it.

He leans forward and captures my lips again, one hand sliding up into my hair. I sink into the kiss, returning it, escalating it. This isn't like the kiss he caught me in when I cast with him. That had been all heat and desperation and a little bit of sadistic glee. This is a slow burn that warms as he nibbles my lower lip, sending thrills of pleasure through me. Gods, but he's a good kisser.

We break for air only to connect again with the fire stoked. My bow and quiver fall to the ground, freeing my hands to slide under his shirt. His are already at the laces of my trousers, and after three days of taking it easy, the need surges hot through me.

Olbric seems happy to oblige. His demanding fingers graze my growing erection as he pulls my length from the slit of my pants. He lets go just long enough that I can tug his shirt over his head and toss it aside.

When we sink back to the soft grass, I end up on top. Olbric's hair has come loose from its tie to lay wild around his head. He grins up at me, and the sight of him makes my blood sing through my veins.

"This is a rather nice change," he says, and I chuckle as I meet his lips again. I ease his trousers down, and he shimmies his hips to help me. He's already hard, and I'm rewarded with a shiver as my hand grazes his heated skin.

"Can't say I'm opposed to it," I say and nip at his lip before moving to his neck. He tilts his head to the side to allow me access as gooseflesh prickles over his skin. Part of me realizes how silly it is to be doing this in full sight of the abjuration tower when there's plenty of perfectly good beds waiting inside. Yet the sight of him so willing, his need matching my own, makes it so I don't want to do anything but what I'm doing right now.

Olbric seems content to let me take the lead. I stroke his length gently, my thumb teasing the head until a bit of precum leaks out. Without access to lotion I'm not able to do what I *really* want to do.

But if there's one thing I've learned at the Crux it's how to be creative. And I *have* wanted to give my mouth a second chance around his cock.

I trail a line of nips and kisses down his chest, but I make him wait, lavishing special attention on his thighs and stomach. His fingers run through my hair before gripping tight as I brush my lips near the crux of his legs. He lets out a needy little groan that makes me melt.

I relent and finally draw his cock into my mouth. I'm rewarded with a stronger moan as he grabs the back of my head like a plea. I slide further down his length, and he rolls his hips just a little as if savoring the feeling.

I *like* watching him, I realize. I like seeing how he reacts, seeing the pleasure snake through his body. I hate to admit it, but before coming here, I was never a very attentive lover. The brief encounters I had around Airedale were an almost selfish act. Trying to get mine, while whoever I was with got theirs. Shame colored every interaction, and the feeling only grew and festered after parting ways.

That's been the biggest shock of coming to the Crux. No one here shows any shame at the acts they do to make magic. In a place like this, the baggage around sex that I brought from home was easy to shed. Like I had been waiting my whole life to be allowed the freedom to just *enjoy* it, and in turn, make it enjoyable for whoever I'm with.

Since coming to the Crux, I've learned to relish making someone squirm, and Olbric puts on a good show, though there's no acting involved. He's open with his vocalizations, soft pants of "please" and "more" feeding back to stoke my own growing arousal. He squirms under me, his face flushed with pleasure. He has his lip held between his teeth as he arches, and I can't help but wish I was the one biting those soft lips.

Without warning, his grip tightens in my hair. His patience has worn out, apparently. He pulls me down, his tongue twining with mine as he kisses me deeply, pouring the heat of his arousal into it. Vaguely, I feel him reach for his neck, and there's a quiet hiss as a focus is spent. When his hand grips my cock, it's slick with lotion.

I pull back and look at him in surprise. "Low-level conjuration can be handy when you learn what to focus on," Olbric says with a grin.

I can't stop a laugh. "You seriously created a spell just to make lotion?" I ask in disbelief.

Olbric leans up to nip at my earlobe. "You'll thank me once you're inside of me."

I can't stop a groan as he finishes stroking me to attention before laying back against the grass. He looks up at me with the single best set of bedroom eyes I've ever seen. For a moment, I can almost forget that we're doing this out in the middle of a field.

I've never played this role with another man before, but it doesn't matter. It feels natural to settle between his legs, sliding my erection up until I find his entrance. I push into him slow. I haven't done much by the way of preparation there, but Olbric's moan is encouraging, and he arches under me as he hooks a leg around my waist, ensuring I can't pull away. He's impossibly tight, and I can't stop my own groan as I thrust leisurely, inching deeper.

By the time my hips are flush against his ass, both of us are panting. My head rests against his chest as I savor the feel of his heat pulsing around me. He clenches down on my length as he arches under me with a quiet sound of need.

"Please," he begs, and I can't say no when he asks so nicely.

I pull out a few inches before sinking back into his willing heat. *Godsdamn*, but he feels incredible. I thrust in again, feeling Olbric's leg tighten around my waist. I set a pace, and he rolls in time with me, taking every inch of my cock as I bury it inside of him over and over again. I reach between us and grab his erection, stroking in time with my thrusts.

Olbric is beautiful like this. I mean - he's always beautiful, but *especially* like this. He shows his pleasure with abandon, arching as his fingers drag down my back. He says my name in a quiet chorus, and I never thought it sounded so good until I heard it from his lips.

By some unspoken agreement, we speed up. Olbric wraps his arms behind my neck as I pull us upright, his legs spread on either side of my lap as I drive even deeper into him. He cries out, his fingers tightening in my hair as he rocks his hips to meet my thrusts.

"Oh fuck, don't stop," he gasps, breathless with pleasure.

He drives me to a frenzy, and soon enough I feel the familiar pressure build. My pace speeds up even more, and Olbric cries out with every thrust, arms tightening around me as he buries his face against my shoulder. There's a crackle of energy between us, and I wonder what spell we'd create if we were trying.

But this isn't about casting. It's more than that. Something intimate. Something special.

Olbric topples over the edge first, his cock erupting under my hand, but I think it's the sound of him that sets me off. He groans against my ear, and the sound of his pleasure sends shivers down my spine. I moan as I thrust deep, embedding myself as my release flows out of me. Olbric shudders again, a little gasp of ecstasy escaping him.

I hold him as he goes limp against my lap. For a moment, I don't want to move. The feel of his passage throbbing around me is bliss. I hold him until my knees start to hurt before I carefully lower us both back to the grass, still connected. He relaxes under me, and I rest my head against his chest, panting in the afterglow.

It's a battle to will myself to move. I let myself savor the feel of him for a moment longer before I catch one more kiss and pull out. Olbric lets out a quiet noise of disappointment that almost starts off round two, but I rein myself in. We're a tangle of half-shed clothes and robes, and there's a shine of sweat underneath the ribbons of cum on Olbric's chest.

He fumbles around for his discarded trousers before pulling out a handkerchief from his pocket. I let him clean us up as best as he's able to before I grab our discarded clothes. I hand him his trousers before re-lacing my own. Somehow I managed to toss his shirt far enough that I have to scoot away from him to retrieve it before I offer it to him.

He pulls it on, but he doesn't let me up. Instead, he drags me back down to the ground, and for a moment, both of us just lay in the grass to stare up at the display the sunset is putting on. It's a comfortable silence that stretches between us. My hand rests on his hip, his own curled up by my cheek. I turn to kiss his fingers, and he meets my eyes, a smile lighting up his face.

"Well, I didn't *mean* to jump you in a field, but you started it," he chuckles. He looks back up at the sky as his smile fades. "I came to tell you that I won't be able to make our casting date tomorrow."

The pleasant post-fuck haze disappears like fog under a morning sun. "What? Why?"

"I'm being called away," he says and waves a hand. "There's been some trouble in the hills. Arlon's sending me to clear things up. Cancassi is even giving me their last longstrider spell to get me there faster."

Trouble? A jolt of fear leaps through me. I knew Olbric was an evoker, but actually participating in a fight? It's at odds with the kind wizard I know. "What's going on?"

Olbric shrugs. "The letter was a request for aid from one of the gold mines in the area. We've had trouble with thugs harassing the miners in the past, though it's never been very serious. My presence there should be enough to deter them. I assume I'll be out for a couple of weeks on guard duty." He must see the unease on my face because he turns to cup my cheek.

"I'll be fine," he promises. He holds up his necklace which has four full strands of charged focuses threaded. "I'm more than prepared. This is an old song and dance for me."

I reach for my own sparse necklace and wonder how much destruction he has hanging around his neck. "Be careful," I say, "I'd still like that evocation lesson you've promised me."

Olbric chuckles and sits up. "If you're so hard-pressed to get a beating, you could always ask Galiva," he points out.

He gets to his feet and offers me a hand. I grab my bow and quiver before taking it. He pulls me to my feet, and I snatch one more kiss from him.

"Who says I'd get the beating?" I ask with a grin.

Olbric laughs at that. "A couple weeks in and he already thinks he's an expert," he teases, but gives me an appraising look. "You know, I wouldn't trust many adepts with the skin on my back, but for you? I'd make an exception."

I'd been joking, but the thought that he'd trust me to cast makes me flush with pride and a little bit of embarrassment. "Well, hurry back then," I say.

Olbric grins and drapes an arm around my waist. "I'll do my best."

Training in Transmutation

T ransmutation: *The school of magic that transforms and modifies matter. Casting methods include objectification and role-playing such as pony play.*

THE TRANSMUTATION TOWER is made of interlocking green-gray stones that fit together like the pieces of a puzzle. It feels like I'm about to cast for the first time all over again as I head into it, my stomach already a knot of nerves. Every spell I've worked has happened in one of the private casting rooms, but for our casting date today Cancassi told me to meet them in the courtyard.

It's a nice day out. Sunny, but not too hot thanks to the lazy clouds that drift overhead. As I step into the transmutation yard, I blink in surprise. It's dotted with some of the strangest trees I've ever seen. The leaves make me think it's some sort of aspen, but the branches droop like a willow. There are others that look like cottonwoods but the trunks have been shaped together into something like a pagoda.

Cancassi waits underneath the woven canopy, and their beautiful face breaks into a smile when they see me. They've abandoned their robe, instead wearing a green short-sleeved shirt and flowing white skirts that cover their long legs. Beside them, they've got a large sack that I assume is filled with casting supplies.

"You're really planning on casting out here?" I ask as I look around the courtyard. The nice weather has drawn people outside, and I spot a couple having lunch under one of the droopy trees while a few others read in the shade.

"Of course. You can't bring a horse into the Crux," Cancassi says slyly.

I can't stop a snort of laughter. "You're really serious about this."

"You have to be with transmutation," Cancassi says and ushers me over as they open their sack. It's full of all sorts of leather straps and buckles that only look vaguely familiar. My trip down from the Hobokins was the first time I had really spent time around horses. The mean little bastard I rode made it a less than great experience.

"Materials are important, but having the correct headspace is the key to transmutation," Cancassi says as they take some of the leather straps out. "It is very different from the conspace high that evocation can give you."

I frown at that. I hadn't realized there was a difference. "What do you mean?"

Cancassi taps a finger against their lips as they think of a good way to explain it. It's an innocent gesture, but I'm having a hard time focusing all the same. Cancassi is so damn beautiful that it's hard to look away from them. An otherworldly sort of attraction. I snap out of it when they start talking, only missing a few words.

" - it like this. When you slip into conspace, it's usually a physical reaction to an intense stimulus like pain. Often, you don't have a choice in the matter - it's just how your body is naturally inclined to react. But schools like transmutation and enchantment rely more on the conduit's internal processing of the stimuli they are subjected to."

They must see my confusion, because they add, "If conspace is a physical high, then a submissive headspace is more of a... mental high. With transmutation, the conduit really has to fall into the role they've taken on."

Thanks to Olbric I know conspace, but what Cancassi is describing reminds me of mine and Galiva's first spell. That calm sort of surrender I felt when she tied me up for the first time. But when I crouch down to get a closer look at the supplies the Maeve's brought, the knot of uncertainty tightens in my gut. I've never been asked to do anything quite like this.

"I'm not so sure about this," I say.

Cancassi kneels down beside me, one long-fingered hand resting on my shoulder. The innocent touch sends a thrill through me.

"It's natural to be nervous," they say. "You've never done anything like this before, and this *is* a mastery level spell. What parts make you nervous?"

I swallow as I pick up one of the leather straps. It's been oiled to a shine.

"Being in public, for one," I say. I'd hoped mine and Olbric's little encounter in the fields would have gone unnoticed, but, as usual, news travels fast in the Crux. I've been catching sly looks all morning. I'm sure news of this will travel even faster, what with it being broad daylight and the fact that we're not even *trying* to hide what we're doing. "And this sort of... role-playing isn't something I have experience with."

Cancassi nods thoughtfully. "I'll start with your second concern, first," they say. "Have you ever seen a play?"

I rub the back of my neck. "We had a troupe of players that would come through Airedale on occasion," I say. "Nothing fancy."

"Good! So when you think of those players, they weren't actually kings or queens or whatever else they were portraying," Cancassi says. "But they played those roles with such conviction that they made you believe it all the same, didn't they?"

"Well..." I think Cancassi might be giving that troupe a lot of credit. As part of the story, the lead man had been sipping from a wine jug, but it wasn't until he got stumble-drunk during the later part of the show that we all realized the jug had actually been full of wine. Really, it had only made the show better. "I suppose that's true."

"Taking on a role for transmutation is similar, but you don't have to make *me* believe it," Cancassi says. "It's just a matter of if you can embrace it and fall into the role. Everyone's experience is unique, but I learned a few tricks casting with Arlon of how to get someone to the right headspace. I'll take good care of you," they say with a wink. "Besides, from what I've heard from Galiva and Olbric, you are a very tractable conduit."

"Rude."

Cancassi chuckles and swats my shoulder. "Take it as the compliment it is," they say. "It's rare we get an adept so willing. And as for your first concern..." They stand up and put their fingers to their mouth before giving an earsplitting whistle. Every head in the courtyard turns to look.

"Sorry all, but could you find a different courtyard? We're going to try a casting, and we don't want an audience today," they call.

There are a few grumbles, but the wizards in the courtyard pack up. I blink as I recognize the busty little enchanter from Arlon's dungeon. Ambra, I think.

"Have fun," she says with a wink before disappearing into the transmutation tower.

"Don't worry about them," Cancassi says and waves off one of the grumblers. "People have the main courtyard for loitering. The tower yards are reserved first for casting."

I look around the now-abandoned courtyard and realize I'm out of excuses. Cancassi comes up, near chest to chest. It's a shock to realize that I'm taller than them. With how confident the Maeve always is, how tall they always walk, I hadn't even noticed. They look up at me, and the excitement in those copper eyes makes me shiver.

Cancassi drags a long finger down my chest, dipping into the v of my shirt. I can't stop a small shiver.

"You say stop, and I stop. I don't want you to feel pressured."

I run my hand over my face. "Alright," I say at last. "I'll try it. I hope I'm not wasting your afternoon."

Cancassi's grin turns sly. "I doubt you will," they say. "Now, if you'd be so kind. Stand up and clothes off, please."

Ever polite. I snort but do as asked. Cancassi takes my robe and shirt before folding them and setting them aside. I can feel them watching me as I turn and pull my trousers off, and I hesitate for only a second at my underthings before I drop them too. I'm sure I'm red to the tips of my ears, but I can't deny that the warm afternoon breeze feels nice against my bare skin. I resist the urge to cover myself as Cancassi walks over to me with something in their long fingers.

They take my hand before sliding a black leather cuff around my wrist. They tighten it snug before fastening it with a little silver buckle. The cuff is lined with fur to let it hug my skin comfortably.

A matching cuff is fastened around my other wrist as they ask, "You've drank enough water? You're feeling alright?"

"Fine," I promise. "I've been taking it easy the past couple of days."

"Good. Be a dear and put these on for me."

I blink as they hand me the strangest pair of shoes I've ever seen. Made of shiny black leather with more of a heel than any I've worn before. The kicker is that there are actual *horseshoes* attached to the bottom of them. I look at Cancassi in disbelief, but they're busy pulling more leather straps out of their supply bag.

Guess we're going all in, then.

I sit down on the soft grass and pull the shoes on. They're a rather good fit and the thick socks Cancassi tucked into them help pad them out. There's no way Arlon and I wear the same size, and I realize they must have been witched to fit. They lace up almost to my knee, and when I stand I'm a little wobbly on the strange heel.

"They fit alright?" Cancassi asks. I nod even as my nerves start fluttering in my stomach.

Cancassi slides a leather harness over my head before tightening the straps snug around my chest. It's lined with fur at the shoulders, and it feels like wearing a travel pack without the weight. I twist a little to be sure it doesn't restrict my movement and am glad to find that it doesn't.

Gods, I feel ridiculous.

"You know, I'm curious what kind of horse you'll be," Cancassi says as they wrap something like a belt around my waist and pull it snug. "Arlon was definitely a work horse, but you, I think, could be something far showier."

I can't stop a small laugh. "Yeah?"

"Well you're only the second person I've cast this spell with, but I assume every person will be just as different as every horse is."

Their long fingers finish securing the belt before they stroke down my back. Something swats the inside of my thigh, a stinging little snap, and I yelp as I spread my legs. When Cancassi circles around to my front, I can see the leather crop they have in their hand.

"You've got good musculature but a lighter build than Arlon. Healthy, if still a little thin, but you've already started filling out since you got here."

Their fingers move down my legs to my calves, squeezing them through the leather boots. "Strong legs and back. I haven't seen you move yet, but I'd bet you're quick."

As one hand squeezes my thigh, another brushes my cock, and I can't stop a quiet gasp. Their long fingers gently knead my testicles and tug down lightly.

"Though fortunately, not gelded," they tease. "We'll just have to see what kind you are."

"You seem to know a lot about horses," I say. "Or... people horses?"

I don't know *what* to call this.

Cancassi chuckles. "The Maeve are renowned for their horses," they say. "Before I left to join the Crux, I trained them. Though it's not *quite* like how I'm going to train you."

Cancassi continues to stroke my cock, and I can't ignore how good it feels. Once I'm hard, they take a thin leather strap and tighten it around the base of my length. A second one goes around my balls, constricting and tugging them down. It's not exactly painful, but it makes me groan anyway. Cancassi ignores me and moves to check my shoes. They pull the laces even tighter until the shiny leather is snug around my calves. I find myself standing a little straighter as I shift my weight from one foot to the other.

Cancassi stands, cupping my cock again as the crop trails up the inside of my thigh. "Ready?" they ask.

The nerves are definitely still present, but trust my idiot cock to keep me distracted. I nod before I can convince myself not to. Cancassi takes my cuffed wrists and connects them to the belt at my waist with a clever little latch.

As soon as the little metal clips are closed, I let out a long breath. I'd noticed it come on when Galiva first tied me up, and again with Olbric, but it's especially apparent now. As soon as I'm bound or restricted, the responsibility is taken off of me. I'm no longer in charge, and instead of being scary it's a relief. There's something freeing in surrendering to someone else.

Cancassi is grinning when they circle in front of me, one long-fingered hand reaching out to stroke my cheek. "There's that compliance Galiva finds so endearing," they say, and I lean into the touch. "Have you ever worn a gag, Dominai?"

I shiver but shake my head. "Other than the silver, no."

Cancassi grabs something from the bag and holds it out for me to see. It's a bridle, but instead of metal there's a leather bit between the two silver rings.

"This is, accurately enough, called a bit gag," Cancassi says. "You could still stop around it, but with transmutation a person can fall into a role deep enough they momentarily forget how to use their voice. If that happens, or if you're not able to get a word out around a gag, stick both of your thumbs out. That acts as a non-verbal stop to the caster, understand?"

"Got it," I say before Cancassi slips the bit into my mouth. It rests between my back teeth before the strap tightens behind my head. Another strap splits over my nose and tightens over the top of my head to help keep it snug in place. It tugs gently at the edge of my lips, and I realize Cancassi's put something on the leather that makes it taste faintly of mint.

The Maeve brushes my hair out of the way of the straps with a dazzling grin. "You look dashing," they say. "But there's one thing we're missing."

They reach into the near-empty pack and pull out a long, black horse tail that's attached to a sizable glass plug. I shiver when I see a focus sealed into the center of the bulb. The vague thought crosses my mind that Cancassi must have been the one who gave Olbric his.

Cancassi moves behind me and coaxes my legs apart with a couple taps of the crop. I obey the silent command, and spread my legs, standing tense and ready. The Maeve strokes a hand down my back, double-checking the straps of the harness before one slicked finger glides into me. I moan around the gag as they ease their long finger in deep, and I cant my ass out towards them as they slide in another.

They twist their digits before spreading me gently, their long fingers opening me to the whole godsdamned courtyard. I whimper, my face red hot as they find that sweet spot inside of me and curl a finger against it. They thrust slowly, taking their time to warm me up.

My cock is hard and red under the leather straps, but Cancassi doesn't leave my hole alone until it starts to leak, a thin trail of liquid oozing from the tip. They finally withdraw, but I'm not left empty as the cool glass of the bulb slides in next. Cancassi gives it a few little thrusts, and I feel myself open around it until the girthy thing settles into place, filling me. I shiver and feel the ticklish swish of the tail fall against the back of my thighs. I stand braced, expecting the bulb to start moving, but it stays suspiciously still.

Cancassi comes around to my front again to slip five focuses down my erect cock. They tingle against my skin, and I bite down on the gag to stop another moan. I'm not sure how to feel about all this. Trussed up like a cart horse in the courtyard, I feel exposed and vulnerable. But fucking hell if it's not heating me up all the same.

I watch Cancassi, looking for some guidance, and they give it to me in the form of a lead rope latched to the front of my belt. Then, they reach into the pack to exchange the crop for a long whip with a little leather switch on the end of it. I take a step back, eyes going wide.

"Good instincts already," Cancassi chuckles. They shake the whip out before resting the tip against the ground. I stand bound and shivering, not sure what to do. But then Cancassi clicks their teeth and points to the right. I hesitate as I look at their finger, uncertain, but the whip flicks up to snap against my ass.

I yelp and start walking in the direction they point. It must be the right thing to do because the whip stays on the ground, trailing through the grass just behind me. Cancassi holds the rope attached to my waist, though they give me about ten feet of slack. They turn in a slow circle, watching as I walk a perimeter around them.

The tail swishes against the back of my legs as I fall into an easy walk. My cock bobs with every step, though the little straps keep me hard. The bulb shifts inside of me, and it makes focusing awful hard. Fortunately, I don't have to focus on much.

A moment later, Cancassi clicks their teeth again, twice in a row. I must not react quick enough because the whip flicks out to snap against my ass again. It's a sharp little jolt of pain that makes me jump to a jog.

The heavy shoes don't make it easy, either. I have to lift my legs higher than I normally would to make up for the extra weight. Out of the corner of my eye, I see Cancassi grin before they tap the whip against the back of my leg.

"Knees higher."

I do as told, even though it makes my cock bob almost painfully with every step. The girthy plug rubs just the right way as I fall into a steady, even jog. Cancassi keeps me at it for a few long minutes until my face is flushed with something other than embarrassment.

Only then do they give a sharp little whistle. I don't need the switch of the whip to know that they're asking me to speed up again. I start to run, my breath coming fast but steady around the gag. Cancassi doesn't keep me at that pace for long before they give a long, low, "Woooah."

I come to a stop, breathing hard. Cancassi folds the whip under their arm and tugs the lead rope to pull me towards them. They swipe my sweaty hair out of my eyes and run their fingers under the harness to be sure it isn't rubbing.

"Are you alright?"

Their melodic voice snaps me back into myself a little bit. For a second, I had forgotten to be nervous. I had focused on the task, honed in on Cancassi's wordless commands. In that moment, the nerves about everything else - of folks seeing me, or screwing it up - vanished.

I look at them in surprise but nod all the same. Cancassi smiles and gives the lead rope a little shake before readying the whip again. I back up and when they click their teeth, they point the opposite direction. I follow their finger and step into pace once more. They put me through another walk, jog and run until I'm breathless and sweating, my mind returning to that quiet, compliant place.

When Cancassi finally stops me again, I'm flushed not just from the exercise but also my own steady arousal. My legs ache from the extra weight of the shoes, but my cock is an angry red under the ties and focuses. The bulb keeps brushing against that sweet spot inside of me, making it hard to think. It's a relief to realize that I don't *have* to think. I just have to obey.

"Good boy," Cancassi purrs, their long fingers stroking through my sweat-damp hair. "You would keep running as long as I asked you to, wouldn't you?"

They don't seem to expect an answer as I lean against their palm. Instead, their fingers wrap around my cock, stroking my hard length even as the focuses spark. I groan around the gag, realizing that I've already started to charge them. With five of them on, I'm not sure how I missed it.

"I should have assumed you'd be more of an endurance creature than Arlon," Cancassi says. "By this point, he was already flagging while you seem ready to go, aren't you?"

I roll my shoulders back and stand a little taller at the praise. I spent years hiking the Hobokins - a little bit of running isn't enough to tire me out. Cancassi gives the rope attached to my harness a little tug, and I follow.

They lead me to the back of the courtyard where a small gate is set into the stone wall. Cancassi opens it and leads me across the small bridge that crosses the moat. My shoes clomp over the wood, and I keep my head down, focused on putting one foot in front of the other and getting my breath back.

Then it occurs to me that they're taking me out of the Crux. Out where *anyone* could see me. A spike of unease breaks through the haze, but Cancassi gives the lead rope another gentle tug, and I obediently follow. They walk ahead of me, humming a quiet tune. With how relaxed they are, my own nerves seem silly. It's easier to let go of them and just allow Cancassi to take the lead.

They guide me to a small, two-wheeled cart that waits just outside of the walls. Cancassi pulls the cart around and sets the poles into my hands before a strap from the cart's handle to my cuffed wrists binds it to me. A few more straps attach to my belt to hold it in place. Finally, Cancassi unsnaps the lead line from my belt before attaching reins to the rings at my shoulders and each side of my gag.

I shift a little as they get me rigged up, trying to watch what they're doing, and am rewarded with their hand snapping against my ass in admonishment. I jump, but I learn my lesson to stay still, eyes ahead, as Cancassi moves out of my sight. The cart shifts, and I tighten my grip on the poles as they take a seat.

They click their teeth, and I don't wait for a flick of the whip to jump to action. The cart isn't as heavy as I thought it would be, and the wheels are well oiled and smooth. It's no worse than a wheelbarrow, and Cancassi's weight is balanced which makes pulling them easier. The end of the whip brushes my back, and I feel the tug of the reins as Cancassi guides me to turn.

Just like before I fall into the rhythm of it, though I'm glad they don't make me jog. Walking I can do forever, even with the shoes on, and Cancassi seems content to let me. The reins keep just enough contact that I know which direction I'm expected to go, and the only time they use the whip is to help guide me or coax my knees higher.

The tail swishes against the back of my legs, the bulb pressing relentlessly against that spot inside of me. But instead of distracting me, it's just another tool to keep me focused on the task at hand. A thin stream of liquid drips from the tip of my straining cock, and the sound of my own breathing is loud in my ears. I barely see the trees and wildflowers we pass, instead focusing on the dirt path ahead of me.

I couldn't say how long we're out, but when Cancassi finally pulls me to a stop by the gate, my legs are shaking, my mouth dry around the bit. I feel Cancassi's weight leave the cart before they come around and stroke my sweaty hair out of my face.

"Good boy," they purr, and I lean into the touch.

They make quick work of unhitching me from the cart before they snap the lead line back onto my belt. They pull the line short as they guide me back into the courtyard and under the shade of one of the strange willows.

"Green broke and already so good," they murmur as they tie my lead line around a tree branch. "I think such good behavior warrants a reward."

Cancassi gives a strange sort of whistle. It seems to ripple through the air around me before shivering through me. I don't know what it means, what I'm supposed to do, but a second later, I realize it's not for me.

The bulb starts to twist inside of me in a deliciously familiar way. I moan around the gag and lean my forehead against the tree trunk as my tired legs start to shake all over again. The ties around my cock and balls seem impossibly tight as Cancassi's hands gently unlatch the bit gag. I lick my dry lips before I let out another low moan. The harness comes off next, and I'm left with my hands still bound to the belt, still tethered to the tree.

I watch Cancassi in a haze as they head over to their pack to deposit the tack. They return a moment later with a jug of water and a cloth. They hold the jug to my lips, and let me get my fill first. It's cold and wets my dry tongue and lips. I take a few big mouthfuls that make my teeth ache before I gasp for breath.

Cancassi uses the jug to wet the cloth before sliding it over my bare shoulders. The cold water is a jolt, but not at all unwelcome. Combined with the things happening inside of me, it feels downright divine. I moan as the water trickles down my hot neck and back.

Cancassi takes their time, humming a nice little tune as they clean sweat off of my face and chest. They're thorough too, tending to my legs as they unlace the shoes and slide them and the socks off. They move up my thighs, leaving me glistening with water before finishing at my cock.

They cup my erection, and I buck my hips against their teasing fingers. Cancassi takes pity on me and fondles my balls as they squeeze the five focuses snug around the base of my cock. The stone sparks, and I can't stop a desperate little shout as I roll my hips into their hand. The little tie around my shaft and balls come off a moment later, and I groan in relief.

"Now this," they say and pull me close with a finger through my belt, "is not something that goes into normal horse training." I can't stop a huff of a laugh. Cancassi unclasps my wrists from the belt and frees me from the lead line. "You've been very agreeable, so I think it's only fair you get to decide. How would you like to finish this spell?"

I open my mouth to try and speak, but they were right - the words just don't want to come out. Instead, I lay my hands on their slender waist, feeling the slight curve of their hips underneath their skirt. Heat rushes through me as I look at them with naked desire.

Cancassi's curious copper eyes widen just before I spin them and press them up against the smooth trunk of the tree. They give a little gasp of surprise that makes the heat surge through me as I lean against the curve of their back to pin them. My freed hands make quick work of pulling their skirts up to rest over their hips. It's a thrill to find that Cancassi is wearing nothing underneath, and I glide a finger over their wet, waiting slit.

"Dominai!" they gasp, sounding a little scandalized though not at all unwilling.

After being driven like an animal for the better part of the morning, I feel like a stallion with a mare in heat. I angle my cock to glide against their slit, and Cancassi moans as they roll their hips back in offering. I grab the mounds of their ass, my thumb teasing at the little pucker of flesh at the center. Cancassi lets out a musical moan, and I can feel how they tremble with anticipation.

This is how I want to finish it. With them moaning underneath me in the shade of the courtyard. I grab their hips, and Cancassi gasps as the tip of my cock slides between their folds. I grab their long, white braid and seat myself deep with a sharp thrust. Cancassi shouts, and it's only then the haze breaks enough for me to realize that I still have five focuses snug around my length.

Cancassi seems to read my mind. "No, no, it's alright," they gasp. "I'm shocked I never thought to do it before. Just... go easy on me."

I grin and press a kiss against the back of their neck before I roll my hips. The tail swishes against the back of my legs even as the bulb continues to twist and spin inside of me, urging me on. I start slow and shallow, an apology for that rough entry.

It's a test of my control not to fuck them flat against the tree trunk, and one that I start to fail under the melodic gasps of "please!" and "more!" Cancassi has a lovely voice, but even moreso when it's layered with pleasure. They arch underneath me, hands gripping the trunk of the tree as I fuck them from behind.

I hold their braid with one hand while the other snakes around their chest to slide under their shirt. I find the small swell of their breasts and grab onto one as I thrust up into their welcoming heat.

With every hard snap of my hips, the focuses shift down my length, adding one more sensation as they spark with charge. Cancassi's body shudders as they let out a shout of ecstasy. I grip their braid tight, pulling their head back against my shoulder as I thrust deep. One of their hands flies back to grab the back of my neck.

"Oh fuck!" they shout, breathless with pleasure.

The muscles of their cunt spasm and constrict around me, and it's my undoing. I groan as I give a few more shallow thrusts before I bury myself to the hilt, my free hand wrapping around Cancassi's waist tightly. My orgasm comes hard, and Cancassi gives a little gasp as I fill them. The constant twisting of the bulb seems to make my orgasm last forever, emptying me and leaving me a little dizzy in the wake of it.

I shiver and kiss the back of the Maeve's neck. It takes me a moment longer to find my voice again. "I'm going to need you to stop this thing." My words come out hoarse and breathless.

Cancassi chuckles before they let out another trilling whistle, and the bulb stills inside of me. I groan in relief and slump against their back. It takes a second longer for me to muster the desire to pull out of them, and when I do, a trail of my seed follows, dripping down their thigh. The Maeve grins at me over their shoulder, face flushed. With their skirts hiked up and cum spilling out of them, they look well and thoroughly plundered, and *godsdamn* if it doesn't make my empty cock twitch again.

Slowly, we get ourselves back together. It's only when we start to clean up that I realize there are only four glowing focuses around my softening length. I take them off and present them to Cancassi. They stare for a second, as if not quite sure what they're looking for before they laugh.

"Oh," they say faintly. "Maybe that's why I've never done that before."

I chuckle as I step towards them. Their back bumps up against the trunk of the tree as they look up at me.

"Here, I'll find it," I say and lift their skirts once more.

"What a gentleman," Cancassi moans, hands braced against my shoulders as I slip my fingers into them again. They're soaked with our combined juices. I tease my fingers through their folds, exploring and twisting until I feel the little ring of the focus, just out of my reach. I hike their leg up over my arm and press my fingers in deeper, making Cancassi's face redden with desire all over again.

I work my fingers into them, teasing and stroking as my other hand finds their cock. I take a second to admire them as they close their eyes and arch in pleasure. Their body is beautiful and not quite like anything I've ever seen before. Their slit rests just between their legs, but where that little button of pleasure should be, their cock juts up proudly. It's smaller than mine, but shaped like it was made by a sculptor.

"You're beautiful," I mutter as I watch them writhe under my fingers.

Cancassi moans as their cock throbs under my grip. "You're not so bad yourself, human," they pant. "Though if you plan on leaving me like this, I'll take back every nice thing I've ever said about you."

I laugh and catch their lips in a kiss as I reach a little deeper. "Wouldn't dream of it."

And I make good on that promise. I thrust my fingers in time with each stroke of their cock, and it doesn't take long to work Cancassi to a second orgasm. They cry out and arch back, their cock swelling before the pressure releases in quick spurts. I feel their walls ripple around my fingers again, and it's just enough to push the ring down so I can reach it. I continue stroking until I'm sure they're finished, and only then do I pull the errant focus out.

Cancassi moans and slumps back against the tree trunk as I set their leg down. They wobble, a little unsteady on their feet. I hold onto them until I'm sure they won't topple over, grinning from ear to ear.

Cancassi lets out a long sigh and smooths an escaped white hair over their pointed ear. I hold the glowing focus out to them.

"Sneaky little bastard," they mutter as they grab it with those long fingers that definitely could have gotten it out without help. "Thank you for indulging me in this. Did you enjoy yourself?"

I smile as I find my trousers. As much as I enjoyed being a horse, I sure do like having clothes. Besides, any longer under the sun and my skin will start to burn. "More than I thought I would, honestly. This was fun."

"You fell into the role beautifully," Cancassi says. "It was a pleasure to watch."

I flush at the praise. "It was certainly good exercise."

Cancassi chuckles. "Be sure you stretch tonight, and drink a lot of water." They step over to me, one long finger trailing up my chest before cupping my cheek. "Can I call on you for future castings?"

I smile and lean into their hand on instinct.

"Absolutely."

Breakthrough

Longer periods of sensory deprivation in the silver can potentially increase the chances of a successful divining.
Please note that this chapter contains mentions of rape.

IT'S JUST PAST DAWN, and the mess hall is abandoned. Most of the Crux tends to sleep in on Saturday, so I grab my breakfast and settle at my favorite table by myself. The quiet is peaceful, broken only by the robins chirping from somewhere outside. I plop down a selection from the ever-growing pile of books Galiva's given me and find the place I left off.

I barely make it through a page before Galiva walks into the mess. Though I've noticed a few other early risers, Gal's not usually one of them. She seems agitated as she walks over to a decanter and pours a cup of the smelly black drink she likes so much.

As soon as her eyes land on me, her pinched face relaxes. She comes to join me, sitting across from me with a sigh.

"Why are you up so early?" she asks.

"I was used to waking up at dawn before some crazed wizards started fucking me senseless," I say. "Y'all are still fucking me senseless, but I think I've finally adapted."

Galiva chuckles and reaches over to steal an uneaten strawberry from my plate. "Cancassi was practically glowing last night," she says as she takes a bite. "Said you were the most fun they've had casting in a while."

I can't stop a small laugh and pick up my tea. "Glad they enjoyed," I say. "I had a pretty good time myself."

Galiva sets the strawberry stem back on my plate before picking up her mug. "You know," she says, "I wouldn't normally suggest this for someone just at the end of their first month, but you're a fast learner. I think you might be ready to start casting in a few schools."

I nearly choke, and I cough to clear tea from my throat. "Seriously?" I ask. "That seems like... a lot of responsibility."

"And it is," Galiva says. "But I wouldn't suggest it if I didn't think you were ready to experiment. Abjuration is a good school to ease into casting. You've read enough of the theory to at least try."

I let out a low whistle as I rub my cheek. Not that I don't like the idea of casting - it just seems like a lot of weight to carry. Besides, I kinda like the spot I've found conduiting.

"You could have someone other than your conduit supervising, if that would make you feel better," Galiva points out, and it's like she can read my mind.

"Gods, that would make me feel a whole lot better," I say and Galiva chuckles.

"Then I'll be sure it happens," she says. "Cancassi, Olbric, and I all have our abjuration mastery. You could cast with one of us while someone else supervises."

"I'd like that," I say, a bubble of excitement forming in my chest. "Maybe once Olbric's back."

Galiva winks. "It's a date then."

I take a sip of tea as Galiva steals another strawberry. "What's got you up this early?"

"Couldn't sleep," she says, but the way she says it tells me that's only a part of it. At my look, she sighs. "I'm worried about Olbric. I don't like that he jumps into these assignments."

"I thought he was being sent away?"

"Arlon never forces anyone to go on assignment, but Olbric was happy to sign on for this one," Galiva says. She finishes that strawberry too, though I get a little distracted watching her lips shape around the bright red fruit. "He's a skilled evoker - one of the best we have. But if you ask me, that skill's made him cocky."

Hearing her concern doesn't do anything to help my own. My breakfast settles heavy in my stomach.

"He'll be alright," I say, and have to believe it. "He's well equipped."

Galiva gives a small laugh. "You got that right," she says. "His libido rivals yours."

"You say that like it's a bad thing."

"No," she says, her grin turning sly. "I just think it means that you two are a good match for each other."

I flush to the tips of my ears. I haven't told anyone about mine and Olbric's non-casting encounter, but the look she's giving me tells me she already knows.

"Olbric's the worst gossip," I mutter.

"Or you two just did it in full view of the abjuration tower. If it was meant to be a secret, you both did a pretty poor job of it." My face gets even hotter as Galiva laughs. "Between this and the spell you and Cancassi cast in the transmutation yard, you're turning into quite the exhibitionist."

"Or you're a dirty voyeur!" I say and snatch my plate away as she reaches for more of my strawberries. "No fruit for you!"

Galiva laughs again and pushes to her feet to gather her own breakfast as I try and fail to rub the blush from my face. She returns a second later with her own bowl of yogurt and fruit and sinks back into the seat across from me.

"What do you have going on today?" she asks. "Still keeping busy?"

I chuckle. "Guess you could say that. I've got another shot at divination with Margeurite," I say. Galiva makes a face, and I can't stop my curiosity this time. "Alright, what's the issue?"

"What issue?"

"The issue with you and Margeurite."

She picks up a blueberry from her plate of fruit and rolls it between her fingers. "It's ancient history," she mutters. I stay quiet and wait for her to continue. She pops the blueberry into her mouth and sighs again when she realizes I'm not dropping it.

"Look, when I first joined the Crux, I wanted to try divination *so bad*. Margeurite had just gotten her mastery and was eager to put me in the silver. Problem is, Margeurite doesn't always realize when she's not in great position to be casting."

Her fingers drum a rhythm against her mug. "She was recovering from a bad cold but insisted she was fine to cast. I was new and didn't know any better, so I went along with it," she says with a sigh. "She had fixed me up with some toys, and then she sat down and... dozed off while I was in the silver."

"Fucking hell!" Galiva shrugs, and I shake my head. "No! I've been in the silver *once*, and even I know that's no shrugging matter!"

"It was an accident," she says. "I still don't know how long I was in it, but it felt like a lifetime. Ever since, I can't go into the silver without panicking."

"Gods damn, I don't blame you."

"It's just... divination was the school I thought I was coming to the Crux *for*," she mutters and takes a sip of her drink. "Both of my parents are master diviners and being so *fucking scared* of it feels like... failure."

I don't like seeing her with that look. She stares into her mug with something deeper than disappointment on her face.

"Alright, here's a proposal," I say before my own fluttering stomach can talk me out of it. "You let me cast with you in divination."

Galiva sets her mug down with a thud and pegs me with a wide-eyed look. When she doesn't immediately shoot the idea down, I keep going and hope I'm not digging myself a deeper hole.

"I'll have Margeurite there to supervise. I-I know I'm not experienced, but that only means I'll be even more careful."

Her fingers are busy against the side of her mug, tapping out a rhythm as she thinks. She gives me a searching look as she chews the inside of her cheek, brows furrowed. I can read the fear on her face, the uncertainty.

"Alright," she says at last. "I'll try it."

WHEN THE TIME COMES, Galiva and I head up to Margeurite's casting room together. I knock, and the ovisari is quick to answer. Her smile falters when she sees who I've brought with me.

"Oh," she says. "Hello, Galiva."

"Hey, Margeurite."

I clear my throat. It doesn't do a thing to cut the tension that thickens the air so I just dive in and tell Margeurite my plan. The ovisari seems less than pleased about it.

"Dominai, we are trying to find our missing wizards. We don't have time for adept experiments."

I bristle at that. "Aside from me, have you had any luck?" The accusation comes out sharper than I mean it to.

Margeurite's ears flatten against the sides of her head like an angry cat. Her curious brown eyes won't quite meet mine as the annoyance fades to weariness. She rubs a tired hand over her face.

"No," she says, and it's only then I notice just how tired she looks. There are dark rings under her eyes, and it sort of seems like she's at that not-in-a-great-place-to-cast position.

"How many others can you turn to for tracking them?" I ask.

Margeurite sighs. "Two," she says. "And after a false try each, neither of them will consent to go into the silver again."

"So, we're your best shot, and yet you won't help me *try* to get Galiva alright with the silver again?" I ask.

Margeurite looks between the two of us before she lets out another long sigh. "Very well," she says at last. "Dominai will cast, and I will supervise. But after, I would still like to put you back in the silver as well. You have been our single source of information so far."

"Deal," I say with a smile. "Thank you."

Margeurite offers a small smile before she opens the door to allow us both in. I take Galiva's hand and give it a squeeze. I can almost feel the nerves radiating off of her. Cancassi talked me down yesterday, so I hope I can do the same with her.

I help her out of her robe and drape it over the lone chair in the room. "What about being in the silver gets to you?" I ask.

Galiva sighs as she ties her mane of hair back. She's quiet for a long moment. "The... inevitability of it," she says at last. "As soon as the silver starts to creep up, I get nervous. I know what's going to happen, yet as soon as I'm in it, I feel like I'll never get back out. I forget someone is out here keeping watch."

With her experience it's a reasonable fear, but maybe there's a way to take the edge off that feeling. Dip a toe into the water before taking the plunge.

Marguerite watches us with her arms crossed over her chest. "When you cast with me, you were able to peel the silver out of my ears and mouth. Can I stop it from covering all of her?" I ask.

Marguerite nods. "The caster can control how much it covers," she says. "But you will never get a successful spell unless the conduit is fully encased."

"I'm less worried about a successful spell, and more worried about Galiva," I say. Good gods, she's single-minded. "I don't want to make this harder by trying to get a spell out of it. If it happens, fine. If it doesn't, that's fine too."

I can almost hear Margeurite's indignation, but the gratitude on Galiva's face makes it worth it. I smile and put my hands on her shoulders.

"So, how's that sound? We get the silver, say, up to your neck and see how you feel from there."

Galiva looks at the two pillars and lets out a sigh. "I'll try it."

I try not to stare as she undresses. It's a losing fight, and even though I've seen her naked before it never fails to get my blood hot. Her beautiful brown skin is peppered with darker scars, and when she lifts her shirt her nipples are a few shades darker still. She eases her trousers down over her curvy hips, exposing the small tuft of black hair that curls between her legs. She's not the tallest woman I've ever met, but even naked she holds herself like a queen.

Finally, she lifts her multi-strand necklace from around her neck and sets it on her discarded clothes. When she raises her eyes to look at me, I can see how nervous she is. But above that, I see trust, and it sends a thrill of excitement through me.

I beam at her before I take her hand and guide her between the pillars. I kiss her cheek and give her shoulders a squeeze. "I'll be right here."

Margeurite comes up behind me and says, "Put your hand on the pillar."

I step away from Galiva and lift my hand to the smooth stone. It tingles under my fingertips, and every hair on me stands to attention. The colors that skitter through the stone concentrate around my fingers and ripple out like disturbed water.

"Now, just focus on it, and guide it," she says.

I swallow and feel the lap of energy under my touch. It's like holding a sloshing bucket of water. I test the weight of it and try to figure out how it moves. As I twist my fingers against the pillar, it starts to cooperate. The silver pours out of the bottom of the stone and pools around Galiva's feet, sloshing up her ankles. It's no slow, easy creep like what Margeurite had with me.

"Sorry, I'll get the hang of it," I promise, and Galiva chuckles.

And I do after a minute. I go slow, letting it slide up her calves and over her knees. I watch her face, but it isn't until it starts to creep up her arms that she tenses. I slow it down the second she does. She gives me a grateful smile before she takes a deep breath, letting her eyes slide closed again. The uncovered part of her shoulders relax, and she lets the silver support her instead of contain her.

Only then do I let the creep continue. Galiva's eyes stay closed, her face calm. I stop it the second it covers her shoulders and smile.

"How do you feel?"

She leans her head back like she's lounging in a chair. "Alright," she says.

"Can I do anything? Move you a little to make you more comfortable?"

She chuckles and wrinkles her nose. "I swear, as soon as I can't scratch it is when my nose starts to itch."

I reach out with my free hand and give it a good scratch. Galiva sighs. "Thanks."

"Any time."

For a moment, I just let her sit, though I can't help but let my fingers wander. I glide my hand over her skin, and am surprised that the silver turns a little translucent. I can see her skin underneath, like the silver is just a dusting instead of a barrier. She sighs as I trail my fingers up her hip and over her chest. Her nipples are hard, and I give the one I can reach a little pinch to perk it up even more.

"Not gonna lie, I've thought of a whole lot of ways I'd like to cast with you," I say. "And this is pretty great so far."

Galiva chuckles and says, "Living up to the fantasy?"

Maybe Olbric's rubbing off on me, because I say, "It'll be better when I can get my tongue in you."

I'm rewarded with her little hiccup of surprise. "Oh, I see," she says, but there's a noticeable smolder in her voice now. I pinch her nipple again, and she bites her lip to stifle a moan.

"Do you think you're ready to go without your ears?" I ask. "I'll take it out to check with you before I do anything else."

Galiva sighs and rolls her neck. "Right," she says. "I think I'm ready."

I focus on the silver again and go slow. It's a little trickier to do than the steady creep, but I manage to split the silver and slide it around her head like a muff. It holds her in place, but she can still see and speak. I give her a wordless thumbs up which gets a grin out of her.

"Can I let go of it?" I ask.

"Yes," Margeurite says. "It stays where it is when you aren't touching it. Your control is admirable for a first-timer."

I take my fingers off of the pillar. "I just hope this helps."

Galiva watches me with heavily lidded eyes. I smile and cup her cheek, running my thumb under her eye before I kiss her. She relaxes under me as I explore her mouth with my tongue before dragging her lower lip through my teeth. When I pull away, I recognize that glazed sort of surrender on her face. It sends a thrill through me to see it.

My hands move to her chest, and when I touch her, it's like the silver isn't even there. Her skin is warm and pliant under my finger. I kiss my way down her neck and am rewarded with a gentle little groan. I nip across her chest until I find one of those perky brown nipples. I roll my tongue around it and look up to see her eyes closed as she bites her lip.

All good signs, then. I reach up and pull the silver away from her ear. "Doing alright?"

"Great," she says, a little breathless.

I smile and nip the skin of her tit lightly. "Ready to go without sight?"

Galiva is quiet for a second as she checks in with herself. "Yeah," she says at last. "I think I'll be alright."

I smile and reach out to touch the pillar again. "I'm right here," I promise before I let the silver cover her ear again. I twist the silver so it crosses her eyes. It covers the top part of her head like a hood but leaves her mouth free to stop. It's enough to constrict movement though - she won't be able to budge her head now.

The nerves start to creep over her face again, but I press my lips gently to hers to remind her I'm still here. My hands stroke down her sides gently before I find my way between her legs. She lets out a quiet moan as I slide a finger between her folds, but I don't press in yet. I just tease her for a bit, exploring the shape of her. When I close my mouth over her other nipple, her moans gets a little louder.

I keep my fingers busy, teasing until her slit is wet before I pull the silver out of her ear. "Still alright?"

"Yes," she gasps, and I can't stop a smile. There's no fear in her voice. Just a yearning that I think I can fulfill.

I kiss her deeply before I ask, "Can I put you all the way in? How does a minute sound to start?"

"Why can't you just keep doing what you're doing?" she says, a whine pitching her voice.

I chuckle and kiss her again. "I'll do whatever you want me to."

She takes a breath to calm herself down. Even with the silver covering half of her face, I can see her thinking. One minute can feel like a lifetime, but maybe it'll be a good one.

"Alright," she says at last. "One minute."

"You're incredible," I murmur against her cheek. "Ready?"

"Ready."

I let the silver fill her ear again before I put a hand on the pillar. I make sure to go slow as I direct the silver to spread out and cover the rest of her face. It pools into her mouth, parting her plump lips. The silver closes fully around her before lifting her a few inches from the ground, suspending her between the pillars. A muffled gasp makes it out from behind the gag, and I put a hand on her chest, fingers stroking down her collar.

"It's alright," I mutter, even though I know she can't hear me. "You're alright."

I keep a silent count as I feel her relax, watch her breathing even out. I smile and trace my fingers down her stomach before sliding between her legs again. A muffled little groan escapes her, and I echo it when I feel how wet she is. Even if she's nervous, this is certainly doing something for her. I gently rub the little button between her legs, though I keep my fingers just shy of entering her until the minute is up.

When I take the silver from her mouth and ear, she's panting. "I'm alright," she says before I can even ask.

I chuckle. "It can be pretty fun, right?"

Galiva gives a small, breathless laugh. "With you doing that thing with your fingers, it certainly is."

I smile and catch her lips again. "Do you want to keep going?"

Galiva takes a few deep breaths before she answers. "Yes."

"Are you sure?"

"*Yes.*"

Pride swells in my chest. "How long do you want to go?"

Galiva thinks on that for a little longer. "Let's try ten to start."

"As you wish," I say before I let the silver fall back into place. I smile and look back at Margeurite. She has an odd look on her face as she watches me. "You're alright?"

Margeurite snaps to attention and gives a small smile. "I'm fine," she promises. "You are very attentive with this. It seems to come natural to you."

I flush a little at the praise as I circle behind Galiva, keeping my hand on her. "I'm just walking her through it like you did with me," I say and glance over Galiva's shoulder. "You set a good example."

Margeurite's smile flickers out as she falls quiet. I want to ask her what's wrong, but a muffled groan from Galiva pulls my attention back to her. I rub her shoulders and feel her relax a little under my hands.

"Is there anything specific I should do while casting?" I ask.

"You're doing well so far," Margeurite says. "Divination is a slow sort of worship. Explore her. See what gets a reaction and indulge it, but not for too long. The silver has a way of letting you know when they're getting close and when it's time to let them finish." A sly smile spreads over her face. "I also brought some things I was planning on using on you, but you can get a sneak peak at them."

I smile at that possibility even as I carefully push Galiva's legs apart. She lets out a muffled squeak that sounds more like surprise than fear. I squeeze the curves of her ass gently and use the silver to my advantage to spread her cheeks apart. Godsdamn, but it's a hell of a view.

"Be careful when moving people," Margeurite warns. "It's possible to stretch them too far. They can't tell you what's too much, but their body will. If you meet any resistance, stop and check in."

"Right."

I kiss the back of Galiva's shoulders even as my fingers work to relax the tense spots in her back. I can tell just by touching her that she hasn't slept well - her muscles are strung tight as a bowstring. I use the rest of the ten minutes trying to work them out, and am rewarded when I finally feel her relax. It's a subtle change. The silver keeps her in the same position, but she sinks into the constraint instead of bracing against it.

When I pull the silver out of her ear and mouth again, she's panting. Her voice has a definite tremor in it when she speaks. "I think I'd like to keep going."

"I hoped you might," I say with a smile. "Anything you don't want me touching or doing while you're in there?"

"You tickle me, and I'll kill you," she says.

I chuckle before kissing her cheek. "Got it."

"No hitting or impact of any kind. Only gentle biting, and don't move me into any crazy positions."

"Deal," I say and kiss her collar. "Penetration?"

"Yes please." This time it sounds more like a plea than a demand, and I chuckle as I give her a quick kiss. "I think I'll be alright."

I can hear the relief in her voice as she says it. My smile feels wide enough to split my face. Whatever barrier that had stood between her and divination seems to have come down, and I'm glad I was able to help.

"How long?" I ask.

Galiva sighs and asks, "What's an acceptable time for divination?"

"An hour is usually the minimum," Margeurite says.

"Fuck, that sounds daunting."

"Don't worry about the spell," I say. "Do what you think you can handle."

Galiva takes a deep breath. "I think I can do it," she says.

"You're sure?"

"I'm sure," she says with a smile.

I kiss her again, letting it linger. I hope she can feel how grateful I am that she's let me try this. "I'm right here."

"I know you are."

The trust in her voice makes my heart skip a beat as I let the silver fall back into place. I keep my hand on her hip but take a step back to look at her. She looks beautiful wreathed in the strange substance, like some sort of statue. I can't stop a giddy little laugh. Behind me, Margeurite chuckles.

I look back at her, a little sheepish. "Sorry, this is... more exhilarating than I thought it would be," I admit.

"It's heady having control over someone," Margeurite says. "It's a large part of what I enjoy with divination."

I sit down at Galiva's feet and start to rub them, remembering how good it felt when Margeurite did it to me. I hear the ovisari's quiet footsteps behind me before she hands me something. It's a charged focus, but it's shaped different than the others I've seen. It looks like an oversized grain of rice that's about as thick around and long as my thumb.

As soon as Margeurite drops it into my hand, it starts to vibrate. "Oh. Now that's fun."

Margeurite chuckles as I trail the little buzzing focus up Galiva's thigh. As soon as I bring it close to the crux of her legs, Galiva's breath hitches. I slide it between the folds of her cunt, and it must feel great because a long moan rattles out of her. I shiver and am glad that the silver only muffles the sounds instead of blocking it. Hearing her pleasure certainly does some things to me.

"Be cautious with that, or you'll end it quicker than you want to," Margeurite warns. I keep it there for a second longer before I pull it away. Galiva's disappointment comes out in an audible whimper.

"Gods, you're not wrong," I say and store the little buzzer in my pocket for now. I scoot closer and gently pull Galiva until she's at the right height. I blow against the inside of her thigh before I press my lips to the spot. I take my time to taste her skin as my fingers tease the folds of her slit. When I finally pull them away, they're soaked with her juices.

I lick her off my fingers, and it makes my half-hard cock stand to attention. She's tangy with a hint of sweetness, and I immediately want another taste. I scoot close and angle her hips before I close my mouth over her slit. I slide my tongue deep through her petals, and she gives a sharp gasp that fades to a long, shuddering moan. She tenses under the silver, wanting to squirm, but the pillars hold her completely helpless.

It sends a thrill through me to know I'm completely in control here. And I'm in no hurry. I push her legs a little further apart and settle into a comfortable spot below her. I lap at the little hood between her legs before I trace the shape of her with my tongue. I suck and nibble at the tender flesh and am rewarded with a wail of pleasure that makes me shiver.

I don't push it too far though. The tingle of the silver covering her intensifies whenever she gets close to orgasm, and it's enough of an indicator to pull away. Every time I do, I'm met with a little mewl of desperation that makes my cock throb.

I go until my jaw starts to ache before I finally pull away. Galiva's gasp is all disappointment. I smile, my thumb stroking over her thigh before my stomach suddenly drops.

"Oh fuck! I've lost track of time."

Margeurite chuckles. "It's a novice mistake, and one we all make," she says before she takes out the watch from her pocket. "You are about twenty minutes in."

I chuckle and rest my head against Galiva's thigh. "Thanks."

"Don't worry, this is why we use a monitor for the first couple of times," she says. "But I'll admit... you're doing far better with her than I ever did."

I stand with a groan and circle around Galiva as I decide what I want to do next. I take the little buzzer out of my pocket and as soon as I do, it starts up again. I trail it over Galiva's chest before focusing it on one of her nipples.

I glance at Margeurite over her shoulder and ask, "Do you want to talk about it?"

Margeurite lets out a gust of a sigh. "I assume she told you about our... mishap," she mutters. "I... hadn't realized how much it had affected her."

I slide the buzzer over to Galiva's other nipple as I soothe the first with my tongue. I pull away a moment later, leaving her brown skin glistening. "Did you two ever talk about what happened?"

"After it happened I apologized, and she accepted it," Margeurite says matter-of-factly. "I thought that was the end of it."

I snort as I give Galiva's nipples a little tug until they're just slightly stretched under the silver. "That's not how it works," I say. "Galiva didn't try divination again until you asked her, did she?"

Margeurite looks away uncomfortably. "No."

I move to lift Galiva's arms over her head, trying to put them in as comfortable a position as I can. "Did you know that I nearly shit myself the first time I saw the familiar I conjured?"

Margeurite looks shocked. "Whyever for?"

"Because a wolf that looked just like it knocked me off a cliff and nearly killed me," I say as I trail my hand over Galiva's shoulders to move behind her. "You don't just... forget memories like those. And even though you apologized, Galiva didn't just *forget* being trapped in the silver. You've been in it - you know how helpless she must have felt."

Margeurite is quiet for a long moment. "I know I made a mistake," she says, and there's a hint of anger in her voice. "Am I to be punished for it for the rest of my life? My casting record has been flawless since!"

"This isn't about you," I say, exasperation giving my voice a sharp edge. I'm glad Galiva can't hear us. "You fucked up, and you said your apologies, and you made sure it would never happen again. You did everything you could, yet Galiva *still* isn't comfortable casting with you because *you* don't get to decide how she feels about it."

Margeurite looks like she's been struck. She swallows and looks at Galiva, her eyes wide. I watch her mull it over, and her ears start to droop.

"You're right," she says through a sigh. "She came to me in good faith, and I was impatient with her. I didn't even realize until I saw how you worked her through it."

"I'm new," I say with a shrug. "Maybe that's an advantage at times."

Margeurite sighs and steps towards me and Galiva. She looks at the woman and reaches out like she wants to touch her.

"There's just so much riding on the success of these divinings, Dom."

I rub Galiva's neck as I trail my other hand down her back. "I know," I murmur. "I know you're under a lot of pressure. It's easy to have tunnel-vision when you're focused on the light at the end of it."

"I suppose you're right," Margeurite says, her fingers just shy of touching Galiva's cheek. "But it's still no excuse."

I offer a small smile even as I wrap my arms around Galiva's waist. I trail my fingers towards the little tuft of hair between her legs.

"You can't make her trust you," I say. "But I think the fact that she was willing to try again here bodes well."

"You do?"

I shrug. "I think the only way you'll know for sure is if you two talk about this."

Margeurite lets her hand fall to her side. "I suppose you're right about that, too," she says, sounding tired.

My fingers find the little hood of pleasure at the crux of Galiva's legs. Her groan has a desperate edge to it this time, and she tenses under the silver as she tries to push against my hand. "But first, we have to get her out of the silver."

Margeurite hums in agreement. "Don't let me distract you."

I chuckle and rub the sensitive spot before tapping it gently with my fingers. It makes Galiva's breath hitch. After the little reprieve I gave her, I feel her brace for whatever comes next. I take the buzzer between my fingers again before I press it against the little hood of her clit.

Galiva squeals as I roll it around, making sure not to focus on one spot for too long so it doesn't get overwhelming. The silver practically hums, and I quickly pull the buzzer away. Galiva wails around the gag as a little bit of saliva creeps out of the corner of her mouth.

"Fucking hell," I mutter, unable to tear my eyes away from her.

"Getting a little close there," Margeurite says through a grin. "You are certainly putting her through it."

I grin and say, "I know that it's worth it."

Margeurite chuckles. "That it is. You still have about half an hour."

I glide my hand over Galiva's stomach and ask, "What else did you bring?"

Margeurite grins as she brings the little bag of supplies over to me. My eyes widen when I see the assortment. There is a collection of phalluses of all different shapes and sizes, a few plugs, some with focuses sealed in them, some without, and even a string of beads like what Arlon had me use for conjuration.

"Gods, you did come equipped," I say even as a shiver in anticipation rushes through me. I know that I'll get a taste of some of these next.

I take the little buzzer and gently slide it into Galiva. I gently pinch the folds of her slit shut, and the silver keeps it there, effectively holding the little thing inside of her. Even though I let go of it, I hear it continue to buzz. Apparently all it needs is the touch of a wizard, and I feel a thrill of sadistic glee to know that Galiva's the one responsible for keeping it going. Underneath my fingers, the silver stays at a steady, even thrum and Galiva moans desperately. Behind me, Margeurite chuckles.

"Gods, as kind as you are, you do have a spark of cruelty in you."

"Who, me?" I say innocently, even as I grab a small phallus from the bag. I move behind Galiva as I slick my finger with lotion. I slide it down the crack of her ass before I push into the little pucker of flesh. Galiva's surprised yelp is like music, but it fades to a shuddering moan as I reach a little further, thrusting gently. I slide a second finger in and the hum of the silver starts to build. I reach down with my free hand to pull the buzzer out of her and am rewarded with a wail of desperation.

"How much time do we have left?" I ask. My cock aches, and I want nothing more than to sink it into her.

"About fifteen minutes," Margeurite says. "Pay attention to the silver. If you start to see colors, then it's time."

I nod and slide my fingers out of her ass before I slick the phallus with lotion. I don't let her stay empty as I ease the shaft into her slick hole. I move slow, knowing how good that tortuous drag can feel. Galiva moans with every thrust, but the thrum of the silver stays steady. It's a bit of a thrill to realize she probably can't orgasm from this stimulation alone.

"Am I allowed to fuck her?" I ask, my own voice thick with desire.

Margeurite comes up behind me, her fingers gliding over my shoulder. "Sure," she says, but her voice smolders as she adds, "But you're going in next, which means you're not allowed to finish yet."

A shiver rushes down my back. How much do I want to torture myself? I look at Galiva and my pulse races. It'll be worth it.

I shift her hips and bend her forward so I can get at her from behind. I keep the phallus in her ass even as I free my cock from the slit in my trousers. I slide the tip of it down her wet slit and Galiva moans, long and low. Even behind the gag, it sounds like pleading.

I twist the phallus inside of her and line my cock up, giving her a moment before I thrust into her wet heat. She feels impossibly tight, and I groan as I seat myself inside of her. I lean my head against her back even as color sparks across the silver. It looks like the Hobokin sky in wintertime, bursting with greens and blues.

I grab the phallus with one hand and take the buzzer in my other to press it back against her clit. The colors flash stronger, brighter. I alternate the phallus and my own cock, filling one hole and then the other as I fuck her slow. Her walls quiver around my length, and I only get three more thrusts before Galiva clenches around me. She cries out as her orgasm comes hard, and I feel the silver shudder as she tenses inside of it. Her walls clench hungrily around my length, and I swear, my balls aching as I stave off my own end by a hair.

I watch the silver reach shades of reds and oranges, sparking beautifully before it finally starts to fade. I wait until it's back to its normal shine before I finally pull out, taking the phallus out as well. Margeurite grabs the toys from me and sets them aside.

"Take her out of it slowly," she says. "Start with her mouth first."

I nod and carefully straighten Galiva back up. I tuck my throbbing cock back into my trousers and put my hand against the pillar, mustering the focus to control it again. I pull the silver from Galiva's mouth, and she gasps like she's surfacing for air. But then I notice the hitch in her breathing.

She's crying.

"Oh fuck. *Fuck.*"

I get her out as quick as I dare. I pull the silver from her ears next, then her eyes, my own panic spiking when I see tears. I direct the silver to slide the rest of the way off, catching her as her shaky legs fail to support her. I help her to the ground, pulling her to me as despair settles in my stomach like a rock.

"Fucking hell, Gal I'm so sorry. Are you alright?"

Galiva waves a hand and wipes the tears from her eyes. "No, no - it's not you," she promises. She cups my cheek and gives me a wavering smile. "Dom, you were amazing. *Fuck* - it's just a lot of emotions," she says with a wet laugh. She leans against my shoulders and takes a few deep breaths before she speaks again. "I-I saw something."

It doesn't sound like a good thing, either. "What?"

Galiva swallows and shakes her head. "After your turn," she promises and my stomach turns. *Really* bad then, if she's not wanting to ruin my headspace with it. Even so, it certainly kills my erection faster than a bucket of cold water.

"Right," I say and tighten my arms around her. For a second, I'd been terrified I'd fucked up. My voice is faint when I ask, "You're sure you're alright?

Galiva lets out a long breath and sinks into my arms. "I'm more than alright. That was incredible," she says. She looks up at me, and her beauty makes my breath catch. Even with the tears stuck to her eyelashes, she's stunning. She leans up to catch my lips, and when she pulls away, she's smiling. "Thank you, Dom."

I brush an errant curl back from her face. "You were incredible."

Galiva gently extracts herself from my grip and pulls me to my feet, yet there's pain just underneath her smile. Unease thrums through me like a warning as I look at the pillars. But I promised Margeurite. Besides that, I *want* to do this. If we can get two successful divinings, maybe we can finally get some real information.

Margeurite drapes a robe around Galiva's shoulders before looking to me. "Ready?" she asks. "I thought we might try for two hours. The longer the time, the more detailed the divinings usually are."

That sounds like a stretch but not an impossibility. "I can handle it."

I strip my clothes off. Even after that unpleasant jolt, my cock is still half hard - idiot fucking thing. I push my nerves aside as best as I can before I step in between the pillars. Marguerite puts her hand on one of the pillars.

"You both staying for this?" I ask.

Galiva smirks a little as she looks my naked body over. "After all you did to me, I've certainly got some ideas of payback."

The silver laps over my feet, and I grin at the challenge as it creeps up my legs. "Do your worst."

Margeurite laughs and says, "You might regret saying that."

The silver reaches my mouth, gagging my reply. I'm plunged into darkness as it covers my eyes and pools in my ears. My feet leave the ground, and I sink into the void.

Hands are on me almost instantly. Not just two, but four stroke over my skin, and it doesn't take long for one of the pairs to stroke my cock hard again. Desire surges in me, hot and eager, banishing every other thought from my head. Last time, Marguerite had taken her time, but there's no slow worship this time. Neither her or Galiva seem inclined to do anything but immediately start teasing the shit out of me.

Lips suck one of my nipples while a finger glides into my ass. I start to regret my challenge to Galiva as a second finger enters me. I already feel like I'm drowning in sensation between the two of them, and we've just started. Two hours of this is going to be unbearable.

Fortunately, both Margeurite and Galiva seem to know how to read me. After my hole is stretched, someone slides a sizable plug into me, effectively blocking off that entrance for now. I sag in relief, a moan escaping me. The bulb rubs against that spot inside of me, lighting my nerves on fire, but I'll take it over the constant teasing of their fingers.

Someone kisses me, taking advantage of the silver parting my lips. It kills me that I can't even budge my tongue to join in. It's Galiva - it has to be. I recognize the way she kisses. She plunders my mouth before pulling away to nip at my lips, and I feel her smile against my skin.

Her fingers stroke through my hair even as I feel Margeurite's hands spread my thighs apart. She teases my balls with feather-light touches that make me want to slam my legs closed. It tickles fiercely, and I laugh miserably into my gag. She doesn't let up until I'm panting and groaning, my whole body taut in the silver.

Then no one is touching me, and for the first time it's a relief instead of something to worry about. I catch my breath, my nerves singing with unmet need. As I get myself back under control, I realize I can hear the phantom voices already. Small trickles of not-quite-conversation.

Someone touches the base of the plug, and it starts buzzing just like the little focus had. I shout into the gag, even as the hands return. They glide over my back and chest, rubbing my body in a way that makes me think that they're distracted by something other than me. For a while, that is all they do, and the part of me that's still able to form a thought wonders if they're talking. I hope so, and not just because it's a nice break.

But no conversation lasts forever, and soon their hands start to explore again. Someone - I've long since lost track of who it might be - grabs my cock. Their hand is slicked with lotion and it feels incredible as they stoke me. Someone else grabs the base of the bulb and starts to pull it out. But as soon as the widest part slips out of me, they push it back in, fucking me, stretching me with the buzzing thing. The hand around my cock continues to pump my length, setting a maddeningly steady pace.

I feel my orgasm start to build, but as soon as I get close the hand on my cock stops. I wail as the bulb slides out of me, leaving me empty and waiting, shivering with anticipation. Then, I feel a hand on my back before I'm bent over. I yelp in surprise, but the silver keeps me from toppling. It's a strange sensation, and it makes me feel that

much more ungrounded. Now more than ever, I feel like I'm floating.

Something else prods at my ass, cool and hard. It was probably
a bad idea to leave the rest of Margeurite's phalluses unused because
one of the bigger ones slides into me next. I moan at the stretch. It
almost feels like Arlon fucking me again, and though I've recovered
from my bout with him, I know I'll be walking funny after this, too.

The hand on my cock starts to stroke again. I don't know who is
in front of me and who is behind, but they work in tandem. Whoever is wielding the phallus goes slow, thrusting it in before dragging it
back out while the hands stroke firmly down my aching length. It's a
strange sort of illusion - almost like I'm fucking myself.

It doesn't take long before my orgasm builds again. I get right to
the ragged edge of no return before the hands around my cock let go.
I wail, but the phallus only fucks me harder and deeper. For a second,
it feels like it'll be enough to finish me off. I groan as the feeling passes, the pressure receding back into my aching balls.

They keep it up until my hole is stretched. Yet when they pull the
phallus out the silver keeps my hole open, drawing attention to how
empty I feel. Then, I notice my cock tingling. I groan, trying to pinpoint the sensation, but it's like nothing I've ever felt before. Whatever they slathered over my length has made me extra sensitive. Every
brush of air, every gentle touch feels amplified.

Then the hands are gone, and I'm left with nothing but my tingling cock and a sore, gaping ass. A hand stays on my hip to remind
me that someone's there, but otherwise they just let me stew. But
the phantom hands have started, and the extra-sensitivity in my cock
doesn't help the matter. I feel like I'm being touched everywhere, yet
none of them are substantial enough to ease the aching need that's
built in me.

When the hands - the real hands - start again, I don't know
whether I want to cry with gratitude or desperation. I'm shifted

again, put even more off kilter. I can't tell which way is up anymore. My arms are pulled behind my back, but the silver holds me stronger than ropes ever could. I feel saliva drip from my mouth even as my legs are spread wider.

Then, my cock is swallowed by the warm heat of someone's mouth. I shout into the gag, and with how sensitive I am, I'm brought right to the edge again. I plead as best as I can. Unintelligible, I'm sure, but I doubt there's a gag in the world that could muffle my need. They pull away just as quick, and I sob helplessly.

It all starts to blur. I'm completely ungrounded, lost in the void that speaks to me in quiet whispers, reaches out to graze me with barely-there touches. I lose track of how many times my ass is fucked. How many times I'm brought to the edge until my balls ache for the release I'm convinced I'll never get. The torment seems to go on forever until I'm too tired to even attempt to fight it. I submit to the silver, give in to the delicious torment. I feel myself moved again, but it's a vague sort of awareness, like experiencing it in a dream.

Something stretches my ass again, re-slicked with lotion, and I can't do anything more than whimper. Then, I feel the brush of skin against my hips before something hot and slick slides down my length. I moan in earnest, knowing it's no mouth this time.

Whoever it is rides me hard, while the other fucks me from behind. The pace has changed now, and as my orgasm builds again, I feel like I might pass out if I'm not allowed to have it. I get to the point of no return and brace for them to pull away. But they don't.

My orgasm rocks through me, and I feel like I'll pass out anyway. I shout into the gag, going lightheaded as the pleasure rushes out of me and into the waiting heat. Just like last time, the phantom colors coalesce into a picture while the whispering voices narrow down to one.

It's Olbric.

He's been gone less than a week, but longing rushes through me at the sight of him. His skin is coated with sweat and ash, and he's breathing hard like he's been running. Something crashes behind him, and his eyes go wide before he takes off again.

His long legs carry him through the woods, darting through trees that look so very familiar. Another crash sounds - louder, closer. Olbric shouts as the earth underneath his feet explodes into a rain of rocks and dirt.

He's pitched to the ground but recovers quick, rolling and scrambling backwards until the trunk of a tree halts his retreat. With a feral snarl, he grabs a focus from his necklace. It sparks out as fire curls from his extended hand. Someone screams as grim satisfaction curls Olbric's lips.

There's a flash of movement behind him. The shine of a naked dagger.

I scream a warning, but the miles between us render it useless. The blade slices through his necklace in one quick motion, sending his focuses tumbling. Olbric shouts in horror, trying to grab one, any one as they fall. But his fingers aren't quite quick enough.

A figure surges out of the fire, and Olbric's eyes widen in shock before a fist connects with his face. It staggers him, but his hands scrape across the ground until his fingers find a fallen focus. It lets loose, flinging his attacker back. I recognize it as the first spell he had cast with me.

Olbric gasps for breath, and hope swells in my chest. It's short-lived. There's another flash of movement before a dagger slides against Olbric's neck.

"*One move and it's your life, wizard,*" a female voice says. As if to prove a point, the woman tightens her grip, and Olbric gasps as a thin line is cut into the skin of his neck. The woman is wearing a dark hood that covers most of her pale face, but her eyes don't leave Olbric as she says, "*Diran, grab the spells.*"

The vision breaks apart and disappears back into the void. I scream again, willing it back, but the darkness doesn't respond. I'm left floating and ungrounded once more.

I thought I knew what it was like to feel helpless, but now I realize that I didn't have a clue.

I'm eased out of the silver carefully. Margeurite and Galiva hold me like I'm some fragile thing that could break at any second. I feel like I might.

I'm sore everywhere, but even the intensity of my time in the silver isn't enough to erase the horror of what I Saw. Margeurite drapes a soft robe around my shoulders, and I pull it close as I lean into Galiva's embrace. She strokes my sweaty hair away from my face, and the way they both look at me says they know I haven't seen anything good.

"Gal," I say, my voice hoarse. "What did you See?"

Galiva swallows, her hand cupping my cheek. "It was Alix - one of our missing wizards," she whispers. Tears well in her eyes. "They were beating him - using him. They were... raping him."

I feel like I've been plunged into cold water. The haze of pleasure vanishes, and I feel sick as my stomach drops like a stone.

It hits me all at once. Wizards are being targeted. And they're being used for casting, whether they want it or not.

I bury my head in my hand, gripping my hair at the roots as I try and calm myself down. But this is no time to be calm. There's not a second to waste.

"Dom?" Galiva asks gently. "Are you alright?"

I shake my head. I don't want to believe it. The thought of it is too horrible to face, but I have to. I know what I saw.

"They've got Olbric."

Revelations

P*lease note that this chapter contains brief mentions of sexual assault.*

GALIVA, MARGUERITE and me find Arlon in his office the second we're dressed. He seems pleased that we have news, but as soon as Galiva starts talking his face falls. I feel sick to my stomach as she recounts what she saw. Every detail could be important and she doesn't leave any out, even if I wish she would.

"I didn't recognize the man doing it. I could hear others there but never caught sight of them," she says. "It was definitely some sort of casting room. Stone, with... tools on the walls."

Arlon's hands are steepled in front of him, eyes dark with fury. "And you?" he asks as he turns his attention to me.

I tell him everything. Galiva's eyes brim with tears as I recount Olbric being attacked. It takes some doing to stop my voice from shaking, and as I finish Arlon's focus sharpens.

"Did you say Diran?" he asks, his voice deadly calm.

I nod, not liking how that anger is focused on me now. I risk a glance at Galiva, but her attention is on Arlon, her eyes wide.

"Oh gods, I knew I recognized one of those voices," she breathes.

"Who's Diran?" I'm almost afraid to speak. Arlon is *scary* when he's mad. I'm suddenly aware that he could snap me like a twig if he cared to.

Arlon's brows furrow, rage settling in every line of his face. "A pathetic excuse for a wizard who came through our doors a couple years ago," he says. "He was expelled after three months for unapologetically violating a stop. His conduit was sent to the infirmary."

Galiva swallows and says, "We tried to have him arrested, but his family is... powerful."

"So what?" I ask.

"So, money speaks where justice should," Arlon spits and kneads his forehead between his fingers. "But at least now we know who we're dealing with."

"So what do we do?" I ask. Every part of me itches with the desire to move. To *do* something.

"Divination can provide visions of the past, present, or future," Arlon says. "What did it feel like when you saw it?"

I swallow. "It felt like it was happening now," I say. "I-I felt like if I could just yell loud enough Olbric would hear me."

Arlon unlocks a drawer in his desk and pulls out the largest strand of spells I've ever seen. It's got eight full strings on it and looks like it weighs a ton.

"Then we don't have time to waste," he says and relief surges through me at the declaration. "We know where Olbric was posted. If we start there, we might be able to follow their trail. Galiva and Margeurite, I want both of you along. We need to gather Cancassi, Ambra, and Thaddius. I'll send for Garrett. I want everyone to reinforce every strand on their necklace with wire before we leave."

My stomach drops when I realize what he hasn't said. "What? No! Arlon, you have to take me!"

The Grandmaster sweeps around to the front of his desk and puts his hands on my shoulders. "Dominai, you are an *adept*. One with undeniable skill, but we are very likely going into a firefight. I can't in good conscience throw you into this."

I muster my courage and don't back down. "Olbric only told me he was going to the hills to defend some mine, but it's the Black Burrows isn't it?"

The only reason I know the name is because folks from Airedale would travel down to work the gold mines every summer. It's about a two week's trip from town and paid well, if you were willing to risk the danger of the job.

Arlon's eyes narrow, and that anger makes me quake, but the need to *act* makes me press on.

"I recognized the woods in my vision - he's just at the edge of the Hobokins, isn't he?"

Arlon sighs and pinches the bridge of his nose. "Dominai-"

"I'm an adept, but I spent my life before this *in those hills*," I insist. "If you can't take me as a wizard, at least take me as a guide! I can track, I can hunt, and I know the Hobokins better than anyone. You want to find them as bad as I do, and I'm your best shot."

Arlon gives me a searching look. I clench my fists at my side to keep my hands from shaking. Speaking up like that makes my pulse race, but I see him thinking. He must come to the same conclusion I have; it's a good argument.

Finally, he lets out a sigh. "You will do everything I say, when I say it."

Relief makes me lightheaded. "Right. Of course."

Arlon pulls a focus from his large string of spells. "You will stay close, and if it comes to a fight, you will take this and stay *down* until it's over, do you understand?"

I take the spell. I've handled enough to feel that it's abjuration, but even stronger than the one Galiva and I cast.

"Understood." I string the focus onto my necklace and look up at him. "Thank you."

Arlon sighs and turns to Margeurite. "Tell the kitchens that we'll need travel rations for eight people. Three weeks, to be safe, though gods willing this won't take that long." He looks at Galiva. "Find Cancassi and have them prepare eight of their fastest horses to leave tomorrow. I'll speak to the quartermaster about supplies."

"Wait, what about the longstrider spell that got Olbric there in the first place?" I ask.

Arlon gives a shadow of a grin. "Unless you want to ride to the foothills with a phallus in you, we don't have enough castings of it. We have to travel the old-fashioned way." He must see the dismay on my face because he adds, "With Cancassi's horses, we'll make it in four days. But I'll keep that spell in mind for the way back."

THE AFTERNOON DISSOLVES into a flurry of activity, and I'm reminded again of just how fast wizards work. News spreads quick, and soon the entire Crux knows that Arlon and a retinue are leaving. By evening, they all know the reason why.

Dinner that night is quiet. The news has spread a pall through the Crux. I make it halfway through my own meal before I give it up as a lost cause. Nerves have effectively ruined my appetite.

I head back to my room to triple-check my pack. The quartermaster Farlan has provided us everything we should need - sleeping mats, oiled wool cloaks for the cold and wet mountain nights, wood axes, flint and steel for fires. In all my years going through the woods, this will be the best equipped I've ever been.

I grab my bow and check the string before packing my backup, just to be safe. I pull out my quiver next and grab my arrows. I go through them one by one, checking the fletching and tips before sharpening them on the small whetstone I brought from home. I'm on my last one when there's a quiet knock on my door.

Galiva gives a small smile as she peeks her head in. "Hey."

I set my last arrow back into the quiver. "Hey."

She lets herself in and closes the door behind her before she joins me on my bed. Her head rests against my shoulder, and I wrap my arms around her before scooting us both onto the too-small mattress.

I already know why she's here. I'm glad for it. Neither of us want to be alone right now.

Her fingers trail across my collar bone as she settles her head against my chest. "I didn't get a chance to thank you," she says, breaking the silence. "I went into that casting room not knowing what to expect, but Dom... you were amazing."

I give a small laugh as I rub her head through her curls. "Thank you for trusting me."

Galiva smiles as she looks up at me. "I'm glad I did."

We fall back into silence, just enjoying the simple pleasure of each other's company. "You ever seen Arlon that angry before?" I ask after a moment.

"I was there when he expelled Diran. Today was nothing compared to that," she says. "He's usually so calm. That was the only time I've ever heard him yell. He takes violation of consent very seriously."

I swallow and think of all the times I've been at someone else's mercy while at the Crux. Every time I've acted as a conduit was a test of trust, and I can't imagine how horrible it must feel to have that trust broken. I tighten my embrace on Galiva, worry twisting my gut.

"Who is this guy?" I ask at last.

"Diran Barclay," she mutters. "The Barclays are a wealthy and powerful family. They're also one of the oldest recorded magical bloodlines, so when Diran arrived he came in like he was the gods' gift to the Crux. He struck me as arrogant and an asshole on top of that, so I never agreed to cast with him. Looking back, it was a good decision." She shivers as I smooth my hand over the curls of her hair. "I was working on my corpimancy mastery, and I helped Garrett stitch up his conduit after he beat her bloody with evocation."

The thought of it makes me hot with anger. "He sounds like a real prick," I mutter but even that's too kind of a word. "I hope Arlon sent him out flat on his ass."

Galiva lets out a tired sigh. "Diran was furious, but he was no match for Arlon. An abjuration held him long enough for Arlon to take his spells and kick him across the bridge. With luck, Diran is still as useless in a duel."

"We can hope," I say, though who knows what sort of tricks he may have learned in the years since.

"It caused a bit of a stir with Straetham for a while," Galiva says. "The Barclays raised a ruckus over his expulsion. They even petitioned King Thermilious to try and allow Diran back into the Crux, but Arlon wouldn't have it. He cited the King's own decree that granted him jurisdiction over magical matters and outright refused."

"Hell of a power move," I say. I don't know much about Straetham politics, but even I can see that much.

"It certainly didn't put him on the King's good side," Galiva says. "But it was the right decision, whether Thermilious agrees or not." Her hand tightens on the collar of my shirt as she says, "In the infirmary, Justinia told me that it wasn't until she begged Diran to stop that he finally did. She left the Crux just a few months after. Gave up magic entirely. And seeing what they were doing to Alix..."

I shudder and tighten my grip around her shoulders. "Gods, Gal, I'm sorry that's what you Saw for your first divining."

She swallows and she tightens her grip on my shirt. "I don't know who else Diran has working with him, but what they're doing is unforgivable."

I press a kiss to the top of her head. "We'll find them," I say, and I have to believe it. "We'll stop them."

Galiva doesn't answer. She goes quiet, and after some time I feel her relax as her breathing starts to even out. I don't much feel like sleeping, but I must. The next thing I know, the early morning sun is peeking through my window and someone is rapping on my door. Galiva blinks and extracts herself from my arms to answer.

Cancassi gives us a smile that doesn't quite reach their eyes. "Time to go."

On the Road

I *llusion: The school of magic that controls and manipulates the sens-*
es. Casting methods include sensory play and deprivation.

WE GATHER IN THE COURTYARD, and outside of a few of
the grooms and attendants, I recognize most of the congregation.
There's a handsome blond man with skin as white as mine that I assume is an unmasked Thaddius talking to Ambra. I head towards
Galiva, but she's beside someone I know I've never met.

He's hard to miss with his ashen gray skin. He stands just a hair
shorter than Arlon, and though he's a little leaner he's just as muscled. Long brown hair is braided away from his strong face to hang
halfway down his back. He's got a necklace that rivals Arlon's in size,
but his most noticeable feature are the two small tusks that jut up
from behind his bottom lip.

No one told me Garrett was an orc.

I push my unease aside as Cancassi grabs me to introduce me to
my mount. They were not kidding about their horses. The ones we're
using were gifted to the Crux as a sign of good faith from the Maeve,
and there's not a nag among them. Even to my untrained eye they
look sturdy and able to cross the miles with those long legs.

The one Cancassi gives me is a gentle gelding with a Maeve name
I can't pronounce, so I settle on the first part of it and call him Mo.
It takes help from Cancassi, but I manage to get my leg in the stirrup

and swing onto his back. The one other horse I've ridden was a mean thing that tried to bite me more often than not and would start to move as soon as you put a foot in the stirrup. Compared to that, Mo is already a blessing. He stands still as I get settled, and I can't help but give his soft brown neck a grateful pat.

Packs are lashed to saddles, rations are stowed, and finally, there's nothing left to do but head out. Arlon's on top of an athletic-looking black mare that he turns around to face us. He's swapped out his robes for sturdy traveling clothes, and his necklace is tucked out of sight under his cloak.

"We're headed into dangerous territory," he says, and what little chatter there was dies instantly. "Our diviners have uncovered information about our missing wizards. We believe that five of our own are being held against their will in an unknown location in the Hobokin Mountains. As of yesterday, the evoker Olbric was taken by this group of rogue wizards outside of the Black Burrow mines. We head there to pick up the trail, and we will follow it until we find them."

He says it with such conviction that I believe it. Entertaining any other outcome is too painful. I don't want to imagine coming back from this trip a failure. Or not coming back at all.

Arlon meets all of our eyes in turn. "The wizards taken were all multi-school masters with a number of spells around their necks. We have to assume that those spells are now in the hands of those keeping them captive," he says. "This is a high-risk assignment. These people have proven themselves to be capable, dangerous, and well-armed. Anyone who wishes to step down should do so now."

No one moves. Arlon looks at the congregation and there's something like pride on his face. "Keep your spells close but covered. We don't need to advertise who we are on the road," he says and turns his horse about. "Move out!"

MO HAS AS SMOOTH A gait as any, but it doesn't make a difference to my sore ass after a full day in the saddle. We alternate walking
and running, but combined with the day I had yesterday, I'm downright miserable by the time we stop to camp for the night. Cancassi
nearly has to peel me off of Mo's back.

"You just have to roll your hips with the canter," Cancassi says for
the fifth time today.

I groan and stretch my stiff legs out. I'm so sore that even walking's hard. "Just because you keep repeating it doesn't mean I'm getting it."

Cancassi squeezes one sore cheek. "Do you need a refresher of
how to move those hips?" they ask.

"Enough," Arlon cuts in. "Now is not the time for casting."

Day two isn't much easier, though Cancassi makes sure to ride by
me. They correct my form throughout the day with commands like
"hips forward!" and "keep your heels down!" I think I finally get the
rhythm of a trot down, but my legs are still sore and shaking by the
end of the day. I roll out of the saddle and swear as my leg bends bad
when I hit the ground.

Mo wickers and nuzzles his nose against my shoulder. I sigh and
scratch the white star on his face.

"Not your fault, buddy," I mutter. "Blame my da for never teaching me to sit a *godsdamned* horse."

"This isn't an easy ride, even for an experienced rider," a voice behind me says. I turn and come face to face with the orc. My back stiff-
ens when I see his hand stretched towards me, but then I notice the
focus he's holding out. "You want something for the ache?"

"I'm alright," I say before quickly ducking away to join the rest of
the camp.

After that, I find myself watching Garrett more than I need to. I'm having a hard time making sense of him. What place does an orc have at the Crux? The only ones I ever heard of would sweep through the mountain settlements on an occasional raid, though they never dared come to a village as big as Airedale.

Apparently I'm not subtle about it. It's the afternoon of our third day when Arlon inches his horse up beside Mo. "Why do you keep glaring daggers at my corpimancer's back?"

"What?" But then it hits me. *Garrett* is the other corpimancer. One of three in the Crux. "I wasn't glaring."

Arlon snorts. "You know, Garrett is also from the Hobokins."

I wonder which settlement his clan drove out. "I'm sure he is."

"He's been working in Straetham as a physician ever since he earned his full mastery. He's non-bloodline as well."

"Obviously."

Arlon continues like he hasn't heard me. "You might find you have more in common than you think."

I doubt that, but I keep the thought to myself. As we're making camp that night, I find Margeurite. "You're from the high peaks, right?"

"I am," she says. "It's been some time since I've been this close to the hills. I can already smell the pines." She sounds a little wistful, and I can't help but smile.

"Do you miss the mountains?"

Margeurite's smile turns a little sad. "Sometimes," she says. "I'm a rare case for leaving. Most with magic in their bloodline tend to stay and study with other tribes. I'm one of the few who decided to come to the Crux, and it's no easy road down."

"I bet it's no easy road up, either," I say. I glance around to see Garrett and Galiva talking by the fire. Galiva says something that makes Garrett laugh loud enough to carry through the camp. "Did you ever have raiders come up from the high plains?"

Margeurite looks at me curiously. "Raiders?" she repeats. "No, of course not. The only people that live on the high plains are the orc clans. We'd trade often enough, but there were never any *raiders*."

I blink in surprise but don't know what to say to that. Maybe orcs only have issue with the humans in the high hills. I try to push the thoughts aside when Arlon calls us around the fire. Rations have been passed out, and as I take my bowl of thin stew I realize just how spoiled the food at the Crux has made me.

"Tomorrow we reach the Black Burrows," Arlon says. "Between Dominai and Garrett, we should be able to pick up their trail."

Across the fire, Garrett catches my eye and gives a small grin. I look away as I take a drink from my canteen.

"Once we are in the Hobokins proper, we'll need to shield our camp at night," Arlon continues. "I don't want anyone catching us off guard. I gave Dominai the last of my illusion barriers. Protections against attack, sight, and sound. Who else has one?"

"Plenty of straight abjuration," Galiva says. "None with that many illusory components."

"I have one," Garrett says and pulls the ring from his necklace before all eyes turn to Cancassi.

The Maeve toys with the end of their braid, looking sheepish. "Illusion sort of got pushed back while I was working on my transmutation mastery."

When no one else speaks up, I say, "I've got one that blocks against attack and sight."

"We need it to block against sound as well," Arlon says with an exasperated sigh. "It wouldn't do to have a disembodied horse wicker if someone is nearby. I was hoping not to cast on the road, but at least we found out now." He gets to his feet with an all too familiar groan. "We'll need two volunteers to conduit for abjuration and illusion."

All of us are tired and sore, but since I'm the only non-master along for this trip, I feel obligated. Besides, it'll be nice to have my ass sore for a reason other than riding. This far off of the main road, there shouldn't be anyone but us around, either.

"I'll do it."

"It's been a bit since I've done illusion," Garrett says. "I'll do it, too."

"Good." Arlon puts a hand on my shoulder before he adds, "Cancassi and I will cast. We need this to be a higher strength spell, so everyone can assist."

Chuckles ripple around the fire as I get to my feet, anticipation already thrumming through my veins. I suddenly feel a lot less sore and tired. Arlon unlaces my leather jerkin and lifts it off before doing the same with my shirt. It's a cool night, and gooseflesh crawls over my skin.

"We'll try not to cut into your sleep too much," the Grandmaster says with that familiar grin.

Behind me, Garrett laughs. I glance over my shoulder and see him toss his shirt on a fallen log, revealing gray skin peppered and crossed with scars. "Awful kind of you," he says. "You've gotten nicer over the years, Arlon."

Arlon quirks an eyebrow. "Then it really has been some time since you've cast with me," he says even as he grabs a pack from the pile of tack by our grazing horses. He flips it open to reveal various casting supplies and a long string of uncharged focuses. He pulls out two long coils of rope and hands one off to Cancassi. "I look forward to giving you a reminder."

Garrett laughs again and I can't help but wonder what their history is. Arlon mentioned that Garrett has full mastery as well, so I wonder if they came to the Crux around the same time. At a glance they might be the same age, but the gray skin makes age hard to tell. How long do orcs live, anyway?

Arlon finds a suitable tree branch that he positions me under. Cancassi guides Garrett to stand in front of me, and it takes me a second to realize I'm doing everything I can not to meet his gaze. Then Arlon takes my hands and puts them in Garrett's.

I blink in surprise. "We're being tied together?" I ask as Arlon loops a rope around both of our wrists.

"Having two conduits for the same spell increases the area of effect," Arlon says. "And we need a large area of effect if we're going to cover us and the horses."

"Right," I say even as nerves settle in my stomach. I'm tense as Arlon carefully binds our wrists together before using the rest of the length to weave down our forearms. I focus on the quick work he makes of the knots instead of looking at Garrett.

This close, I can feel the heat of the orc's breath, and I'm all too aware of him watching me. Arlon tosses the end of the rope over the branch overhead and ties it so our arms are pulled tight over us. It makes me stand tall, though it's not quite enough to put me on my toes. I try and fail to stop my chest from bumping Garrett's.

"You have a problem with me, don't you?" Garrett says at last.

Behind me, I hear Cancassi's little "oooh" and flush. I don't have a problem, and I think it's mighty forward of him to say so. Instead I say, "I don't *know* you."

Garrett chuckles, and the deep sound rumbles through me. "Well, we're about to get very well acquainted."

I flush but keep my head down even as Cancassi pulls my boots and breeches off, underthings following soon after. They do the same to Garrett, and I shiver as I feel his sizable cock brush mine. The cold that's doing nothing to help me doesn't have the same effect on him.

Arlon rummages through the supply bag and asks, "Dominai, do you know how to stop when you have a gag on?"

"Thumbs out, right?"

"You got it," he says and he pulls out a handkerchief and a strip of leather. "This will undoubtedly be a new kind of gag for you, so if at any time you have trouble breathing, you know how to let us know."

I nod, and Arlon balls the handkerchief up before he shoves it into my mouth. My cheeks bulge around it, but then he straps the leather over my mouth. It covers from the bottom of my nose to my chin, and a buckle around the back of my head secures it firmly in place. I groan and it's well muffled.

I glance up just in time to see Arlon do the same to Garrett. With the gag on he looks a little feral, like he's been muzzled so he can't bite. I can't think on that long as Arlon ties a blindfold tight over my eyes.

All the while Cancassi continues with the ropes, tying us ankle to ankle. I hear the snap of a branch, and our legs are spread apart. Ropes tie us to either end of the stick to keep our legs wide. It leaves us just enough freedom that I can move my hips, though I have nowhere to go but directly into Garrett.

He's taller than me, and I already feel his hardening cock rub against my stomach. I shiver as my own responds, even as I try to forget who I'm tied to. With the blindfold on, it's pretty easy to do.

"Careful how you cast," Arlon says. "We're not doing evocation."

"Boo," Galiva says, her voice suddenly very close to me.

"Shame we can't use his mouth," says Ambra. "From what you've told me, Dominai is pretty good with his tongue."

"We're not doing enchantment either," Arlon says, exasperation coloring his voice.

Ambra and Galiva's laughter sounds around me, and I shiver. Being able to hear all that's being said about me while I'm gagged and blindfolded is new. It puts me into a good headspace almost immediately, and I stop worrying so much about Garrett.

Hands start to explore my skin, giving me goosebumps for a reason entirely separate from the cold. They're gentle, and I'm grateful for it as fingers massage the sore muscles of my legs and back. All the while, they talk about us. Without my eyes, I can't even tell which comments are about me.

"He's got the best ass, doesn't he?" Cancassi says.

"It's durable, too," Margeurite adds, a bit of mischief in her voice.

A voice I recognize as Thaddius says, "I've never cast with either before. Apparently I'm missing out."

Through his gag, I hear Garrett's deep groan by my ear. The sound does things to me I don't really care to admit, but my cock's not nearly as good at keeping a secret. I feel myself getting hard even as the hands on my ass spread me wide. I shudder in anticipation.

Ambra gasps. "You'd think he was a virgin!"

"Told you he was durable," Margeurite says, and I flush to the tips of my ears.

"And Margeurite did not go easy on that ass," Galiva adds.

Arlon sighs. "What did I just say about enchantment?"

"Sorry," Ambra says, though she doesn't sound sorry at all.

But then someone's finger is in me, and I suck in a breath through my nose as someone else grabs my cock. They tease my length before slipping a snug focus down to the base. Three more follow, and I'd swear they're tighter than the others I've had on. I groan as my cock throbs inside of them.

My hole is still a little sore from my time in the silver, but the lotion-slicked fingers feel amazing as they massage me inside and out. I feel Garrett tense before he rests his forehead against mine. Whatever they're doing to him wrings a long low moan out of him before deteriorating into little noises of pleasure, his breath puffing hard and fast.

"I never realized orcs had the most perfect cocks," Ambra says.

"Half-orc," Arlon corrects, "But you're not wrong."

A second finger presses into me, stretching me gently even as they add more lotion. I groan and find myself nuzzling against Garrett's hot neck as those fingers curl against the sweet spot inside of me. When they pull away, I can't stop a little noise of displeasure.

"He's so eager," Thaddius says, and I feel a hand trail over my ass, like he's resisting the urge to swat.

"Let the suspension out a bit," Galiva says. The ropes holding our arms up loosen even as another pair of hands grabs my hips and pulls my ass out so I'm no longer chest to chest with Garrett. I yelp and nearly lose my balance, but there are enough hands to steady me. Garrett rests his head on the back of my neck.

My sore legs are getting a good stretch, but after three hard days of riding the fatigue in my muscles catches up quick. I tremble as I feel a cock prod at my well-slicked hole. Without my eyes I have no idea who it is, and the thought of being passed around lights my nerves on fire.

The focuses around my cock spark as whoever it is eases into me. I wail into the gag and hear Garrett moan in response, deep and guttural. Whoever it is sets a slow, leisurely pace that makes pleasure race up my spine. My cock bobs with every thrust, hard as a rock. Other than those first few strokes, I'm acutely aware that no one has touched it since.

"Gods, he's so sensitive," Thaddius says, and I'm finally able to put a voice to the cock inside of me. "And so *tight*."

"He's a very agreeable conduit," Galiva says, and I feel her fingers stroke through my hair.

Garrett jerks sharply, a grunt of near pain making it past his gag. Whoever is behind him has set a brutal pace, and I feel him jerk with every punishing thrust. His moan rattles out of him as his head butts against me. Despite my soreness, I want to shout at Thaddius to go faster. He spears me slowly, reaching deep, and as sore as I am, I wish he would just *fuck* me already.

I hear Arlon's low groan. Garrett's body stills, and he presses his face against my cheek, breath hissing in and out of his nose.

"Maybe that'll remind you of the kind of caster I am," Arlon growls. The heat in his voice makes me shiver even though he's not talking to me.

Thaddius starts to speed up and I moan loudly to goad him on. His cock slides deep into me, dragging across that spot as his hips slap against my sore ass. His fingers dig into my hips as he buries himself deep. I feel him empty himself inside of me and whimper even as Garrett starts to move again.

"I'm glad you brought these," Margeurite says, her voice holding a hint of a moan. I vaguely wonder what she's talking about before Thaddius pulls out of me, a trail of wet following him. I remember the first time I saw him - hooded and gagged in Arlon's dungeon with cum spilling out of him. Funny how things change.

Then someone else is at my hole, though I can tell it's no real cock. A phallus, I realize, and I feel familiar hands grip my waist.

"Are you alright?" Galiva asks as she kisses down my back. I manage a nod and feel her smile against my skin. "Good," she purrs before she thrusts into me. The focuses spark again as she rides me far harder than Thaddius had. If anyone knows my limits it's her, and I wail as she pushes me right to the edge of them.

I hear her moan, long and low, and wish I could see what she was using that felt as good for her as it does for me. My head bumps against Garrett's chest with every thrust as I submit to the thorough fucking. She takes a little longer than Thaddius had, and it's a relief when she tenses and moans behind me, rolling her hips twice more in long, slow thrusts. Yet as soon as she pulls out of me, someone else takes her place.

"Finally," Cancassi says as their hands grab my hips. My whimper barely makes it past the gag. Their cock is smaller than the phallus Galiva used, and I'm grateful for it. For a second, I thought I was going to have to suffer Arlon, and I don't think I could have kept my thumbs from going up.

As Cancassi works their slicked length into me, I feel someone brush my cock. I jump just as Garrett does, a surprised squeak coming from him that seems very out of place. I can't stop an exhausted laugh, but it's gone the second a mouth closes around my cock. Gag or no, my moan is loud, relief flooding me.

The focuses spark hard, and I feel the warmth of a tongue teasing the skin between them.

"Not yet," Arlon says.

The mouth over my cock stops, and both Garrett and I wail in unison. Chuckles ripple around us even as Cancassi speeds up. They cum with a little sigh of pleasure before pulling out and leave my hole dripping and spread wide.

I'm shaking with need, and I'm not the only one. Garrett shivers against me, a muffled mewl of pleasure sounding as he rests his cheek against mine. Apparently even after gaining full mastery, one can still be reduced to a cum-filled mess during a casting.

Then I feel something stretch my hole again and realize that it's a string of focuses, just like what I used during my conjuration. Five marbles slide into me, filling me up in a way that a cock or phallus never could. I whimper, almost dreading how intense my orgasm is going to be. Almost.

Then, the mouth around my cock starts again in earnest. My focus is too ruined to even try and guess who it is, so I just enjoy it. Whoever it is does an expert job of it, and it's not long before I feel my orgasm build. The focuses around my cock and inside of me spark, making me see stars behind my blindfold.

I howl as my orgasm overtakes me. Someone starts to pull the string of focuses out of me, and I moan until I run out of breath, shuddering as each marble pops out of me. It adds another layer of pleasure to my release, making me feel lightheaded. The lips around my cock continue to suck until I'm well and fully spent.

Vaguely I hear Garrett's cry echo mine, and judging by the sound of it, we had no trouble charging all of the focuses Arlon put on us. Finally the mouth pulls away, and I sag into the ropes, feeling Garrett's heaving chest thump against mine again. He buries his face into my hair, and I can't do much else but rest mine against his collar, panting as I try to regain my senses.

The blindfold is peeled from my eyes, and I blink as I blearily focus on Galiva's smiling face. She holds up the string of marbles, all of which are glowing softly.

"Plus the four on your cock, I'd say that's a new record for you," she says.

I give a muffled laugh and let my head fall back against Garrett's chest. I don't stay there long as someone pulls my head back to get the gag undone. I'm forced to look up, and I find Garret's gray eyes watching me, expression still hazy in the aftermath of pleasure. Even with the gag still on, I can tell he's smiling. For a second, I just stare as a thought creeps its way into my pleasure-addled mind; I've been a *shit* to him.

"Well done," Arlon says as he frees us from the ropes around our wrists. Someone else frees our ankles, and Arlon drapes a blanket around my shoulders before giving them a gentle squeeze. Garrett is given another, and I notice Arlon press a kiss to his cheek before motioning for us to go sit by the fire. Someone already has a pot of water warming for us to wash with. I check it with my finger, but it's tepid at best.

Instead I take the seat next to Garrett and shiver as I finally start to feel the night's chill. Behind us, the others laugh and chat as they walk down to the creek to clean the focuses and casting equipment. For now, it's just me and Garrett.

"You hear that?" Garrett asks, breaking the silence between us.

I glance up at him. "What?"

"That's the sound of wizards being happy in their work," Garrett says as I hear Cancassi's trill of laughter echo up from the creek. "That's how it *should* be. With all the terrible things we've learned lately, it's nice to be reminded."

I nod and pull my blanket a little more securely around my shoulders. I want to say something, but I can't find the words. I'm still having a hard time gathering my thoughts after having them thoroughly fucked out of me. Garrett doesn't seem to have the same problem.

"You're alright?" he asks. "That was a pretty intense spell for an adept."

"I'm fine," I say with a sigh. I'm not sure if it's true, but it certainly doesn't have anything to do with the adrenaline drop after the casting. After a moment, the words come tumbling out. "Look, I'm sorry. I've been an ass to you. It's just that-"

Garrett holds up a hand and my words shrivel in my mouth. "It's just that you're a human from the Hobokins and I'm a half-orc from the high plains," he finishes for me. A moment of quiet stretches between us as Garrett seems to weigh what to say next. "Let me ask you this - you ever met an orc before?"

I swallow. "No."

"You ever met anyone who's *actually* met an orc before?"

I think back, remembering all of the my-cousin's-friend's-neighbor's stories with a sinking feeling. "No," I say at last.

"Didn't think so," Garrett says blandly. "Wanna know why that is?" He doesn't seem to expect my answer. "Because about five or so generations ago, orcs were driven out of our settlements in the Hobokins by humans. We were forced up to the high plains, but you bet your ass we tried to fight to get our land back," he says, an edge cutting into his voice. "But we also saw the losing fight for what it was. You all breed like mice, and the fight became too costly for my ma's folks to keep up. By then, we'd inherited the plains and they were a defensible enough position that we didn't *have* to deal with humans anymore.

"So now, we fight off aggressors, protect our borders, but let me tell you - our desire to take back the rest of the mountain has long passed. Guess you could say humans won that territory war," he scoffs. "But you know what's funny? While humans have the shorter lifespan, your memories last *forever*. It never ceases to amaze me how your kind hold on to prejudices from a conflict that's been over for *decades*."

I swallow, guilt settling in my gut. When I first came to the Crux, I was afraid I'd be taken as some ignorant mountain boy, but it's only now I've proved it.

"I'm sorry," I say quietly. "I was being stupid."

Garrett nods sagely. "You were," he agrees. "But I accept and appreciate the apology. It's better than the rocks some folks offered me when I first came down the mountain with a human woman. At least in Straetham, I'm more of a curiosity than a menace."

A silence falls between us, only slightly more comfortable than it had been. "You can tell me to fuck off, but if humans and orcs don't do a lot of mingling... then how'd you come to be?"

Garrett laughs. "Because humans that have been ostracized from their villages tend to wander," he says. "If they make it up to the high plains and prove they're not a total fucking asshole, we'll let them in. My da was kicked out of Airedale for thieving. My ma's clan found him half-dead and frostbitten, so they took him in. He proved that he wasn't a total fucking asshole and a pretty good hunter on top of that."

He looks a little sad as he adds, "He died never even realizing he had magic in his blood. If he had, he never would have had to steal in the first place."

I run a hand through my hair, my curiosity getting the better of me. "How'd you find out you had magic?"

Garrett chuckles and says, "It was kind of a, ah... low time for me. After I left the high plains, I slept with a human prostitute in Frostcliff who also had a spark of it. She was the only one who'd bed a half-orc, but I think we're both pretty glad she did. She left that hellhole of a brothel the next morning and we came to the Crux together. Neither of us have ever looked back." He has a fond smile on his face and adds, "You probably haven't met Bridgette - she's been working off-site as a conjurer and herbalist for a few years now." He takes a drink from his canteen before offering it to me. "You?"

"Was working as a forest guide and Allisande hired me," I say and take a long drink. "I chased off some goblins one night, and she, ah, thanked me."

Garrett chuckles, and I have to admit that I like the sound of it. He's got a deep, resonant voice that has a way of shivering over my skin. "Sounds like Allisande," he says before his smile fades. I know where his mind's gone because mine keeps looping back to the thought as well.

The chatter of the others starts to get louder as they head back up from the creek. "We have seven heavily armed wizards and two people who know the Hobokins inside out," I mutter. "I don't think these monsters stand a chance. We'll get them back."

Garrett nods in agreement. "We'll get them back."

The Black Burrows

The next morning, we reach the hills proper. Our road gets steeper, the trees thicker and more wild. We deviate from the main road to follow a rough cart path, but Cancassi's horses handle the rugged terrain without complaint and only a few missteps. By early evening, we reach the Black Burrows.

The entrance to the mine would have been easy to miss if it weren't for the signs of destruction in the surrounding woods. Trees are toppled and scorched, the earth torn and cracked. That and the twenty or so dirty-faced miners clearing the debris are a pretty good sign that we've made it to the right place.

"Who the hell are you?" one of the miners shouts as we approach. Others grab their pickaxes as they catch sight of us and hold them like they're readying for a fight. Then, I notice the graves, some dug, some open and waiting for the bodies that are lined up just a little way from the mine's entrance. The mine's security, I assume, judging by the armor that a few of the miners were stripping off them.

"We're wizards of the Crux," Arlon says as he dismounts. "My name is Arlon Kalisson. I'm Grandmaster of the towers."

It does little to put the miners at ease. They glare at us, but the man who first spoke takes a few steps towards us. Another behind him spits disdainfully.

"The last ones claimed to be from the Crux, too," the first man growls, but I'm too busy looking at the spitter.

Then it hits me. I stumble off my horse with a laugh. *"Walter?"*

The man blinks and looks at me with new eyes, recognition lighting up his face.

"I'll be damned. Is that *Dom*?" He laughs and some of his work-mates scowls soften a little. "You running with wizards now?"

"Needed a change of scenery," I say through a grin. "Why you working the mines?"

Walter sighs. "Da's herd fell sick. We lost more than half of them before we got it under control," he says. "We needed the extra coin, so I came here for the summer."

"Fucking hell, I'm sorry to hear that." Behind me, Arlon clears his throat. "Right. Look, we got word that there was some trouble out here. We sent one of our own to help a little over a week ago but we... heard something happened." I look around at the destruction. "What's gone on here?"

The first man who spoke seems to be the leader of the little group and he walks forward, wiping sweat from his forehead.

"You're Olbric's people?" he asks, and when I nod, he lets out a sigh of relief. "Good - turns out the security the King sent were less than useless. Olbric was the only one who even stood a chance against the folks that have come sweeping through."

"Bandits?" Arlon asks.

The man shakes his head. "No bandit crew around is carrying that amount of firepower," he says. "They claimed they were from the Crux, and we believed them right up until they tried to raid the mine."

Arlon frowns at that. "Going after gold ore seems like a waste of magic," he says.

The miner shakes his head. "They weren't after the gold," he says. He reaches into his pocket and pulls out a white stone that I recognize instantly. And I'm not the only one. I feel the ripple of shock go through our little group.

It's a focus.

Raw and uncut, but there's no mistaking that curious shine. "We hit a vein of this not three weeks back. As soon as we started hauling it out, this group showed up. They were coming back for more when Olbric tried to stop them. Hate to say it, but I think your wizard's dead. We never found his body."

I flinch at that, my heart tapping an anxious beat in my chest. He can't be right. *Please* don't let him be right.

Arlon steps forward and takes the raw stone from the man's open palm. "What's your name?" he asks.

"Regis, sir," he says, adapting a much more formal tone now that Arlon's standing right next to him. The Grandmaster definitely has a presence that others take notice of.

"Regis, do you know what this is?" The man shakes his head, and he has the look of someone who wished he had never pulled it out of the ground. "This is a magically conductive mineral called magiline. It's the only material we've found that can store magic indefinitely, and until now, the only known source of it was the main tower of the Crux in Straetham."

Galiva comes up beside us and takes the chunk from Arlon. "How much of it did they take?" she asks.

Regis looks Galiva over curiously. "Not sure," he says. "A cart-load, at least."

Arlon says something in a language I don't recognize, but it's easy enough to spot a swear. "Then they aren't limited by the number of focuses they've stolen from our missing wizards," he says. "They're working to create their own stockpile."

The Grandmaster looks at Garrett, and some unspoken conversation seems to happen between them. Arlon lets out a long sigh. "We'll camp here tonight. I need to get a Sending back to the Crux and to King Thermilious."

A shiver of unease runs through my spine at the thought of that. Whatever distrust the King has of wizards is only going to grow if there are rogue ones running about with their own store of focuses.

Arlon's not finished. "Cancassi, I need you to seal the entrance to this mine until a time we can reopen it securely."

"Hey now, we've got a job to do!" Regis protests.

Arlon reaches into his cloak and pulls out a letter with a crest that even I recognize. It's the royal seal - a rearing gold griffin on a field of red.

"On matters of magical importance, I have authority," he says and hands the paper to Regis. "As of now, this mine is closed until it can be properly secured. You and your men will be paid for the season, plus extra compensation to get you all home safely. Ambra?"

"Got it, sir," she says and rummages through our saddle packs until she finds a bag that jingles in a telling way.

Regis looks from the paper to Ambra's large bag with wide eyes. "Oh," he says, sounding a little faint.

Arlon turns to me next. "Dominai, I need you to find our trail," he says. His words feel like a physical weight. If I'm not able to do it...

Garrett's hand lands on my shoulder, a comforting presence. I take a breath and meet Arlon's eye. I muster every bit of confidence I can. "I'll find it."

THE PATH OF DESTRUCTION isn't hard to read. Trees with trunks as thick as a person have been snapped like twigs while others are scorched to embers along with the ground around them. Thank the gods it's been a wet summer so far. The fire wasn't able to spread.

Olbric had led his attackers away from the mine. To keep the miners safe from the firefight, no doubt. With their security dead, they had no one but him and their own pickaxes to rely on.

The trail goes on for nearly a full mile, and I gain a whole new appreciation for what evocation can do. They really went at it. Olbric held his own for quite some time but when the destruction stops, it stops abruptly. I see the wrecked earth that had sent Olbric tumbling to the ground, see the cone-shaped irregularity in the pine needles from where he sent his attacker flying.

I find the trunk he was backed up against when the knife found his throat. The ground around it has been searched well. I don't find a single focus, but I do find the broken strands of leather that had held them all in place. I pick it up, an ache settling in my chest.

"He was right here." My voice barely reaches a whisper, but Garrett hears me all the same. He straightens from where he's examining the torn earth.

"From the damage, I can spot evocation, transmutation, and a bit of conjuration," Garrett says with a sigh. "It's impossible for me to tell what was theirs and what was Olbric's though."

I nod and put my hand to the ground, feeling the soft earth. Thank the gods the ground's damp enough to hold a trail, and fortunately it hasn't rained since Olbric was taken to wash it away. I pick out the indent of their boots, and the scrape of earth where they must have dragged him.

"There are four sets of footprints aside from Olbric's," I say. "My guess is three wizards, and one regular ol' human."

"Why's that?" Garrett asks.

"Because the woman I saw in my divining only had a dagger," I say. "She may have had some spells hidden around her neck, but if she did, why not use them? Magic's got to give you a whole lot of other ways to disable someone without getting into arm's reach."

We follow the trail, making sure not to trample the tracks as we go. It's maybe a quarter mile later when the tracks deviate from their straight line. A scuffle, I realize. Olbric had fought back, tried to throw them off, but then I find the dried blood splattered across the nearby rocks.

Anger settles like a hot coal in my stomach, but the trail continues on, further into the hills. "It's a good trail," I say. "They weren't trying to cover their tracks."

Garrett looks up where the sunlight is quickly dwindling. "Then we should head back," he says. He offers me a hand, and I let him pull me to my feet. "We'll start fresh tomorrow." He claps me on the back. "Good work, Dominai."

THE NEXT MORNING, WE get an early start. The sun is just over the horizon by the time our camp is packed and the horses loaded. The miners, pockets jangling with coin, are just as eager to get out of here and get home. Walter and a few others are headed towards Airedale while most come from a village further down the hill.

"Good luck," Walter says and shakes my hand. "Olbric was a good guy. I hope you all can find out what happened to him."

I swallow and put on a smile I don't feel. "Me too. Say hi to your da for me."

We pick up the trail again, and on horseback we make it to the spot where Garrett and I had to stop much quicker. The footprints continue on for a few miles before I notice another spot where Olbric must have tried to escape again. His tracks trail off to the left, into the thick of the woods, but over them are spots where someone dragged him back - kicking and fighting the whole time by the looks of it.

There's no blood, but Olbric's tracks disappear. "Search for a body," Arlon says, and my heart stops in my chest. I don't think I breathe again until we've canvassed the whole area to rule that out. We have to assume whoever took him carried him. I'm not sure what subdued him this time, but it leaves a sour feeling in my stomach.

Our trail leads us further up into the bluffs. The path gets rockier, and as the sun starts to go down the footprints get harder to follow. It's only after I lead us on a false trail for nearly half a mile that Arlon calls a stop. We set up camp for the night, and I fall asleep discouraged despite Garrett and Galiva's attempts to reassure me.

I'm up before dawn, and as soon as it's bright enough, I find where I went wrong. We're reaching a rocky area. The footprints are few and far between, but a muddy shoe print sets me on the right path again. I follow it and am reassured when I see other tracks along the route.

My hope is short-lived as the terrain gets worse. I dismount and lead Mo on foot, panic starting to creep at the edges of my mind. There's a rock flat up ahead, and the last print I can see is a muddy mark on the edge of the gray granite.

I hand Mo's reins off to Cancassi, eyes scanning the ground for anything, any scuff or print, but there's nothing. I feel numb as the realization sinks in; I've lost the trail. No matter what way they went, it's nothing but rock fields for at least a mile. Even if I knew which direction they had gone, picking up the trail on the other side would be nothing but dumb luck.

I reach into my pocket, grabbing the leather strands that had held Olbric's focuses, as if that will somehow point me the right way. It feels like we're so close, yet at the same time still a million miles away.

Despair creeps through me, sapping my strength. That's it. I've failed.

Tears sting at the corner of my eyes as I reach for my necklace, fingers finding the spell Olbric and I cast without thought. Then my thumb brushes the one next to it, and an idea blooms like hope.

I grab the spell and release it just as I had in the courtyard with Arlon. My wolf appears in a flash of light. She looks at me with those intelligent gold eyes, expectant.

Behind me, a couple of the horses hate the shit out of what I've just plopped in front of them and make their displeasure known. Cancassi's rears with a scream of alarm while a few others balk, legs braced to run.

"Wooaah, wooaah, easy," Cancassi says as they get their mount back under control. When they do, the others seem to fall into an anxious sort of quiet. Cancassi lets out a sigh and brushes a wayward hair behind their pointed ear. "Maybe warn us before bringing a predator into a herd of prey animals?"

"Fuck, sorry," I say, even as I pray to whatever gods might be listening that this works. I walk up to my wolf and hold out the remains of Olbric's spell necklace. "Can you track this smell?"

My wolf looks at it curiously before she leans in, wet nose snuffling at the leather. She sticks her nose in the air, sweeping her head around before she puts it to the ground. She wavers for a bit, moving back and forth before she settles on one direction.

I take Mo's reins and follow her, though the gelding makes sure I stay a good distance behind. Ahead of us my wolf moves more confidently now, which I hope is a good sign. We follow her for about a mile before the rocks start to fade back to dirt, and as they do, the three sets of prints re-appear. I lean against Mo's neck, relief making me lightheaded.

I turn back to the others who trail even further behind us. "This way!"

We don't stop for lunch, and it's like all of us can sense we're getting close. My wolf leads the way, her nose still to the ground. Around mid-afternoon, she stops abruptly. Her hackles raise, and she looks off to the left, baring her teeth.

I have my bow off my back and an arrow nocked in an instant. A twig snaps, and then something in the shadows moves. Whoever it is takes off at a run just as the others catch up.

"What's going on?" Arlon asks.

"Stop them," I say to my wolf. "Don't kill them."

She lunges into the woods, and it's not a second later I hear a shout of alarm before my wolf yelps in pain. Arlon and Galiva are off their horses in an instant. I move to follow them as they hurry into the brush, but Arlon rounds on me.

"Stay *put*, Dominai."

I swear, but do as I'm told. Through the brush, there's a flash of light. A voice I don't recognize shouts, "What the hell!"

"It's alright," Arlon calls back to us. Cancassi takes Mo's reins, and I hurry forward with Garrett and Thaddius to see what's going on.

Galiva has a glowing focus between her fingers, and on the ground in front of her is a woman. A shimmer of red surrounds her, keeping her arms pressed flat to her sides. She struggles against the magic before she shouts in pain and falls still, glaring up at us from under her hood. Beside her my wolf lays dead, a bloody gash in her neck. I step forward to put a hand on her shoulder and she vanishes into a swirl of light. I glare at the woman, and the memory of her face makes my heart lurch unpleasantly.

"Who are you?" Galiva demands.

"A hiker," the woman sneers.

"It's her," I say. "The woman who put the knife to Olbric's throat."

Arlon reaches through the flowing red energy and searches her, pulling out three daggers from the folds of her dark cloak. The woman turns her gaze onto me, head tilted curiously.

"Ah," she says. "Reinforcements have finally arrived."

"Where is he?" Galiva demands and the red energy around the woman intensifies.

The woman grimaces, and I realize this must be the spell Galiva had cast with Olbric. I wonder if she was ever able to test it. Well, no time like the present.

"In the caves," the woman spits through gritted teeth. "About half a mile up the hill."

Galiva rolls the focus between her fingers. "How many of you are there?"

"I'm not one of them," she spits. "They hired me."

Thaddius scoffs. "A mercenary."

"Doesn't matter," Galiva snaps. "How many are there?"

"Five," she snarls. "Though three of them are away."

"Where?"

The mercenary glares her hatred at Galiva. "Do I look like their fucking keeper?" she snaps. "They're away."

Galiva gives a long-suffering sigh. "Do you expect them *back* any time soon?"

"Who knows?" the woman says. "They come and go as they please. I'm just here to keep an eye out for anyone approaching."

Arlon glares down at her. "Who are you?" he demands.

"Isa," she says simply. "If you want your thots back, now's your time. I've already been paid. I got no stakes in what happens next save for my own life."

Arlon's eyes narrow, and I see the barely contained anger simmering behind his expression. "We'll take her back with us to face the King's justice for kidnapping," he says at last. It's a mighty kind sentence, especially when Arlon undoubtedly has a couple dozen ways to kill someone hanging around his neck. "Thaddius?"

Thaddius grabs one of his focuses, and it winks out with a flash of yellow light. Though I don't see the spell, it slams into Isa like a physical blow, shuddering through her body. Her face goes slack, eyes glassing over.

"You're going to stay here," Thaddius says even as Galiva takes some of our rope to bind her to the nearest tree. "And you will not leave until we come back for you."

Isa gives a listless nod. "I'll stay here," she says, her words slurred. "And I'll not leave until you come back for me."

Arlon nods in approval. "We'll leave the horses here under illusion with her."

We're quick to loosen cinches and tie the reins off. Cancassi sets the spell and the horses all blink out of sight, as if they were never there.

Arlon looks around at us, grim determination written in every line on his face. "Let's go."

The Cave

Wizards of the Crux base all of their magical studies and practices around the concept of consent. Rape or coercion are anathema and grounds for immediate expulsion.

Please note that this chapter contains allusions to rape, brief visual of sexual assault, mention of non-consensual drugging and brief violence.

WE FIND THE ENTRANCE to the caves just where Isa said. Half a mile up the hill, set into a rocky outcropping. There's signs of inhabitation. A full clothesline is strung between two trees, and a cold fire pit is circled with sitting stumps. Nearby, I hear the trickle of a creek. Beside it, there's a makeshift wooden tub for bathing. We creep closer, but to all appearances no one's home.

Arlon turns to me. "This is where you stay," he says, voice pitched low.

"Arlon, *please-*"

The Grandmaster puts his hands on my shoulders and squeezes. "No. You have done more than enough," he says, his tone gentle. "Your resourcefulness has led us straight to their lair. And that same resourcefulness will someday make you a wizard to be reckoned with. But today, I need you to stay here, and stay *down*."

I nod, but I can't meet his eye. It feels too much like being a kid again, told to stay behind while the adults do the important work.

Arlon squeezes my shoulder again before he searches my necklace. He finds the abjuration spell he'd given me, and pulls the focus off. With a quiet whoosh, he releases the spell before setting it on my palm and closing my fingers around it.

"If we're not out by sunrise, you go back to the horses and you return to the Crux. Is that understood?"

I swallow, dread settling in my stomach as I squeeze the magiline ring. I don't want to think about going back alone. Even so, I nod. "Understood."

Galiva kisses my cheek, and I pull her into a tight embrace. "Be safe," I whisper, holding on for a second longer before I let her go. My traitorous thoughts remind me that this could be the last time. We outnumber them, but who knows what waits inside of that cave?

Arlon turns back to the assembled wizards. He detaches a string of spells from his necklace and wraps it around his fist. A few others copy him, readying for the fight.

"On my lead we go in, we find our people, and we don't hesitate against those who would stop us. Understood?" There are nods all around, and Arlon lets out a quiet sigh. "May the gods watch over us."

Then, without another word, they vanish from sight.

I don't hear them leave, but something changes in the air, and I know they've gone in. I duck a little further back into the trees and let out a shaking breath, my nerves alight. Even under the protection of Arlon's abjuration and illusion, I stay still and quiet. It's more habit than anything, even though I itch to pace, to *do* something. It feels wrong to be sitting here while they're all risking their lives inside of that cave.

The minutes tick by, a slow torture. I pull my bow down and nock an arrow. The weight of it is a comfort in my hands. Somewhere to my left, something small shuffles through the underbrush. The birds chirp their songs overhead, oblivious to me and my churning thoughts. I block them out and watch the dark entrance of the cave, waiting for movement, ears strained for any noise.

It feels like an eternity, but when movement comes it doesn't come from the cave. My fingers tighten on the string of my bow, and I duck low as laughter makes its way up the hill. A minute later, a small group of people emerge from the trees not twenty feet from where I'm crouched.

Three men with full strands of spells hanging heavy around their necks. Between them is a young woman with her wrists bound in front of her. The colorful skirts she wears are ripped, and a part of it makes the bright gag that's tied into her mouth. Tears wet her bronze cheeks.

One of the men gives her a shove, and she stumbles. At first, I think she's shaking from fear. But when she turns to scream muffled obscenities at the man, I see nothing but plain fury on her face.

"Look at that, Diran," one of the men laughs. "She's a fierce one, ain't she? You'd think a bandit's bedwarmer would have learned something of fear by now."

I don't know what I expected Diran to look like, but I'm surprised by how... average he is. White-skinned with short brown hair. One could squint and call him handsome, but the sneer on his face makes me want to knock some of those white teeth out. He's wearing well-made traveling clothes and sturdy but muddied boots.

He steps forward and grabs a fistful of the woman's black hair, yanking her to her knees. She shrieks into her gag, and I draw an arrow back to my ear.

"She will soon enough," Diran says.

My arm shakes. I want to let the arrow fly straight through the man's eye. But *fucking hell*, I can't take three of them with a bow. Not when they're armed to the godsdamned teeth.

Diran pauses before he looks around the clearing. He tosses the woman to the ground. She yelps as Diran delivers a sharp kick to her leg.

"Shut up," he snarls, and the woman huddles into a trembling ball, arms lifted to protect her head.

Diran looks back towards the woods - towards *me*. He takes a step in my direction, mud-brown eyes narrowed to a glare. My instinct is to run, but I'm frozen like a deer. I don't have a choice but to trust Arlon's spell.

I hold my breath, but Diran's gaze passes right over me. Instead, he focuses on the trampled grass the others had walked across. He kicks at one of Arlon's footsteps that's sunk into the soft ground.

My stomach drops into my feet. I'd been so focused on following a trail, I hadn't even considered hiding our own.

Diran smirks, and he's so close that I can see his crooked front tooth catch the dry skin of his lip. He follows the others' footprints to the entrance of the cave and kneels to brush away a layer of dirt. Underneath, a glowing focus pulses.

"Someone's here," he says. He sounds almost pleased. Then his gaze turns back to the woman. Her eyes widen with fear as he reaches for a spell. His fingers pick out the one he's looking for, and when the focus flashes out, the woman flinches and throws her hands up. But whatever attack she was expecting doesn't come.

Instead, a cold gray barrier appears around her like a cage. She gets to her feet, slamming her bound fists against the wall. It sparks bright under her attack, but holds. She rips the gag out, but the abjuration blocks whatever hatred she shouts.

Diran smiles and puts his fingers to his lips. "Don't worry," he says. "We'll be back for you, little dirt blood."

The woman yells something else at him, and just to make her disdain clear, she flips a rude gesture with her hand. Diran just chuckles and turns to his two companions.

"Let's go," he says, and all three of them wink out of sight.

My stomach drops. Even if the others have taken down the wizards inside, they have no idea what's coming towards them. I can't stay here. I can't just wait.

I step out of the trees and creep towards the mouth of the cave. Arlon's spell kept me hidden from Diran, and it holds strong as I walk past the caged woman. She slumps against the barrier of the spell to sink back to the ground. Even though I walk right past her, she doesn't give any indication she's seen me. Instead, she buries her head in her hands and starts to sob.

We'll come back. We'll get her out, too. We have to.

The tunnel is dark. I follow it until I reach the first torch that's set into the wall about ten feet in. As the darkness of the tunnel closes around me, the stone walls seem to do the same. I walk past the torch, moving further into the tunnel. The path constricts enough that I have to crouch down before it widens again.

It's not long before I reach a fork. A breeze rushes up from one of the paths, cooling the sweat on my face. Gooseflesh prickles over my neck as I look at the dark path that yawns open to my left. I imagine Diran's smirking face striking out from the shadows, and the fear turns sharp, tightening around my lungs.

I choose the path with the torch instead.

The sound of my footsteps are covered by Arlon's spell, and maybe that's what makes it seem so eerily quiet down here. You'd think sound would bounce off the stone like an echo chamber, but the paths twist and branch so much, sound seems to get trapped in the maze.

I cross a few more dark paths, and every time, I expect an ambush. It's only when I reach one tunnel that stinks that I realize what this place is.

These pricks have set up shop in a godsdamned *goblin hovel*. Yet somehow, these wizards are still the worst things down here. Whatever colony existed here appears to have cleared out. Or were killed, judging by the sickly-sweet smell that wafts up from the darkness.

My skin crawls when I pass another dark tunnel, but it tries to break into a run when the path moans.

I spin and slam my back against the stone wall. My quiver clatters, and my bow twangs against the wall as I stare at the darkness. My own breath is loud in my ears, but nothing attacks.

Idiot. Good fucking thing I'm shielded from sight and sound or I could have alerted the whole place. But what the *fuck* was that?

Slowly, my eyes adjust to the gloom. A short, straight path goes on for a couple meters before it ends in a heavy door, bolted straight into the stone. I steel myself and creep towards it, my heart in my throat. There's a plank of wood set against the wall, and I see where it usually rests to bar the door closed. Like some sort of prison.

Everything is telling me to get as far away from here as possible, but I can't. Not yet.

I reach out and grab the heavy metal handle. The door groans quietly as I push it open. And inside, chained along the walls, illuminated by nothing but a single torch, are the missing wizards.

Allisande looks up at the sound. To her, it must look like the door is slowly opening on its own. She looks right through me, but flinches as another long, low moan comes from further inside the room. Allisande clamps her hands over her ears, making the heavy manacles around her wrists clank. She shuts her eyes tight, and I realize the other three wizards have already done the same. A man with copper skin and black hair cries quietly where he's curled into his corner.

I hear the moan again, louder this time, and my gut drops.

"Get *off* me."

His words are thick and clumsy, but I'd know Olbric's voice anywhere. I hurry to the back of the room, brushing past Allisande close enough that I'm sure she feels me.

I find a narrow path through the stone of the back wall. From beyond the little hall, there's a sound of tearing fabric.

"Please," Olbric moans. He sounds exhausted, defeated. It makes my stomach twist, but the sight that greets me as I squeeze through the narrow passage is worse.

Olbric is shackled and hanging a few inches from the ground by nothing but his wrists. His face is bloodied and bruised so bad that his left eye is swollen shut. Blood drips from where the manacles bite into his wrists, his arms wrenched at an awful angle.

The man that stands in front of him rips at the fabric of his shirt. One last tear gets it all the way off before he tosses it aside. Olbric kicks feebly at him, but it's like his body won't cooperate.

"Begging already, huh?" the man sneers. "You know how much I've been looking forward to some payback?"

Olbric moans, his head rolling loose on his shoulders. He blinks hard, like every time it takes more effort to keep his eyes open.

My stomach drops. They've *drugged* him.

I check my arrow and draw my bowstring to my ear, taking careful aim.

"Get off of him."

The second I speak, there's a shiver of magic across my skin, and I know I've just broken the spell that kept me hidden. I can't quite stop my voice from shaking.

"Get *off* him."

The man whirls, and the sight of his face makes me want to recoil. The skin on one side is pink and raw, glistening from where one of Olbric's spells must have burned him. His lip is curled into a permanent sneer, but it only grows more pronounced as he focuses on me.

He ducks behind Olbric's hanging form. One hand closes around Olbric's throat while the other pulls a knife from his belt. The man jabs it under Olbric's chin, and a new trail of blood slides down his neck.

"Hope you're a good shot," the man sneers.

With him using Olbric as a shield, only part of the burned half of his face is visible. It makes him a narrow target. His eyes flick off of me for just a second, and I follow his gaze to his spell necklace. It's laying in the corner with his shirt. The man tenses, ready to lunge for it.

I don't let him get that far. Rage steadies my hand.

"I am."

I let my arrow fly, and it flies true. The meaty thud of impact makes me feel sick to my stomach. It's so like shooting a deer, and yet not like it at all. The man barely makes a sound as the arrow pierces through his eye. He gives a little grunt of surprise before the knife drops from his hand. The man takes a staggering step back and collapses, dead before he hits the ground.

I sling my bow over my shoulder as I rush forward, doing everything I can not to look at the man I just killed. Olbric is limp as I grab him around the waist and lift. It takes a second, but I manage to get the link of his manacles off the hook that's screwed into the rock above. He shouts as I lower him to the ground, and his shoulder lets out a sickening *pop* as it slides back into place. I swear and cup his cheek, tapping gently.

"Olbric, can you hear me?"

Though one eye is swollen shut, his other flutters open. It rolls in his skull, disoriented. When he finally finds me, his face twists with pain.

"No," he gasps, his voice hoarse. Tears well to his eyes and spill down his cheeks. "Not you, too."

I pull him into a tight embrace, careful of his shoulder. "It's alright, it's okay," I say. "They didn't get me. We're here to get you out."

It's hard to say what gets through to him. Whatever they've given him has looped him up good. He rests limp in my arms even as his entire body shakes like a leaf. I pull back and kiss his forehead.

"You're alright. I'll get you out of here, I promise."

The last thing I want to do is leave him, but I *have* to. I might already be too late.

I scoot past the dead man and snatch the string of focuses from on top of his pile of clothes. I drape it around my neck before I give Olbric a gentle shake. He blinks hard and clutches my arm as I gently ease him to his feet.

"C'mon."

He struggles to get his legs underneath him but I pull him to lean against me, my arm tight around his waist. I half-carry him out of the room, squeezing us both through the narrow tunnel.

Allisande's gasp snaps me to attention. She stares at me with wide eyes, a hand closed over her mouth. She lowers it just a little as she whispers, "Dominai?"

The sound of my name on her tongue again makes my stomach do a little somersault.

"Hi, Allisande." I lower Olbric to the ground beside her as careful as I can. "I'm here with Arlon and a few others. We're here to get you *out*."

I take the dead wizard's spells from around my neck and hand them to her. Her hands shake a little as she takes the string. She's still looking at me like I'm a specter that might vanish at any second.

"How?" she asks, and it's only then I notice the other wizards have tuned in. They're all watching me with a desperate sort of hope. I put my hand over hers and squeeze gently to assure her I'm real.

"It's a long story that starts with your letter," I say with a strained smile. "I'll tell you the whole thing soon." A smile flickers onto her face, and it seems like it's been a long time since she's done it. I press a kiss to her fingers. "I'll be back with the others. I promise."

Olbric makes a distressed noise when I pull away from him, but I don't have time to waste. I move back out the door and down the short hallway to follow the torches. I move as quick as I dare. There's no spell keeping me hidden now, but a second later, I realize that it doesn't matter if I'm quiet anymore.

As I turn a corner, Cancassi's musical voice screams in pain. Light flashes from around the corner, and a crack of thunder makes my heart leap into my throat as the walls around us shake. Up ahead, there's a crash of rock as something gives.

"Get *down*!" Arlon shouts.

I move forward, arrow nocked. I barely notice the body I step over, except to note that it's someone I don't recognize. A bloom of crackling red light brightens the tunnel ahead, and I round the corner to see Diran lift a spell to shield himself as fire and debris rain down.

Galiva stands over Cancassi and Garrett. She has an abjuration up to shield them, and good fucking thing too. A chunk of the ceiling gives way a second later. Chunks of stone and dirt clatter off her shield as she looks at the ceiling with wide eyes. I can only pray that more of it doesn't decide to go. Garrett kneels next to Cancassi, spells winking out even as blood pools to stain the Maeve's white hair.

Behind them, I see Ambra's back as she raises an abjuration that shimmers like ice. Thaddius is crumpled at her feet while Margeurite stands poised and ready beside them.

In a flash, I understand what's happened. Diran and his cadre split up. They must have ambushed the Crux wizards from two different tunnels, trapping them in the middle.

Further down the tunnel, there's a flash of light. Ambra shouts, and her shield cracks and disappears. But in the second before she raises another Margeurite shoots off an attack with a snarl. Arlon echoes her with a roar as he aims a spell at Diran that crashes against his abjuration like thunder.

Diran's back is to me, but I see him tense, his legs threatening to buckle under the force of Arlon's spell. He holds with dogged determination, a smirk tugging at his lips.

They can't break through. Diran and his two cronies have closed in on them like the jaws of a trap. Arlon looks like he's throwing a punch, and a focus around his knuckles winks out. The spell cracks against Diran's shield in another ear-rattling *crash*.

Diran spreads his arms, focuses glowing from the string of spells wrapped around each of his hands. The spell concentrates in front of him, and the shine of magic makes a wall between him and Arlon. He's so focused on it that he doesn't even notice me.

I raise my bow and draw, aiming straight for the middle of Diran's back. Arlon's gaze jumps to me, and our eyes lock in a moment of brief surprise. Then Arlon gives a curt nod.

I let fly, and Diran screams as it punches into the flesh of his back. His concentration on the wall falters, and when Arlon slams another attack against it, the light of the abjuration flickers and cracks.

Diran snarls and keeps one hand raised to the wall even as he half-turns to glare his hatred at me. He holds his other hand out towards me, palm crossed with dozens of glowing rings and marbles. I fumble for an arrow, but my fingers are too slow.

In the split-second before one of his spells flashes out, I can't help but think that it's been a real fun time. Shame it was so short.

But there's no impact. No fire or pain. He doesn't blast me.

Instead, he runs.

There's a sharp *snap*, and Diran vanishes from sight.

One of Diran's mates shouts in despair. "That son of a bitch!" he snarls, just before Margeurite's well-timed spell crashes into him. I don't see what it does, but I hear him scream all the same.

Arlon spins, stepping past Garrett and Cancassi as he throws another punch. He snarls, and one of the spells on his hand flashes out before there's another deafening *crack*. There's an echoing crash, a final shout, and the tunnel falls quiet.

In the breath of silence that follows, Arlon sweeps down the hall. I hurry forward to see the Grandmaster strip the two downed wizards of their spells. Neither of them seem to be in any condition to stop him. I can hear that they're both still alive - if feeling pretty miserable about it.

It takes me a long second to unclench my fingers from the grip of my bow. Galiva keeps the shield up, but she looks far happier about it now that the thunder has stopped rumbling the tunnels around us. Ambra crouches by Thaddius, but the man groans and pats her hair. She helps him to his feet, and though he's moving gingerly, at least he's moving.

Cancassi whimpers as Garrett does something, but I let out a breath when I realize that the Maeve's alive. For a second, I had thought the worst.

Then, Arlon turns his furious gaze to me. I swallow and stow my bow, raising my hands as he sweeps towards me. For a split-second I see my da storming up to deliver an ass-whooping, but instead, Arlon pulls me into a bone-crushing embrace.

"Are you alright?" he asks, deep voice rough with relief. "I thought I was going to see the end of you."

"I'm fine," I promise. My frayed nerves finally relax, and I feel myself start to shake. "I-I saw them come in and couldn't just *wait*."

"They caught us by surprise," Arlon admits. "Their spells were stronger than we anticipated."

I shudder when I realize it's probably because they didn't give a damn about their conduits while casting them. Allisande's haunted face and Olbric's wrenched shoulder are still fresh in my memory.

"I found them," I say, and I can't stop the tremor in my voice. "I found all of them."

Arlon cups the back of my head and presses a soft kiss to my fore-head. "Show me."

I LEAD EVERYONE THROUGH the tunnels before I push the spooky door to the prison open. As soon as we're through, Margeurite lets out a cry of joy. She runs to Allisande, throwing her arms around the other woman as they crash together. Allisande sobs as she returns the embrace, holding the ovisari like she'll never let go.

Galiva hurries to Olbric, and I follow. "They had him hanging by his wrists," I say. "The man who did it is dead."

"Good," Galiva says. She peels Olbric's eyes open, gets a look at his dilated pupils and swears. "They've drugged the shit out of him." Her fingers are gentle as they touch the bruised skin around his eye, wringing a miserable little sound out of him. "But I don't think they broke anything." She moves to the cuts around his wrists and the new one under his neck. They've stopped bleeding, but the knife line that Isa had drawn when they first captured him is red with infection.

I smooth Olbric's tangled hair back from his face, and his good eye flutters open. He blinks as he looks up at us, unfocused and con-fused.

"You're safe," I promise, and it must be enough because his eye slides closed again.

Once Galiva has patched his wounds, she moves to help Garrett with the others. I stay by Olbric as the rest of them are freed from their shackles. Other than some very telling bruises and cuts they're physically alright, but I can see the shadows behind their eyes. What-ever they've endured here is worse than anything I want to imagine.

The reunions are quiet, and I keep a hand on Olbric as I watch them happen. There are tears all around. Even Arlon, who's as stoic as they come, sheds a few as he pulls Allisande and the shorter black-haired man into a tight embrace.

Spells are redistributed so the found wizards have something to carry. While Arlon takes Ambra and Margeurite to search the tunnels, Garrett and Galiva make sure all are hale enough to travel. They even tend to the rogue wizards, mending burns and sealing cuts, though I don't think they deserve it.

We search them to make sure every spell and weapon is out of their hands before shackling them in the same manacles they had used to keep the Crux wizards captive. Once the tunnels are cleared of magiline and supplies, we take them with us when we walk out of the caves.

The woman that Diran had dragged through the woods is still at the entrance, trapped behind the abjuration. She's managed to work her hands out from the ropes, and as soon as she catches sight of us, she straightens up. Arlon breaks the barrier around her with a spell of his own, and she looks braced to run.

"More godsdamned wizards," she spits.

"We're not here to hurt you," Arlon says and holds out a canteen to her. It's only then I realize they have the same charcoal hair, same sun-bronzed skin.

She looks from him to the canteen before she snatches it out of his hand. She drinks all of it, water leaking from the corner of her mouth. When she finishes she wipes her mouth on her sleeve, and only looks a little less wary.

"Who are you all?"

"Wizards of the Crux," Arlon says. "I assume you are not here willingly?"

The woman spits at the feet of the two rogue wizards Garrett's holding.

"A bandit crew overran my caravan in the Hobokins a few weeks ago," she says. "Killed my family, but took me alive. They were doing work with this lot when Diran paid for a night with me. Then decided he had to *keep* me," she hisses as she glares at the two. "You kill him?"

Arlon sighs. "No. Unfortunately, he made an escape."

"Shame," she says. "I would have liked to put a knife in his back myself."

Arlon looks her over. "You're Tinari?"

She straightens and gives him a similarly searching look before she answers. "Yes."

I blink in surprise. We had a few Tinari caravans come through Airedale, though outside of trade they wanted little to do with us. They're a close-knit community that never stay in one place for long, choosing to travel the roads with their horse caravans instead.

Arlon hums as he looks her over. "Your road is your own to choose, but it would be safer to travel with us - at least until we are out of the Hobokins."

Her wary gaze travels over all of us, but her eyes are drawn back to Arlon. She tilts her head curiously. "What's your name?"

"Arlon Kalisson," he replies, and I see something like surprise cross her face. "Yours?"

"Orabelle Burgess," she says. She looks him over once more before she comes to a decision. "I'll stay with you for now."

We return to where we left our horses only to find one of them missing, and Isa along with it. The ropes that had bound her are neatly cut.

"How the fuck?" Thaddius asks. "That domination spell was incredible!"

Arlon sighs and runs a hand through his hair. He looks as tired as I feel.

"Apparently her will was stronger," he says, displeased.

"I could track her," I offer.

Arlon shakes his head. "We have more important things to worry about."

He's not wrong. Cancassi and Thaddius were both hurt bad, and the recovered wizards are weak from their time in the cave. We help them onto the horses, and I offer to sit behind Olbric on top of Mo to hold him in place. I keep my arms tight around him, whispering quiet words of comfort into his ear as we start the long road down.

Behind us, Arlon and Garrett keep a close eye on the two captive wizards. From the snippets of conversation I catch, they know one of them. Lucien is his name, and he's another who had been expelled from the Crux, though he'd been kicked out nearly five years ago.

We make camp about half way back to the mine. Even though we set an illusion to hide our camp, we take shifts to keep watch over the rogue wizards. After losing Diran and the mercenary, Arlon isn't taking any chances with these two.

I sleep like the dead before I'm woken for the last shift, just before dawn. The two rogue wizards have fallen into an uneasy sleep, but I jump when Olbric wakes beside me with a quiet gasp. In the light of our dying fire his good eye stares up at the starry sky in confusion, as if he's not quite sure how he got here.

"Olbric?"

He blinks and tilts his head to look up at me. His eye glosses with tears as an uncertain smile spreads across his face.

"Please tell me I'm not dreaming," he whispers. "I-I've had so many nightmares recently."

The fear and uncertainty on his face makes my chest ache with sympathy. I scoot closer to him before I bring my lips to his. He relaxes under me, and I stroke his cheek as I pull away.

"It's no dream," I promise. "Do you remember what happened?"

Olbric clenches his eye closed, as if he's trying to piece together the fragmented memories.

"They overwhelmed me outside of the mines," he says. "It was three against one. I-I didn't stand a chance. And then that woman snuck up behind me." He swallows, a hand going to rub against the bandaged cut on his neck.

"They dragged me up the hill. I fought back. Almost got away once, but then they forced something bitter down my throat and things get... fuzzy," he says. "I remember a cave. I remember Alix yelling my name. I think they tried to feed me, but I couldn't keep anything down. More bitters... and then pain." His hand reaches up to grab mine, "But then you were there." He looks up at me, his brows furrowed. "How did you find us?"

I squeeze his hand gently. "Divination. Galiva Saw what they were doing with the captured wizards. I Saw that woman cut your necklace," I say. "We got here as quick as we could. I found your trail, and we followed it until we got to the cave."

Olbric is quiet for a long moment. "They were using me for a casting, weren't they?"

"Yes." I swallow, my thumb stroking down his cheek. "He had you hanging by your wrists. I put an arrow through him."

Olbric swallows, and when he opens his good eye again, he looks scared. "I don't remember what all they did," he whispers. "And I don't know whether I should be grateful or not."

My heart twists, and I don't know how to answer. I don't know what to say that will make it better. I don't think there's anything that can.

"The first time they brought you into their casting room was the same time Dominai brought you back out," Allisande says quietly, and we both look over. She's laying on her side, Margeurite's arm slung over her waist. She watches us with a sad smile. "You're alright now, Olbric. We all are."

Olbric looks at her, and something in his expression crumples. Anger and guilt and relief all blur together on his bruised face. Tears spill from his eyes, and he rolls onto his side, burying his head in his hands. I scoot down beside him and wrap my arms around him holding him tight as his shoulders shake with silent tears.

Long Road Home

The trip back to the Crux isn't easy. Olbric spends the first few days sicker than a dog as whatever the rogue wizards drugged him with works its way out. The bouts of dizziness make it hard for him to ride without help, and I hold his hair back more than once as he retches off the side of the path.

The road home seems to stretch forever, and the trip back takes us nearly three times as long as the trip out. With the amount of people we have, we run out of rations before we're even out of the foothills. Arlon and Garrett have a few conjurations that create enough food to last us a couple of days. I hunt what I can, but feeding sixteen people is no small task. We go through the deer I take down quicker than I thought possible, and all of us eat a little lean those last few days on the road.

The Tinari woman, Orabelle, stays with us the whole way. I had my suspicions about her having magic in her blood, but Arlon must have convinced her to come to the Crux to confirm. She's seen what magic can do. After sex being used as a weapon against her, I imagine it must be tempting to see how she could use it back.

Arlon spends a lot of time with the recovered wizards as well. He takes them aside one by one, and they linger at the back of our group to have their quiet conversations. I'm not sure what he says to them, but all of them seem to come out of it red-eyed but smiling. Like some bit of normalcy has been restored after their months-long nightmare.

We just reach the last fork in the road for Straetham when Allisande walks Mo up beside me.

"So," she says. "You decided on a change of scenery after all."

I smile as I glance up at her. "Wish I had done it a lot sooner."

She raises an eyebrow curiously. "How long have you been at the Crux?"

I rub the back of my neck, trying to think back. "Little over a month, now?"

Allisande laughs, and I remember how that sound had won me over the first time I heard it. "And in that time, you've helped uncover a plot against the wizards of the Crux, led a retinue to a hidden lair, and helped take down a band of rogue wizards," she says. "That's quite a list of accomplishments for a month-green adept."

I flush and keep my head down. "I guess none of it would have happened if those goblins hadn't tried to nab you that night."

Allisande hums thoughtfully. "Even without them, I think I would have found some way to seduce the handsome ranger that was kind enough to guide me through the woods."

"Wouldn't have been hard," I say, but my thoughts circle back to the cave, as they have so often these past few days. "Allis, I'm sorry I took so long to get to the Crux. Maybe if I had come sooner, we could have found you-"

Allisande must also ride because she nudges Mo's haunches into me, checking me into silence. "Dom, you saved my life and the lives of everyone else who was trapped in that cave," she says matter-of-factly. "You owe *no one* an apology. Frankly, I'm already tired of hearing apologies." Allisande turns her hard gaze on the two rogue wizards we've captured. "What they did to us was unforgivable, yet you don't hear *them* apologizing. Diran is still out there, but at least Jaret and Lucien will face justice for what they've done."

That shuts me up quick. The closer we get to Straetham the worse the two rogue wizards look. They seem to know what's in store for them, and I don't have a shred of pity to spare. Not when Alix and Marvin start awake from nightmares, or when Iona gets that far away look on her face. Not when I see the crow's feet etched around Allisande's beautiful blue eyes and the bruise on Olbric's face. No, they've earned whatever's coming their way.

"What'll happen to them?"

"They'll be brought to the King," she says. "My cousin already has a dislike of magic, but magic that was wrought unwillingly? They'll be lucky to have a painless death."

Behind me, I hear Lucien stumble with a short grunt of surprise. I suddenly feel faint. "Your *cousin?*"

Allisande's smile is sharp as a blade's edge. "Some bloodline wizards have a more recognizable family name than others," she says. "Once we're inside of the Crux, there's no real need to share a family name unless there's a worry of incest."

"Why keep it secret?" I ask, still reeling at the fact that I've slept with *royalty*.

"It's not that it's a secret," she says with a shrug. "It just... doesn't matter so much. Once you're in the Crux, everyone there becomes family." She gives a small laugh as her eyes land on Marguerite who's walking just ahead of us. "Closer than family, actually."

I can't stop a smile as it sinks in just how true that is. Wizards work quick, and in the span of a month, I realize that I'd die for any one of the wizards of the Crux. Nearly did, even. And after seeing how they rallied to get their own back, I think they'd do the same for me.

The question comes out before I can stop it. "Then why did you leave?"

Allisande is quiet for a long moment before she lets out a long breath. "Because even families fight," she says quietly, her eyes traveling to Marguerite again. "I made a rash decision because I felt like I was being stifled at the Crux." She gives a small laugh and shakes her head. "I can't even remember all of what we argued about. I just know that I still have a lot to apologize for."

I put my hand on her knee and squeeze gently. "You got nothing but time now, right?"

She smiles and puts her hand over mine. "I suppose you're right."

WHEN THE CRUX FINALLY comes into view, a cheer goes through our little caravan. As we draw closer, I see that our home-coming hasn't gone unnoticed. A call must have gone out through the towers, because it seems like the whole place has come out to welcome us home. There are over a hundred people crowding the court-yard and hanging from windows to cheer us as we enter through the gates. It's a bit of a jolt to realize that I've only met a fraction of the population of the Crux.

The missing wizards are welcomed back with tears and open arms. Arlon finally has to call the mob off to allow the wizards to be gently ushered towards the infirmary. Physical injuries from their time in the cave can be healed, but I have a feeling they all have a long road ahead of them. For now, seeing the joy on their faces at coming home is enough. At least whatever comes next will happen on their own terms.

I help Cancassi off of their horse, steadying them as their injured leg tries to fold. Garrett and Galiva did what they could for them, but they're in for a long recovery.

"Thanks, Dom," Cancassi says. They kiss my cheek as I hand them over to Galiva.

A few grooms take the horses from us, servants grab our packs, and just like that, our responsibilities are over. I stand there with my bow and quiver still slung over my back, a little unsure what to do. Arlon catches my eye over the quartermaster's shoulder, and as soon as their conversation finishes he comes over to me.

"Walk with me."

I fall into step beside him, a little uncertain. He leads me through the main atrium and into the conjuration yard. It's empty, but as the summer starts in earnest, the strange vines that creep up the walls have started to blossom. Blue and yellow petaled faces turn to follow us as we pass by. Arlon's silence starts to make me nervous before he finally speaks.

"You've done an incredible thing this past month," he says. "Your divinings not only told us our missing wizards were alive, they helped us find them." I feel my ears getting hot, but Arlon isn't done. "Do you know how you earn a divination mastery?"

I hadn't really thought about it. It would have to be different from what Cancassi had to do for their transmutation mastery just because of the nature of divination.

"No, sir."

"You prove you can use the silver safely when you cast with me," he says. "But then you have to uncover information pertinent to the future of the Crux. Divination is all very imprecise - it takes focus on the part of the conduit, and even then, it usually goes awry. It can take years to accomplish, but you... honed in. It came naturally to you. On top of that, you eased Galiva back into the silver, which is something she declined to let me even *try*."

"Oh." Galiva hadn't told me that part, but it makes her trust in me that much more meaningful. I can't stop a smile even though I'm sure my face is as red as the setting sun.

"So, with all of that in mind," Arlon says and holds a small band of purple ribbon out to me, "I have decided to confirm your divination mastery."

I falter, mid-step. *"What?"*

"You've proven you are responsible with the silver, and your divinings helped restore five precious assets back to the safety of the

Crux," Arlon says and folds the little ribbon into my palm. "You have demonstrated everything I would have tested for."

I blink at it before looking up at him, shock numbing my tongue. "Arlon, I can't accept this," I say at last. I've been in the silver twice and cast *once*! I'm no master.

Arlon squeezes my shoulder and tilts my chin up when I try to look away. "Dominai, we had given those four wizards up for dead, but *your work* helped bring them back to us," he says. "Just because you are new does not mean you are unworthy of this. You've earned it."

He closes my hand around the little purple ribbon. I don't know what to say, so I say the only thing I can. "Thank you."

Arlon smiles and cups the back of my neck before pressing a chaste kiss to the top of my head. "You know, most newcomers wouldn't fight me like you did when I said you weren't coming. I'm grateful that you did. Bringing you along was the best decision I almost didn't make."

I worry the soft little ribbon between my fingers as my face grows even hotter. I feel like sinking into the ground just to get him to stop before I catch fire.

Then Arlon continues. "But at the cave, you still disobeyed a direct order from the Grandmaster of the Crux."

I recognize that tone. I swallow and glance up at him. "I suppose that's true," I say, a little uncertain.

Arlon has an amused grin tilting his lips. "Unlike previous grandmasters, I don't require total obedience. I'm not foolish enough to think I'll never be wrong, and I like to be challenged when someone thinks I am," he says. "But know that when I give you an order, I *will* punish you for breaking it."

I bite the inside of my cheek as a shiver creeps its way up my back. "What kind of punishment?" I ask, my tone matching his in implication.

Arlon hums thoughtfully. "You still haven't tried enchantment," he says at last. "Is there a reason for that?"

I can't stop a small laugh. "I probably would have gotten to it eventually," I say. "I'm willing to try anything twice."

"Good to know," Arlon says. He grins as he thinks, and I'm starting to realize he only shows teeth when he's feeling particularly sadistic. "I think I'll make you a target."

"Ominous," I say, though something about the way he says it makes my gut tighten in anticipation. "What's that mean?"

He reaches for his necklace, and a spell flashes out. "It means that until I decide you have served enough time as a target, your robes will be red. And while they are red, that is a signal to the rest of the wizards that you can be used for casting at their whim."

My stomach does a somersault, a thrill of anticipation going through me. "Oh."

"You always have permission to stop, for any reason," Arlon says, his tone sobering. "But consider this a chance to... get to know the other wizards in the Crux. Agreeable?"

I chuckle, my face flushes hot red. It's a tantalizing idea. I can't lie and say that being passed around in the woods didn't make me feel some kind of way.

"Alright then," I say as I try to rub the blush from my face. "I think that's an acceptable punishment."

Arlon chuckles and presses a kiss to the top of my head. "I hoped you would."

AFTER NEARLY A FULL two weeks of warmed river water and streams, all I want to do is take a bath. And apparently, I'm not the only one. When I head down to the basement that night, I find that most folks from the road have found a pool to occupy.

Thaddius and Ambra are sharing a pool with Iona, who rests wrapped safe in their arms. Garrett snores quietly while a silver-haired woman I don't recognize is nestled against his chest. Margeurite and Allisande are in a pool in the far corner, talking in low voices with tears in their eyes. I don't disturb them and instead take my favorite pool that's left empty in the back.

I swear as I sink into the water. After two weeks of hard travel, every part of me aches. I savor it. The sting of heat reminds me what Olbric had said during my first evocation lesson about tempering pain with pleasure. Evening out the bad with the good. It feels like one small step to getting back towards good.

I take my time to wash and shave before I sink into the pool up to my neck. The steady trickle of water lulls me to doze, which is only broken when I feel someone's eyes on me. I lift one eyelid and blearily focus on Olbric. He's watching me with a fond smile on his face.

"Fuck, I fell asleep," I croak and rub my eyes. I feel dry as a husk.

Olbric gives a huff of a laugh and offers me his canteen of water. "It's been a long couple of weeks," he mutters. "Can I join you?"

"Silly that you think you gotta ask," I say and take the canteen. I drain half of it in one breath before I set it on the lip of the tub.

Olbric hangs his bathrobe up on the hook on the wall before he sinks into the water with me. The injuries from the cave have only faded so much on the road home. His shiner has turned to a puddle of yellow in the bag under his eye, but his wrists and right shoulder are still dark with green and yellow bruises. The cuts, at least, have more or less healed.

"Galiva gave me the all-clear," he says with a smile that doesn't quite reach his eyes. "Whatever they drugged me with doesn't appear to have any lasting effects."

I slide around the pool to sit next to him. With him naked, it suddenly makes me aware of a whole new level of vulnerability on his part.

"Can I touch you?" I ask.

Olbric grins, but underneath it he looks relieved. I've seen how some of the others treat the recovered wizards like they'll break if someone so much as grazes them.

"Silly that you think you gotta ask," he says, imitating my accent with surprising accuracy.

I smile and slide my arms around him, careful of his shoulder. He's solid and warm and anything but fragile. He sinks against me, his head resting against my collar.

"According to my friend Walter, you made a good impression," I say. "I think his exact words were 'Olbric's a good guy,' which is a high compliment in Airedale."

Olbric grins at that. "They were nice people. Shared their beer with me that first night," he says, but his smile fades. "Wish I had done better by them."

I tighten my embrace. "You did everything you could," I say. "The ones that got away with their lives are grateful to have them."

Olbric sighs and sinks further against me. He's quiet for a long moment, his finger drawing idle patterns through the hair on my chest. "This was my first real firefight outside of sparring," he says. "I've been sent in to quell mobs, fight back brigands and marauders, but I've never felt like *this* after a fight."

I scoot us over to the stairs that lead into the pool and pull myself up on a higher step to cool down a bit. Olbric settles in front of me, using my knees as an arm rest. My fingers start to pick the grass out of his long hair. It's tangled to knots in spots, but I'm careful not to tug.

"You've never been overpowered before," I say. "You said yourself that with three against one you didn't stand a chance. Besides, in those other fights you were an obstacle. In this one, you were the goal. That's bound to fuck with your head."

Olbric shudders, though I can't tell if it's from my fingers or my words. "I don't think I've ever been so afraid," he admits. "I always assumed if I died in a firefight, it'd be quick. When Diran and the others were bearing down on me, I thought I *was* dead. But then they took me alive." He swallows and pulls his knees up to his chest. "They were promising... a lifetime of misery in that cave."

I drape my arms around him and press my lips to the side of his neck. "You're safe," I murmur against his skin.

It's not the first time I've said it, and I know it won't be the last. Olbric lets out a long breath and relaxes against my chest. It feels like he might be starting to believe it. For a long moment, I just hold him.

"Up in the infirmary, Galiva mentioned that you tracked us," he says.

I carefully work through a knot, trying not to tug at his scalp. "You all left a good trail."

"I'm safe - we're all safe - because of *you*."

I flush as I pull a twig from his hair and set it on the lip of the pool. "People keep saying that. Like I'm some sort of hero."

Olbric chuckles and leans his head back onto my lap to look up at me. His dark hair floats in a halo around him. "That's because you *are*." When I can't meet his eyes, he tilts his head curiously. "You have a hard time taking praise, don't you?"

I give a short laugh and give a knot a bit of a yank to try and distract him. "I guess you could say that."

"Why?" Olbric asks, and I should have assumed that wouldn't work against an evocation wizard. He doesn't even flinch. "Because you don't think it's deserved?"

I feel my face getting hotter. "I - no, it's not that," I say even though it's *exactly* that. I let out a sigh. "Before coming here, I wasn't exactly doing anything worthy of praise."

"I think Allisande would probably have an argument for that, but."

I scowl at him before looking away again. "I guess what I'm saying is I'm just not used to it."

Olbric reaches up and cups my face before guiding me down to a gentle kiss. It lingers, making my lips tingle with the contact. When he allows me to pull away, he's smiling. In spite of the bruised eye he looks like himself again.

"I'll get you used to it. Because you deserve it, Dom."

I swallow and rub my reddened face, wishing that we could talk about anything else. "You know," I say, "if you hadn't gotten nabbed, we never would have found the cave. So, hey, thanks for being great bait."

Olbric chuckles and lurches up out of the water to catch my lips in a much less gentle kiss. "Ass."

I smile and grab a jar of hair soap from the lip of the pool before scooping some of it into my hand. I slather it into his wet hair and use it to carefully untangle the rest of the knots. He relaxes with a sigh of pleasure and lets me do as I please. The silence that stretches between us is a comfortable one, but my excitement from my talk with Arlon bubbles up.

"You know, Arlon confirmed my divination mastery for my vision of you," I say. "So thanks for that, too."

"You're kidding me."

We both look up to see Galiva walking towards our pool. I smile as she discards her bathrobe and slides into the water with us.

"He said I've done everything he would have tested for," I say with a shrug. "I thought it was crazy, too."

"It's not crazy," she says. "It is definitely a new record though. Adept to first mastery in a month." She glides towards me and kisses me gently. "Congratulations, Dom."

"Uh, excuse you, it's now *Master* Dominai," Olbric says, and Galiva swats his shoulder. "Hey, I'm injured! You yourself told me I couldn't cast until the bruises are gone."

"And you can't," Galiva says as she rolls her eyes before she catches his lips. "But it's good to see you acting like your normal foolish self."

Olbric gives a lopsided grin. "I'm glad that I'm starting to feel like my normal foolish self again," he mutters. "But seriously - congratulations, Master Dominai. We'll have to take a trip to the Devilish Boar to celebrate."

"I may have to wait on that," I say. As much as the idea of being jumped on a whim sounds appealing, I'd rather it happen within the tower walls. "As, ah, punishment for disobeying him at the cave, Arlon's made me a target."

"Oh *has* he now?" Galiva asks with a sly grin. Her and Olbric share a look that screams trouble. A jolt of anticipation travels straight to my groin as their eyes turn to me, but Galiva just leans back against the lip of the pool and closes her eyes. "Good to know."

Target

Enchantment: The school of magic that can entrance or beguile others. Casting methods include humiliation, degradation, and other forms of mental manipulation.

WHEN I DON MY RUBY-red robes the next day, folks certainly take notice. Eyes follow me through the halls like they had after my first day. The catcalls I get are enough to make me feel like I'm going to catch fire, but at first, folks keep their distance. I wish they wouldn't. No one so much as touches me until I nearly run into Garrett coming in from the anterior courtyard that afternoon.

The half-orc must be coming from the infirmary, but as soon as he catches sight of me, a predatory grin splits his face. Without warning, his hand tightens around my forearm. I yelp as he spins me around before pinning me face first against the nearest wall. It's so sudden, so unexpected, that my fight reflex kicks in. I struggle against him, but my pulse spikes as he presses his knee between my legs.

"Oh fuck," I gasp.

"Alright?" Garrett rumbles, amusement coloring his deep voice. I give a wanton moan as I grind down against his thigh. It must be answer enough. "Good," he purrs before his mouth closes over the side of my neck.

My legs turn to water as his tusks scrape my skin before biting down gently. The suddenness of it all, the sheer rush of doing this

249

right in the main atrium makes my cock throb. Garrett grinds against my back, letting me feel his sizable bulge through the fabric of his trousers.

I squirm under him with a whimper as I roll my hips back. His finger trails around the waist of my trousers before he closes his mouth over the skin of my neck and sucks. I yelp as a bruise pops up before Garrett soothes the spot with his tongue.

He hums against my skin, considering. "Hmm, not yet."

His weight lifts, and I barely manage to keep my feet under me. I turn to look at him, but he's already continuing on his way through the atrium. He looks back to wink at me before disappearing down the hall towards Arlon's office, leaving me with my heart thudding in my chest and my cock aching between my legs.

Yet Garrett is just the start of it. The next morning, I'm grabbing breakfast when someone pinches my ass. I jump, my bowl of hot oats clanking as I set it abruptly onto the serving table.

I look back to see that it's the little blonde enchanter, Ambra. She smirks as she says, "Eyes on me, fuckboy."

With my pulse racing, I do as ordered and turn around to face her. Even though she's a few heads shorter than me, she's got a presence. She backs me up to the table as she positions herself between my legs. Her pretty blue eyes look up at me as her hand trails up between my thighs to cup my already hardening cock through my trousers.

"Oh, you like this," she purrs. "I bet you want me to ride you right here on the breakfast table, don't you?"

I gasp as her hand dips under the hem of my trousers to grab my swelling length. "F-fucking hell," I moan and thrust into her grip. "Please?"

Ambra's smile is pure mischief. "I like how you ask so politely," she says. "Why don't you show me how you beg?"

Heat rushes to my face, and I'm aware of every eye in the sparsely populated mess hall watching us. Ambra loosens the laces of my trousers as she strokes me to full attention. I can't help but rock against her hand.

"Fuck - please, Ambra," I groan. "Would you please ride me on the breakfast table?"

The look she gives me smolders. She reaches up to grab my chin before pulling me down to catch my lips. Her kiss is gentle, light and teasing, yet when she pulls away I'm breathless all the same.

"No," she purrs as her hand slides out from under my trousers. "Not today."

I can't stop a groan of disappointment, but Ambra's finger settles over my lips. "No complaints, fuckboy," she says.

I'm not sure what possesses me, but I run my tongue over her finger before I draw it into my mouth. Ambra's surprise is quickly eclipsed by something else. For a second, I think I might just get ridden on the breakfast table after all, but Ambra just grins as she pulls her finger away.

"See you around, Dom," she says with a wink before heading to meet Thaddius at one of the tables.

I swear and take a second to catch my breath. When I tug my laces closed, my cock gives a disappointed throb. Breakfast is a struggle to get through, especially when Ambra trails a finger over my shoulders as she gets up to leave.

After that, I start to get a little desperate. I find Olbric for some much-needed relief, but even though I'm *supposed* to be available for use he turns me down.

"I can't, Dom," he says, doing a poor job of hiding his smirk. "Galiva said no casting until my bruises fade."

When I go to Galiva, she seems equally amused by my desperation. "Not tonight, Dom," she says through an unconvincing grin. "I've got a headache."

The teasing only gets more insistent as the days creep by. Wizards that I haven't even met yet will grab me in the halls or slide in to join me while I'm bathing. Yet no matter how badly I want them to, no one takes it further than some not-so-innocent groping or some filthy words whispered in my ear.

When Arlon made me a target, I had a very different idea of what it was all about. I had expected to be passed around, not teased to madness. Yet it still feels like I'm waiting for the other shoe to drop.

Around me, however, things begin to tilt towards normal. I hear rumor that Cancassi has finally been released from the infirmary. I start to see the recovered wizards at meals. After the chaos, the Crux is starting to settle again.

As I reach week two of being a target, things start to ramp up. No one has cast with me, but I can barely leave my room without being accosted, and sometimes not even then. I don't have the luxury of a lock on my door like Olbric does, so when Margeurite and Allisande burst into my room as I'm winding down one evening, they get an eyeful of me trying to relieve myself.

My eyes widen in surprise, my face flushing hot, but the twin smiles they wear only grow when they catch sight of my hard cock in my hand. I'm not given a second to recover as the two women descend on me. Allisande grabs my hand off of my cock and pins it to the bed as she straddles my waist. My other hand is pinned shortly after, her fingers twining with mine.

"We came to say goodnight," she purrs.

"Not ready to go to bed yet," I gasp, only to moan as Margeurite's hot mouth wraps around my cock.

"Shh, you'll wake the hall up," Allisande says before she claims my lips.

I whimper into the kiss, the heat surging in me. The redhead has my hips pinned so I can't do much more than squirm as Margeurite swallows me. My already sensitive cock throbs, aching for release, and the ovisari is downright merciless.

Her nose brushes my stomach, her throat rippling around me. I throw my head back with a gasp as Allisande latches onto my neck, adding a second bruise to my growing collection.

"Fucking hell, I'm so close," I gasp.

But it's like Margeurite was waiting for that. She pulls away, leaving my cock glistening with her spit. Allisande chuckles as she kisses my cheek.

"You didn't really think we were going to go easy on you, did you?" the redhead purrs even as she sinks down to join Marguerite between my legs.

"I really, really hoped you would," I groan.

She smirks up at me before running a long lick up the side of my cock. Margeurite mirrors her, teasing over my head. My eyes go wide at the sight of them.

Since we brought Allisande home, something has changed in Marguerite. The ovisari's curious brown eyes smolder as she looks up at me, and it's like there's a liveliness in her that I don't remember being there. Like getting Allis back has rekindled a fire that had gone out. It makes my heart soar to see that she's finally reached her light at the end of the tunnel.

And the sight of them, radiant and eager, is nearly enough to undo me. Allisande grabs the ovisari's horn, and my eyes get wider when the redhead pulls her into a messy kiss around the head of my cock. My hands fist in my covers as I stare, my pulse roaring in my ears.

"This is cruel." My voice emerges in a croak. "You two are *cruel*."

Allisande chuckles as her teeth graze the tender head of my cock. "Aww, poor boy, you don't know cruelty."

And she's right, because they proceed to show me what it really is. The two women take turns holding me down while the other works my cock. They use their mouth, their hands. At one point,

Allisande even pulls down the collar of her nightdress to allow my length to slide through the cleft of her tits while Margeurite laps at my tip. I'm brought to the edge of orgasm more times than I can count, but they always manage to pull away before they topple me over into bliss.

"Please!" I shout, at the edge of my endurance. "F-fucking hell, please let me finish!"

Margeurite smiles as she trails a line of kisses over my heaving chest before catching my lips. "Hmm, not tonight," she says.

Allisande slips off of my bed as she straightens her nightdress. "And don't go finishing yourself off after we're gone."

Before I can really catch up to the fact that they've *stopped*, I get a kiss on each cheek. They slide off of my bed before they sweep out of my room, and I'm left with my cock resting hard and unsatisfied against my stomach. The door snaps closed, but I can still hear their laughter echoing down the hall.

I must either be a masochist or an idiot, because I obey Allisande's parting order. And regret it almost immediately.

When I make it to the baths the next morning, Cancassi is there. The Maeve smiles at the sight of me and beckons me to join them with one long finger. The wordless command draws me forward, and I drop my bathrobe before I sink into the water of their pool.

I slide into the water, and they grab my spell necklace to pull me close. I carefully straddle their waist as they drag me into a kiss. It starts out hot, but softens almost immediately as I slide my hands up to cup their face. I let out a small, contented sigh against their lips.

The trip home was hard for everyone, but no one else had to do it as hurt as Cancassi. This is my first time seeing them since they were released from the infirmary, and even through the ripples of the water, I can see the rough, red scar that stretches over their left hip and down their thigh. A stark reminder of what happened in the cave.

I'm just so relieved to see them.

My hands tangle in their loose white hair as they deepen the kiss. Their tongue tangles with mine, our breath mingling in the steam of the baths. When we finally part, we're both breathless. Their copper eyes meet mine, twinkling with mischief.

"Nope," they declare and abruptly shove me away. "I won't be the one to ruin it."

"Boo!" I groan. "Ruin what?!"

I'd have to be blind not to see that something's up, but I'm getting fed up with this whole target punishment all the same.

The Maeve chuckles as they kiss my cheek. "You'll see."

But apparently no one is in a hurry to show me. I haven't had an orgasm in two whole weeks. No one has actually cast with me - by asking or otherwise. Part of me wonders if they're just waiting for me to let my guard down, though with how tightly I'm strung I doubt that's a possibility.

Not knowing when or where it's actually going to happen is enough to drive me mad. I'm starting to get a little jumpy about it all, truth be told.

As I enter the mess hall, people immediately look up from their dinners. I swallow as I watch them, just waiting for someone to spring at me. No one does, but I'm quick to gather my dinner slip into a seat across from Olbric and Galiva before someone changes their mind. Fortunately, the two of them are too busy to pay me any attention.

"The bruises are gone!" Olbric says, exasperated. "Now you're just wanting to torture me."

Galiva rolls her eyes. "Your shoulder's still tender. Last thing you should be doing is letting someone tie you in an arm binder."

"Doesn't *have* to be an arm binder," Olbric says. "They could tie me up in some other ways."

Galiva looks unamused. "No conduiting," she says. "Casting only until I say so."

Olbric chuckles as he leans forward. "Oh, is that an invitation? Been a while since I've heard you mewl."

I eat my dinner in silence, and I'm kind of glad that people seem to be preoccupied with things other than me tonight. I relax a little and let the conversation happen around me as I enjoy the stew and fresh bread the cooks have prepared for tonight. It's kind of nice to be left alone for once.

Next to me, Cancassi and Ambra are talking excitedly about a new enchantment spell they're wanting to try. Down the table, Thaddius lifts a bite of bread to Iona's lips, and the woman's smile stands out stark against her ebony brown skin as she takes it. From further down the bench, I hear Garrett's booming laugh. After Cancassi got out of the infirmary I thought he'd gone back to his medical clinic in Straetham, but maybe I'm wrong.

I finish my bowl and push it away before I pick up my water cup. I debate getting up for another helping when Allisande leans over and whispers something to Margeurite. Her blue eyes lock with mine, and her lip quirks in a grin just as I register someone big behind me.

I turn a second too late. Arlon's muscled arms grab me, wrapping around my torso in a bear hug to pin my arms to my sides. Adrenaline spikes my pulse. Fight or flight kicks in, and since I can't run, I fight. Arlon swears as I thrash, but Garrett hurries to help, and they overpower me easily.

Then my brain catches up with what's happening. I pull my kick right before my foot can connect with the half-orc's testicles. Relief and excitement surge through me.

Fucking *finally*.

Olbric and Galiva grin at me, yet after making me wait two godsdamned weeks, I decide I'm not about to make this easy for any of them.

I struggle as my robe is pulled off, and I might have broken free if it weren't for Galiva. She sweeps my legs out from under me, and it gives Arlon and Garrett just enough leverage to pin my chest against the table, making the remaining mugs and plates rattle.

"Fucking hell, he's slippery," Garrett says, and I'm pleased that he sounds a little winded.

The bench grinds against the stone as it's pulled away from the table. Then someone is tugging my trousers down and off.

"You should see me when I'm trying," I pant and kick out, only to have two more people grab my legs and pull them wide apart. They don't treat my underthings nearly as nice. The cold metal of someone's dinner knife slides against my skin before it saws through the fabric. When they come off, I'm left exposed from the waist down to the whole godsdamned mess hall.

"That's enough of that," Olbric says and leans over to gag me with my own underwear, shoving the bundle into my mouth.

There are cheers from across the room, and I notice that those who were finishing up their dinner have stayed to watch the show. I even catch a glimpse of the cooks and servants peeking out from the kitchens. There's people and laughter all around me, and I flush all the way to the tips of my ears.

Arlon adjusts his grip on my arms to pin my wrists to the small of my back, but he leaves my hands uncovered to give me a way to stop. Good thing I don't want to. Mortification at being stripped in front of the entire Crux is quickly eclipsed by arousal as someone grabs my cock.

I blink, and suddenly Garrett is in front of me, hand gripping my hair. He releases his gray cock from the slit in his trousers as he yanks the gag out. I barely get a breath in before he thrusts deep enough into my mouth that I nearly choke.

"Suck," he orders, and it doesn't even cross my mind not to obey.

Behind me, someone slicks my hole with lotion even as the hand continues to tug at my cock, so rough it borders on painful. I'm having a hard time keeping track of who all is around me. There are hands everywhere, groping at my ass and thighs, pinching and teasing.

Garrett's sizable cock fucking my face isn't helping my concentration either. His thick length makes it so I have to concentrate not to gag.

"You know, someday I'll have to test how much his ass can take," Margeurite says from somewhere behind me.

"Today might be that day," Galiva chuckles.

I shudder as a finger presses into me, but the teasing little thrusts aren't enough. After two weeks of being denied I'm desperate, my nerves already on fire with need. I wiggle my hips even as the hands on my thighs pull me open a little further. A stinging slap cracks against my left cheek.

"Don't be greedy," Galiva admonishes. "You'll get plenty."

The promise of that makes my cock throb, but whoever was giving it such attention suddenly lets go. My cry of disappointment is muffled by Garrett's cock, but apparently the vibrations do something to him.

"Fuck," he gasps. His sizable girth swells in my mouth before erupting. I brace, ready to swallow what he gives me, but he catches me off guard when he pulls out. I gasp as cum hits my face, hot and wet.

A full-bodied shudder rushes through me. My head swims, like I'm suddenly punch-drunk. It saps the last of the fight away from me, throwing me deep into a headspace. It's *humiliating* but my cock throbs with need at the degradation.

"Gods he's got a talented mouth," Garrett pants as he tucks his cock away.

"Talented fingers, too," Cancassi say. Their hands run through my hair to grip at the roots before they thrust in to use my mouth next. Even though my jaw is already aching from the half-orc's girth, I'm not exactly in a position to complain. I give them as good as I gave Garrett and am rewarded with their musical little moan as my tongue plays with the cock.

Then, someone is pushing into me from behind, stretching me. I recognize Olbric's cock, but I'm only certain it's him when he snaps his length sharply, burying his last few inches inside of me.

I shout around Cancassi as I hear Olbric's moan, and I forgot how much I had missed that sound. He sets a fast pace, and the table shudders underneath me with every hard thrust. For a tortuous minute Cancassi and Olbric work in tandem, fucking me from both ends.

Abruptly Cancassi pulls away and gives their cock a few hard strokes to bring them over the edge. This time I'm expecting it, but I still shudder as the Maeve's cum hits my cheek. The gag is shoved back into my mouth to muffle me as Olbric shifts for better leverage, fucking me deeply. His hands grip my hips hard enough to bruise as his hips stutter to a stop. I moan as he holds my ass flush against his hips as he fills me. I'm barely given a moment to savor the feeling before he pulls out, leaving me empty and dripping and wanting.

"Flip him over."

I yelp as I'm scooted further onto the table and turned suddenly onto my back. My shirt is stripped off as they do, leaving me fully exposed to the room. With this many people, they move me like I weigh nothing.

Someone grabs my hands and pins them to the table over my head. I'm so deep in my own submission to what's happening that I've lost any desire to fight it. Strong hands grab my legs and yank my ass just to the edge of the table before another cock slides into me. At least this time, I can see that it's Thaddius.

Margeurite crawls up onto the table beside me and pulls her skirt up. "Let's put that talented mouth to better use," she says and pulls the gag out again.

She straddles my head, and I glimpse the folds of her pussy framed by neatly trimmed hair before she sits. I barely get a breath in before her slit grinds against my face. I know what's expected of me, and I lick and suck her folds like my next breath depends on it.

And it might. I start to feel a little lightheaded before Margeurite lifts herself up. I gasp, drawing in a ragged breath only to have it forced back out of me as Thaddius shifts my legs and thrusts in at a new angle. I'm left reeling as Margeurite smothers me again.

I suck and nip gently, focusing on rolling my tongue around that little button of pleasure at the crux of her legs. It feels like an eternity before her thighs tighten around my head. Her moan rattles out of her as she grinds against my face, milking every last second of her pleasure from me. When she pulls off of me again, I gasp like I'm surfacing water.

Thaddius tenses, and I arch with a shout as he fills me again. I'm panting hard as Galiva and Ambra float into my field of vision.

"Are you alright, Dom?" Galiva asks.

I'm far past the point of being able to form words, so I just nod. I shudder as Galiva finds a dry spot on my cheek and kisses it.

"Of course you are," Olbric says, and I blink, realizing that he's the one holding my wrists pinned. "You're far more durable than that, aren't you?"

I shudder as Thaddius pulls out of me. My cock aches, jutting up hard and untouched. Galiva takes mercy on me as she slides five focuses down my length, one at a time. As soon as they touch my skin, they spark and start to charge. I shout in surprise as she scoots them down until they're snug around the base of my cock.

"We got very lucky with him," Arlon says.

"He really is a treasure," Margeurite says from somewhere to my left.

"Gods, look at that *face*."

"He's deep in it."

"A perfect conduit," Garrett says, and I feel his fingers pick a glob of seed out of my hair. "Yet I can't wait to see him start casting."

I shudder as I feel the tip of Arlon's slicked cock press against my leaking hole. Galiva crawls up onto the table and lifts her own skirts aside as Ambra does the same over my face. I draw in a breath, but it's immediately robbed as all three of them descend at once. Arlon splits me open as Galiva envelopes my length. Ambra smothers me, and I will my aching tongue to action one more time.

They ride me mercilessly, pushing my endurance past the point I thought I could take. My thoughts have slowed to a crawl, leaving me mindless with the sensation. As exhausted as I am, apparently my tongue is still able to do its job, because I bring Ambra to climax first. She cries out, fingers tangled in my hair as she shudders. When she finally pulls off of me, she leans close enough that her lips brush my ear.

"Gods how I'd like to get you to myself," she purrs. "The ways I could violate you."

I whimper, not sure how much more violated I could get, even though part of me wants to find out. As Ambra moves aside, I look up at Galiva, seeing her haloed by the light behind her. She smiles as her eyes meet mine, rolling her hips leisurely. Her hand travels up my neck to cup my cheek even as Arlon starts to speed up, his cock thrusting wetly into my well-worked hole. The feel of him splitting me open, the heat of Galiva quivering around me - after everything else, it's too much to take.

"Please," I beg, and it's the only word I'm capable of forming. "Please, *please*."

Galiva stills her hips and looks at Olbric thoughtfully. "What do you think? Should we let him have it?" she asks.

Olbric hums and looks down at me. He's got both of my wrists clamped under one of his hands, but his free thumb strokes a bit of cooling seed from my cheek.

"I think he deserves it," he says with a smile.

Arlon groans as I feel him seat himself deep inside of me. He cums hard, and I can't stop an anguished little cry, my ass aching and sore from all the rough treatment. He pulls out of me, and I feel a trail of wet follow him. Round focuses are slid into me a second later, and they don't even need lotion to slick their entry.

Olbric leans down and catches my lips, plundering my mouth with his tongue as Galiva starts moving again. I lose myself between them, ecstasy racing through my exhausted and used body. It builds and builds, and when I finally break under the sensation I scream, my vision going fuzzy.

My hands clench under Olbric's grip, entire body tensed as the pleasure overwhelms me. The focuses spark, and I arch as the string of marbles are pulled out of me one by one, adding one more sensation to the overwhelming flood. My hoarse scream of bliss is echoed by Galiva as she curls against my chest, shuddering with her own orgasm.

Then, it's over. Everything goes still. My nerves sing as I float just outside of my body, exhausted and satiated.

I don't know how long I stay in that comfortable place before I'm vaguely aware of someone scooping me up. Voices surround me. I'm too tired to keep my eyes open, but I still hear the quiet praise that's whispered at me.

"So very willing."

"And so full of potential."

"He's going to be an incredible wizard."

The person carrying me chuckles, and I recognize Olbric's voice say, "He already is."

I feel the brush of air cool the seed on my face, and the voices start to fade away. Soon, steam caresses my skin, and I moan as I'm lowered into hot water. Then someone's arms are around me, holding me secure as someone else starts to bathe me. The gentle brush of a washcloth strokes my face, cleaning me off. They handle me carefully, as if in apology for all the rough treatment. It helps coax me back into my right mind. I start to sink back into myself, my thoughts returning after they'd been thoroughly fucked out.

My eyes flutter open, and I'm greeted by Galiva's dazzling smile. She cups my cheek, her thumb stroking under my eye.

"Hey."

I blink and glance back, seeing that I'm reclined against Olbric's chest. Somehow we've made it down to the baths. I can't quite form words yet, but Olbric leans down and kisses the tip of my nose.

"You fell into it pretty deep," he says. "Don't worry, you'll come back out."

"You're safe," Galiva says as she wipes the washcloth over my forehead.

I close my eyes and sink back against Olbric, just enjoying their gentle attentions. My body aches, my jaw and hole sore from the rough use. Underneath that, I'm so satisfied I can barely muster the energy to open my eyes again. When I finally manage it, I'm a little confused.

"Where is everyone?" I ask, finding my voice at last.

Olbric chuckles and brushes a lock of hair behind my ear. "They didn't want to overwhelm you more than they already had," he says. "They left the aftercare to us."

"Though expect them to check in on you anyway," Galiva says. "Arlon was afraid we'd pushed you too far."

I can't stop a small laugh. "I'm sore in ways I didn't think possible. Does that count?"

Olbric chuckles and nuzzles against my neck, his arms tightening around my shoulder. Something about the tenderness of it breaks me. It hits like a falling brick, overwhelming me all at once. Tears prick at the corners of my eyes. Galiva must see the change, because she moves forward to wrap her arms around me as well. I sink against the both of them, feeling like they're the only thing keeping me grounded as tears streak down my face.

"What are you feeling?" Olbric asks gently.

My shoulders shake as I try and sort through it all. Through my tears, it takes a moment to find the words. "Grateful?" My voice shakes as it comes out. "Guilty."

"Why?" Galiva prompts.

I wipe my eyes with the heels of my hands, but the tears won't stop. "Because I'm a fucking nobody! I-I don't belong here. Who the hell am I? Just some penniless idiot who walked down the damn mountain and got lucky." I shake my head, trying to get the torrent to stop, but the insecurities all come pouring out. "I'm not worthy of this place! I don't deserve any of your praise, don't deserve *any of you*. I keep thinking I'll wake up and someone will get wise to it and kick me out."

Galiva silences me with a kiss that steals the breath from my lungs. I shiver when she pulls away, and Olbric tilts my head up so he can kiss me next, his fingers stroking lightly down my neck.

"You are worthy, Dom," Galiva murmurs, her lips brushing my cheek.

Olbric smiles, his hazel eyes looking straight into me. "One of the most endearing things about you is how humble you are. But I've also noticed that you sell yourself short every opportunity you get." He tightens his embrace around my shoulders. "If the past couple of weeks have taught me anything, it's that we can be our own worst enemies. Don't let that idiot part of you convince you that you don't belong here."

"You belong here, Dom," Galiva says with a smile. "You're one of us."

Part of me knows how absurd it is. Arlon didn't make me a master of the Crux for no reason. No one is going to kick me out. Maybe all the rest of the things they said about me during casting are true, too.

Galiva strokes my hair away from my face. "I think you've just experienced your first drop," she says gently. "Arlon may have been right. We pushed you a little too far."

I shake my head as I scrub the tears from my face. "No - no," I say. "That was... fuck. I didn't know anyone could make me feel like that. It was... incredible."

"Did you have fun?" Galiva asks.

I give a wet laugh. "Absolutely. It's the type of fun that'll make me sore for a week."

Olbric chuckles. "I'm glad you enjoyed it," he says. "You know, we don't plan an elaborate gang bang for just anyone."

That startles another laugh out of me, but this one doesn't want to stop. I laugh until my sides hurt. Both of them tighten their embrace on me as I bury my face against Olbric's shoulder to try and stifle it.

"My God, he's still loopy," Olbric teases.

"We did fuck him to oblivion and back," Galiva says. "Though I am curious to see how strong of an overwhelm spell you created."

"Oh *that's* what that was? If that's not the most literal spell I've ever conduited for."

The whiplash of emotions slowly starts to subside, leaving me exhausted and satisfied once more. I sink against them, feeling safe and secure wrapped in their arms. I close my eyes with a sigh.

"You were amazing," Olbric says.

"You *are* amazing," Galiva adds.

I smile. Coming from them, I might finally be able to believe it.

Available Now

Main Series:
    Initiation, Sex Wizards Book 1
Mastery, Sex Wizards Book 2
Championship, Sex Wizards Book 3

SIDE STORIES:
    Storm Night, A Sex Wizards Story
    Divination Practice, A Sex Wizards Story

COMING SOON:
    Starshine, A Straetham Story (Garrett and Bridgette's backstory)
    Odyssey, Sex Wizards Book 4

About the Author

Alethea Faust is a writer of kinky, queer, erotic epic fantasy. Things you can expect to find in their works are risk-aware consensual kink, hard BDSM, non-toxic masculinity, kind and emotionally mature adults, and a lot of butt stuff.

They also have a Patreon, where you can find exclusive stories in the Sex Wizards world as well as early access to future books in the series.

They can be found on Twitter @AletheaFaust

Read more at https://linktr.ee/aletheafaust.

Printed in Great Britain
by Amazon

41928809R00158